GRACE NOTES

D0030897

by the same author

SECRETS
LAMB
A TIME TO DANCE
CAL
THE GREAT PROFUNDO
WALKING THE DOG

GRACE NOTES

BERNARD
MAC LAVERTY

W. W. Norton & Company

New York London

First published as a Norton paperback 1998
Copyright © 1997 by Bernard MacLaverty
First American edition 1997

All rights reserved
Printed in the United States of America

The publishers gratefully acknowledge the Society of Authors, as
the Literary Representative of the Estate of James Stephens, for
permission to use the poem "The Shell."

For information about permission to reproduce selections from
this book, write to Permissions, W. W. Norton & Company, Inc.,
500 Fifth Avenue, New York, NY 10110.

The text of this book is composed in Bembo
Manufacturing by The Haddon Craftsmen Inc.

LIBRARY OF CONGRESS CATALOGING-IN-PUBLICATION DATA

MacLaverty, Bernard.
    Grace notes / Bernard Mac Laverty. — 1st American ed.
    p.   cm.
    ISBN 0-393-04542-0
    I. Title.
    PR6063.A2474G67   1997
    823'.914—DC21   97-22090
                                                         CIP

ISBN 0-393-31841-9 pbk.

W. W. Norton & Company, Inc., 500 Fifth Avenue, New York, N.Y. 10110
                    http://www.wwnorton.com

W. W. Norton & Company Ltd., 10 Coptic Street, London WC1A 1PU

    2   3   4   5   6   7   8   9   0

For John

PART ONE

SHE WENT DOWN the front steps and walked along the street to the main road. At this hour of the morning there was little or no traffic. If there was a car, then it sounded just like that – a car going past in the wet – there was no other city noise. It was still dark and the street lights were reflected on the road surface. She tucked her hair back and put her collar up as far as it would go. The raincoat was creased as if it had just been unpacked. She made her way to the bus station on foot carrying a small hold-all.

She was early at the airport stance and walked up and down the concrete pavement. It was lined and felt, through the soles of her shoes, like hard sand close to the water's edge. It was a way of not thinking – to concentrate on her surroundings. Somewhere a man was whistling – at least she assumed it was a man. Women rarely whistled.

In the bus she chose a place towards the back and put her knees up against the seat in front of her. The bus was empty and warm. She watched the chrome seat rails vibrate in unison as the engine idled. If she stared at things, then it helped block out stuff. Like Anna. She did not dare think about that. Two people got on. She noticed that her fists were clenched and she consciously relaxed them, turned her hands palm upwards on her lap to see if it would make a difference.

3

On the motorway they drove towards the January dawn, a sky of yellow light and dark cloud. Then as the bus careered through the rain and spray thrown up by the growing traffic, at seventy miles an hour, she began to cry. It came over her and she just let it happen. She tried to make as little noise as possible but the others on the bus heard her and looked round. It helped her to stop when she saw her distorted face reflected in the window. She had done it before – used the bathroom mirror in the same way. You just looked so awful, you stopped.

In the airport she bought her tickets with the money Peter and Liz had lent her. She sat in the middle of the concourse trying to think of nothing, trying not to listen to the airport chimes, the flight announcements. People walked around her but she did not look up. She continued to stare at her feet. She was wearing brown court shoes and denim jeans. Somehow talcum powder had got on to her left shoe and dulled the leather. She wondered how it had survived the rain.

At one side of the lounge men were building a staircase, hammering incessantly. Somebody was sawing wood by hand – better than the scream of a power-saw. She thought the sound nostalgic – like the hee-haw of a donkey. Somewhere a baby was crying. It was very young – a week, maybe two. The exhalation of each cry seemed infinitely long. She did not dare to think of babies.

She needed the toilet. Beside the sign for LADIES and GENTS was one for a BABY CHANGING ROOM. If only it was as easy as that. 'Don't particularly like this baby, would you mind changing it?' Afterwards, washing her hands, she looked in the mirror and saw her eyes puffy with crying.

4

An airport was the place for such things. People meeting and people parting. Tears of one sort or another. Some things were too painful. Offspring and what they did to you.

Everybody said she took after her father. The urge to cry came over her again but this time, facing herself in the mirror, she controlled it. She wondered what it would be like to face the mirror in a moment of joy. But this seemed such an impossibility. She took one of her red and grey capsules and washed it down, gulp-swallowing water sipped from the arc of a drinking fountain.

Outside the toilets school parties from France and Germany stood in stiff groups photographing themselves. They talked loudly without removing their Walkmans. Their headsets sizzled and tished. Two policemen went past in shirtsleeves – one hugging a machine-gun close to his chest.

Her flight was called and she went through Security and then through Special Security for those people travelling to Northern Ireland. The body search the uniformed woman gave her was close to being offensive. Breasts and buttocks flicked by her touch. A Special Branch policeman looked at her ticket.

'The reason for your trip?'

'I'm going home.'

'Business or pleasure?'

'Neither.'

He looked at her, his fingers playing with the ticket.

'For what reason?'

'A funeral.'

'Someone close?'

She nodded. He handed her back her ticket.

'Sorry. On you go.'

As the plane turned, the runway lights formed a squat triangle to the horizon. The window was covered with shuddering droplets of rain. The engine note changed, went up an octave, as they raced for take-off. Being pressed back into her seat as they accelerated was a kind of swooning. At this speed with the engine note almost a scream the rain droplets became minute, with tails streaking across the glass – like individual sperm.

On holiday her father wore an Arran sweater, full of cable and blackberry stitching, knitted with untreated wool – he said the untreated nature of the wool repelled the rain. Her mother said it repelled her too. The smell of it was something awful. Like a wet dog.

His voice was one of the greatest things in the world – just talking. He had a big Adam's apple which bobbed when he spoke. When she was very young she would sit on his knee and reach out a finger to touch it as it moved – the sound he made, guttural, so deep it resonated with her insides.

When they dropped down through the cloud at Aldergrove she saw how green the land was. And how small the fields. A mosaic of vivid greens and yellows and browns. Home. She wanted to cry again.

The bus into Belfast was stopped at a checkpoint and a policeman in a flak jacket, a young guy with a ginger moustache, walked up the aisle towards her, his head moving in a slow no as he looked from side to side, from seat to opposite seat for bombs. He winked at her, 'Cheer up love, it might never happen.'

But it already had.

On the bus home she watched the familiar landmarks she used as a child pass one by one. Toomebridge, her convent school, the drop into low gear to take the hill out of Magherafelt.

The bus stopped at a crossroads on the outskirts of her home town and a woman got off. Before she walked away, the driver and she had a conversation, shouted over the engine noise. This was the crossroads where the Orangemen held their drumming matches. It was part of her childhood to look up from the kitchen table on still Saturday evenings and hear the rumble of the drums. Her mother would roll her eyes, 'They're at it again.'

It was a scary sound – like thunder. Like the town was under a canopy of dark noise. One summer's evening she'd been out a walk with her father and they'd come across a drumming match as it was setting up.

'Oi oi, Catherine, would you look at this nonsense.' He held her hand tighter. Land-Rovers and vans had been drawn up on to the grass verges. A party of men was gathering. A couple of drums were being taken from the back of a Land-Rover. The drums were two to three feet deep as well as huge in circumference. They were so big that it took two men to help each drummer struggle into his harness. They hung the drum around his neck and each drummer leaned back as far as he could and supported the drum against his stomach. Then they handed him two long rods. There was a thin drummer and a fat one. Both were hatless and in shirt-sleeves. The fat one had a tanned face which stopped at his hat line. Above that, his skin was white. He rattled the rods against the skin of the drum, testing it. The drum was so big in relation to the man that Catherine thought of a penny-farthing.

'They're made of goat skin,' said her father. 'King Billy-goat skin. You could smell the stink of it from Omagh.'

When she'd heard the drums in her home their rhythm had been fudged by distance and the sound had become an indistinct rumble. Now here, close up, it was a different thing altogether. Her father leaned over to her ear as if to shout something above the noise of the drumming, but instead shook his head. When the drums ceased, he whispered to her, 'They're supposed to be able to play different rhythms, different tunes – *Lilliburlero* and what have you – but it all sounds the same to me. A bloody dunderin. On the Twelfth they thump them so hard and so long they bleed their wrists. Against the rim. Sheer bloody bigotry.' Catherine stared at the flailing sticks, felt her eardrums pummelled. 'They practise out here above the town to let the Catholics know they're in charge. This is their way of saying the Prods rule the roost.'

But Catherine was thrilled by the sound, could distinguish the left hand's rhythm from the right. She tried to keep time with her toes inside her shoes. There were slaps and dunts on the off-beats, complex rhythms she couldn't begin to write down – even now, never mind then. The two sticks working independently. The hands tripping each other up. A ripple bouncing back and interfering with the other ripples which had first started it. The drums were battered so loud she felt the vibrations in her body, was sure the sky and the air about her were pounding to the beat. It

8

didn't exactly make her want to dance, more to sway. But there was an edge as well – of fear, of tribal war drumming. The gathering of men turned to stare across the road.

'Come on,' said her father. 'You're looking at a crowd whose highest ambition, this year and every year, is to march down streets where they're not wanted. Nothing to do with the betterment of mankind or the raising of the human spirit.' Her father's hand tightened on hers so that it began to hurt. 'It's their right, their heritage. God love a duck. Bowler-hatted dunderheads. Gather-ups. The Orange dis-Order, I call them. And the politicians that lead them are ten times worse, for they should know better. The whole problem, Catherine, is racist. I've heard Protestants saying, "The one side is as bad as the other". It's just not true. It's the Protestant side's bigoted. The Catholics are only reacting to being hated. And it's a polite kind of hatred, too. Around the Twelfth the Prods'll say, "Hello." Any other time of the year they'll say, "Hello, Brendan." And it's not just the guttersnipes. If anything, the bloody lawyers and doctors and businessmen are worse – men who've been educated.'

In the town itself she was surprised to see a Chinese restaurant and a new grey fortress of a police barracks. She stood, ready to get off at her stop. There was something odd about the street. She bent at the knees, crouched to look out at where she used to live. It was hardly recognisable. Shop-fronts were covered in hardboard, the Orange Hall and other buildings bristled with scaffolding. Some roofs were covered in green tarpaulins, others were protected by lath and sheets of polythene.

'What's happened here?' she asked the bus driver.

'It got blew up. A bomb in October.'

'Was anybody hurt?'

'They gave a warning. The whole place is nothing but a shell.'

She stepped down on to the pavement and felt her knees shake. A place of devastation. The bus pulled away and turned the corner. The sound of its engine was drowned by the hammering, the scouring roar of cement mixers. A lorry with a crane reached round and lifted a pallet off itself. Unburdening itself. How was she going to get through the next couple of days?

She passed Granny Boyd's house, the door boarded up. It had always been open when she was a child. Catherine would skip across the street.

'Who's that?'

'It's me.'

Granny Boyd had a cat. Catherine liked to stroke its head and stare into its yellow eyes until it began to purr. She always bent down so that her face was at the same level as the cat's. Purring was the funniest thing, like a motorbike in the distance.

'Catherine, don't you dare. I've told you about kissing cats.'

'I wasn't going to kiss it. I'm just playing with it.'

When Granny Boyd was upstairs the boards squeaked and the light bowl trembled. There were dead flies in the light bowl. When Granny was out of the room, Catherine would look under all the sofa cushions and chair cushions to see if there was anything there, but there never was.

The pub was on a slight hill. When dogs pissed at the

door the dark lines ran diagonally to the gutter. The main double doors were closed with a black-rimmed card pinned to them. An Intimation. What a strange word. Her eyes flinched away from reading what it said on the card. She went in by the side door. Her father's name was hand-written above it – black on cream. *Brendan McKenna – Licensed to Sell Wines and Spirits.*

They had always lived over the pub with its buzz of voices. Bar talk. It had a door of grey glass which had a rim of clear glass to peep through. She hated having to go into the bar – the way all the men looked up and, seeing a girl, would stop talking. When she was fifteen she had come home one night from the school concert just about closing time. Men were coming out on to the street and she could hear her father's voice calling time. She had heard this scene every night from upstairs and been afraid of it – the loud voices, the shouting, the maleness of it. This was the first time she had ended up in the middle of it. Twenty or thirty men of all ages thronged the pavement. Fuckin this and fuckin that – before anyone saw her. Two guys were pissing in the shadows and their streams were ribboning out across the pavement. In the dark at first they didn't know who she was. There was some wolf-whistling and growling.

'Hello darlin.'

'Fancy going a dander up the road, love?'

'Show us the colour of your knickers.'

One man shoved another younger lad for a joke and he cannoned into her. Everyone smelled of stale smoke and Guinness.

'I'm sorry,' he said. Catherine ran in the door and up the stairs. She heard somebody say, 'That's Brendan's girl.'

'Aw fuck – no.'

'Catch yourselves on.'

After that she made sure never to be around at that time. She would wait and be later rather than run that gauntlet again.

The building had started life in the 1900s as a bank with living quarters above for the manager. And the joke in the town was to say, 'I'm just away down to the bank.' Wives would say, 'Why don't you rob it instead of giving that McKenna all our money?' Now as she climbed the stairs she smelt again the leftovers of stale smoke and Guinness.

She stood, trying to regulate her breathing. She opened the door and went on to the landing. Quiet talking was coming from the kitchen. For some reason she knocked.

'Come in.'

Catherine pushed open the door. Women were sitting at the table buttering stacks of bread. She saw her mother among them. In five years her hair had gone grey and she looked too old to be her mother. A changeling. Someone had taken her real mother and substituted this older, uglier version. The air was full of the smell of egg and onion. Her Aunt Mary, who sat with her back to the door, twisted round to see who was coming in. Everyone stopped what they were doing. Her mother set down the buttery knife and got to her feet.

'Catherine,' she said. She opened her arms and stood like that. Her chin went lumpy and she began to cry. Catherine went to her and they held on to each other. Both women were crying.

'I'm sorry – I'm sorry,' Catherine said over and over again. It was her mother who broke the embrace – to get at the hanky in her sleeve. She blew her nose loudly. The sound seemed to break the spell and one of the other women said, 'We'd better make ourselves scarce, girls.'

'Stay where y'are,' said Mrs McKenna. 'We'll go into the other room.'

Catherine set down her bag and she and her mother went out on to the landing.

'Where is he?' said Catherine. She hung her raincoat on the hall stand.

'In there.' Her mother nodded to the front bedroom. 'Your old room.'

The door was slightly ajar and it was obvious from the faint light that the curtains had been pulled. Catherine turned away and they both went into the living-room. There was a young woman cleaning. She wore yellow rubber gloves and was tipping ashtrays into a bin.

'Geraldine, can you finish this place later?'

'Surely Mrs McKenna.' Geraldine turned and saw Catherine. Her face brightened, 'Catherine.'

'Geraldine Scully.'

'The very one,' she grinned. Then she stopped grinning. 'I'm awful sorry. About your father.' As she went out of the room she touched Catherine's hand. It left a damp rubber feeling.

The room was littered with empty bottles and glasses.

'Would you look at this place?' said her mother. 'There was some crowd in last night.'

'Did you stay up all night?'

'No – till about two. The doctor gave me a pill to

knock me out. I just went to bed and left Paddy in charge.' They sat down. Catherine cleared her throat.

'Paddy?'

'Paddy Keegan – our barman. He's been great. Just took over. One of the world's most genuine men. I don't know what I'd have done without him. He put the notice in the papers – worded it nicely and all – got Carlin's, the undertakers – drove the whole way to Cookstown to register the death. Aw, Paddy's been great – he's away home for a sleep now.'

'When's the funeral?'

'From here tonight at seven. Then in the morning at ten. From the church.'

They both nodded. Her mother massaged her hands. Her fingers were shiny with butter. She said, 'How are you?'

'I'm fine.'

'So you've moved off the island?'

'Yeah.'

'To Glasgow?'

'Yeah. How did you get my number?'

'Paddy spent the whole day on the phone – contacting everybody. He's a gem.'

Again they both nodded. Outside, a lorry climbed the hill in low gear. The street seemed to be full of a constant hammering.

'What happened?'

'A massive heart attack. He'd had one or two wee warnings but . . .'

'Where was he?'

'He said he wasn't feeling great. Yesterday morning.

Was it yesterday or the day before? God, I don't know which end of me is up. Anyway, he felt sickish and had a bit of a pain across here.' She touched her chest. Catherine noticed the rings, the gold ring and the engagement ring. 'And he'd been having these pains in his upper arm, of all places. I told him to take his tablets. And off he went, down to open the bar. The next time I saw him he was dead. They'd put him on two tables, rather than leave him on the floor. Malachy McCarthy and Jimmy were the ones who were with him. The early drinking crew.'

Catherine stared at her mother, then got up and went to her and put her arms around her. Her mother laid her grey hair against her daughter's breast. There were no tears now.

'This is getting us nowhere,' said Mrs McKenna rising to her feet.

Catherine said, 'That was terrible about the bomb.'

'I like the way you phoned to check we were all still alive.'

'There's days go by, weeks maybe, when I never see the news. I just didn't know.'

'We missed the worst of it. It went off further up the street. Your father was so angry about it. "It's our own kind doing this to us". That's what he kept saying.'

'The IRA?'

'Who else?'

'It's awful.'

'It's a policy they have now. Blowing the hearts out of all the wee towns.'

The two women stood facing each other.

'You're looking well.'

15

'I don't feel it,' said Catherine. Her mother's face became concerned.

'Is anything wrong?'

'No – no . . . apart from my father being dead.' Catherine smiled a sad kind of a smile.

'You'd better come in and see him.'

'I don't know whether I can. Whether I want to. I've never seen anyone dead before.'

'Did you not see Granny Boyd?'

'No. You wouldn't let me.'

'Well . . .' Her mother began to wipe the butter off her hands with her apron. 'Maybe a cuppa tea, first?'

Catherine nodded. They went back into the kitchen. The women making the sandwiches did not say much – there was just the sound of knives and an awkwardness in the silence. A fear of saying something out of turn. Geraldine, still wearing the yellow gloves, said, 'Is that you two finished in there?'

'Yes, love. I'm making more tea.'

'Some of us have work to do.'

Geraldine lifted her bucket and walked to the door. She spoke to Catherine and waggled the yellow fingers of her left hand, 'How's the piano playing going?'

'Fine,' Catherine smiled.

Mrs Gallagher said, 'Open another tin of salmon there.' Catherine looked around for the tin opener but another woman beat her to it. 'We'd be far better off giving everybody a couple of quid and sending them down to the Chinaman's for chips with curry sauce.' Everybody smiled.

'What's it like?' asked Catherine.

'Very handy. He's open all hours.'

'He didn't do chips in the beginning – but it was the only way he could stay in business.'

Another of the women, Mrs Steel, was baking. She had taken a baking tray from the table and had eased fluted paper buns from the hollows with a knife. She spooned a little white icing on each and sprinkled coloured hundreds and thousands on top.

'There you are now. A feast fit for a king.' The carton she was shaking from went silent in her hand. 'Aw, don't tell me.' She shook it over her upturned palm. A last coloured speck fell out. 'Would you look at that. There's only one left. And I've another two trays to do. Imagine having only one hundred and thousand left.' They all laughed.

'Our kids call them prinkles.'

'That's far nicer.'

'The sole survivor,' said Mrs Steel, still staring at the speck on her hand.

'The individual matters,' said Mrs Gallagher. 'I *was* that hundred and thousand.' Then she turned to Catherine. 'Sorry love. I hope we're not upsetting you with our gabble.'

'No – no.'

Mrs Gallagher leaned over and whispered, 'We're here to get your mammy through it.'

Her mother, with her back to the company, made tea. Catherine remembered the spoon which always lay on the top of the dry tea leaves – more a scoop than a spoon. It had a coloured coat of arms on the handle.

Once when they'd nearly run out she'd been sent for a half pound of Nambarrie. She emptied the packet into the tea caddy before taking the spoon out. The next time her mother went to make tea she'd shouted, 'It's like a bloody lucky dip.' She'd put her hand into the dried tea to grope for the spoon. The sound of her mother's hand husking around in the tea caddy – a hollow scuffling – had stayed with her.

Mrs McKenna poured the tea and handed the cup to her daughter.

'Milk?'

'No.'

'Sugar?'

'No.'

'Changed times. I mind when you took three. I was always washing the sugar out of the bottom of your cup.'

The sound of a Hoover whined and roared from the living-room. Mrs Gallagher said, 'That Geraldine's a great girl. She can do the work of ten.' All the others nodded.

'I'll get my sleeves rolled up later,' said Catherine.

The room fell silent. Next door the sound of the Hoover went on and on. The smallest woman at the table, a Mrs Curran, the only one buttering brown bread, said, 'Your da had a way with words, Cathy, didn't he? Do you mind the night there was the fight in the bar – the night Barney Neary was in . . .'

Mrs Gallagher looked at Catherine and said, 'Barney Neary's a dwarf from Newtownstewart. Not that height.' She put out her hand at the level of her waist. All the women except Catherine were smiling and chuckling.

Mrs Curran went on, 'And a battle royal started. Bottles and ashtrays were flying all over the place. And Brendan

18

said — "The only man who hadn't to duck was Barney Neary".'

'I can just hear him saying it.' They were all laughing now.

' "She's an oul model and there's no parts for her". That's what he said about Nan in the Post Office.'

Catherine's mother was smiling. She said, 'He heard all these sayings in the bar.'

'There's manys the one can hear the things but never tell them the way Brendan did.' Mrs Curran looked at Catherine. 'Your father was a character.'

Catherine finished her tea and went to the sink to wash her cup.

'Maybe I should go and see him,' she said. 'Get it over with.'

'You'd never forgive yourself,' said Mrs Gallagher.

Her mother said, 'Who's in with him now?'

'Bella.'

'Do you want me to go in with you?'

'I'll be all right. Stay where you are.'

Catherine went out on to the landing and stopped. Then instead of going to her old bedroom she went into the living-room. Geraldine had her back to the door and was still Hoovering the carpet. Catherine spoke her name, then had to reach out and touch her.

'Geraldine — do you mind for a minute?'

'What?'

She switched the Hoover off and waited for Catherine to speak again.

'I want to go in and see him.'

'And?'

'I don't want the noise . . . you know . . .'

'I understand . . . love. Is there still tea in the pot?'

Geraldine moved off to the kitchen. Catherine went across the landing and pushed her bedroom door gently. A woman, whispering her rosary, looked up. Seeing Catherine she stood and cascaded her beads from one hand into her other palm. Catherine said, 'Mrs McCarthy.'

'Aw darlin.' Mrs McCarthy awkwardly touched Catherine's hand and slid past her, out of the room. Catherine stepped over the threshold. Think of something else. Don't look. She'd always slept in this room. The light coming through the drawn curtains was yellow. The window was open about an inch and the curtains moved in the draught. Nylon and slithery. The coffin was on the bed. She kept her eyes away from it. It rested on one of the patchwork quilts Granny Boyd had made. The design of the quilt had an odd name which she could not remember. It was either *Grandmother's Flower Garden* or *The Drunkard's Path*. The lid of the coffin was propped upright beside the wardrobe. His name had already been etched on the brass plate. How did they do it so quickly? On the wall – all her music certificates. It was her father who'd insisted they be framed. When she was young she'd accepted them but later they just embarrassed her. There was a wooden crucifix, the wood of the cross dark, the Christ figure pale. Two candles burned on the bedside table. The room smelt strongly of perfume. She traced it to a bowl of potpourri on the mantelpiece. Were they trying to mask the smell of decay? She must look at him. She stepped nearer and the floorboard at that side of the bed squeaked as it had always done. Outside the hammering and sawing continued. Men shouting to one another. She made herself look directly into the coffin at her father.

'Aw Jesus . . .' It was him and it wasn't him. Another changeling. He was robed in a white shroud, his hands joined as if in prayer. His fingers were waxy, yellowish – interlaced and tied in that position by rosary beads. He looked strange lying on his back like this. Everything seemed exaggerated – his nostrils were cavernous, his nose looked more hooked, his eyebrows bushier. His lips were blue-black and his skin was darker than she had ever remembered it. With his eyes shut the face had lost all its animation, did not seem like her father. A dead face. The face of a dead man was exactly what it was. She imagined him behind the bar smiling – throwing back his head and laughing. She would never see that again. Ever. Her father was dead. The last time she'd seen him was at Larne. On her way to Glasgow for her post-grad year he'd driven her to the Stranraer boat and waved her goodbye from the quayside. He was always making fun – this time he took out a white hanky and waved. Then he operatically dabbed his eyes with it, then, such was his grief, he pretended to wring it out.

In a story she'd read once a madman called Lenz had put out his hand to touch a dead child in the hope of a resurrection. How futile. How disturbed he must have been. And then she was crying. The tears were spilling out of her eyes and running down her cheeks and her nose was bubbling. She heard herself repeating over and over again the word daddy. Her own handkerchief was elsewhere, in her raincoat pocket. She stood until the spasm of crying stopped. When it did she wiped away the tears from her face with her right sleeve, then her left.

Out on the landing she hesitated. She went into the bathroom and reeled off several sheets of pink toilet roll. She blew her nose and looked at herself in the mirror. The paper dropped into the bowl, flattened and went dark. Now that she was in the bathroom she felt the need to go. She snibbed the door and sat down, stared ahead. Facing this way, she noticed a new shower above the bath. Apart from that everything was much the same. The long turquoise stain on the bath enamel was still there. From a previous dripping tap. But somehow it was as if she was seeing it all for the first time.

She heard the cascading noise of the flush and the long slow refilling of the cistern. She did not go back to the kitchen but instead went into the living-room. Geraldine had opened the window and the place smelt better. Catherine moved about, looking – touching. The black upright piano. The piano stool with the squeaking strut. She lifted the padded seat to look inside. The stool lid had a brass support which sounded like scissors as it opened. It clicked into place to prop open the seat. The topmost piece of sheet music was 'Down by the Sally Gardens'. She opened the lid of the piano. The keys were more yellowed than she remembered. She pressed a three-finger chord, pressed it so gently that the hammers did not engage. Silence.

One day, when she was only three or four, she'd slipped away from the kitchen as her mother baked and listened to the radio. On this particular day the piano lid was open. Catherine had reached up above her head and pressed the keys as softly as she could. No sound came from them. She had to press harder to make the sound come. It frightened her when it did. Dark, deep, thundery. The booming faded away and the noise of the birds outside came back. She tried further up the piano where the notes were nicer, not so frightening. She pressed a single note, again and again. It wasn't the note which made her feel funny – it was the sound it made as it faded away. The afterwards. It made her feel lonely. She was scared that, no matter how hard her mother tried, she would never find her in this room. And she would always be lost. She would always be isolated. The piano stool had a lose strut. There was no glue in the socket and it could be twisted so that it made a dry squeaking sound. She would do this until she tired of it. People who came into the house and played the piano took the music sheets out of the seat and put them on the front of the piano, looked at them and played. Sometimes they sang at the same time. Sometimes people came in and could play without any sheets. Like Frankie Lennon. Then she heard her mother's voice calling her from the kitchen. She didn't dare answer because her mother sounded angry. Her mother flung open the door and saw her standing at the piano. She strode across the room, picked Catherine up and slammed the lid of the piano shut so hard it made the whole instrument tingle and hum. Then she banged the seat of the piano stool closed.

'Fingers,' she shouted. 'A child could lose her fingers through sheer bloody carelessness. And then where would we be?'

She was surprised to see a CD player and a dozen or so CDs stacked beside her father's records. She tilted her head to read the spines of the flat perspex boxes. Opera mostly. Martinelli, *Great Duets*, McCormack, *Duets from Famous Operas*, *Divas*. Repeats of what he had listened to on LP. She opened the drawer of the player. There was a CD in it. The first track was 'Au fond du temple saint'. Sung by Jussi Björling and Robert Merrill. From the depths of the holy temple.

In a room behind the bar, at the centre of the house, was a safe. When her father showed it to anyone he always said, 'Isn't that an almighty door?' Her father had to use both hands to turn the handle – a brass fist clenching a baton – then slowly swing the door outwards. It was the height of an ordinary house door but made of metal, the thickness of a human being.

'A man could hold his head high and still walk through that door,' her father had said. 'It's not a safe, it's an iron room.' Even on well-oiled hinges the door had to be pushed, almost shouldered open. And Catherine, the child, would peer into the dark room beyond the door from behind her father.

'It's stiff.' He had a container of Three-in-One oil in his hand and he put the plastic nozzle to the hinge and pressed. The tin made a hollow double noise. Toc-tic, toc-tic. 'But a squirt of the old Father, Son and Holy Ghost should fix it.'

'I like that noise.'

'Did you ever hear tell of the writer Lynn C. Doyle?' She shook her head. 'Well that's not his real name. It's a pen name. A joke name. Because it sounds the same as linseed oil. They're homo-phones. Homo – same, phono – sound.'

'What?'

'Things that sound the same. Lynn C. Doyle and linseed oil. Get it?'

She nodded to please him. If he were here now she would say to him Bartók and bar talk. But he was dead, lying in the other room and would never chuckle at her discovery.

'It's like a thing can be its opposite,' he said. 'How can a thing be its opposite? Eh – answer me that. Hearing things means you're hearing noises? Right?' Catherine nodded again. 'But if you're watching TV and you think the phone's ringing your mother'll say, "Ach—you're hearing things". To mean you're hearing nothing at all.' He squatted down and wiped some oil off the red floor tiles. 'D'you want me to lock you in?'

'Noooo . . .' And she would run away through the empty bar. That was a thing which could be its opposite – safe. Why was she terrified by both the place and the word? Locked in the safe. In isolation. Airless, black, soundless. A cascade of suffocation. Anything but safe.

Her father was strict about her musical education. He thought pop music a kind of noise pollution. When the other girls in the school talked about groups and lead singers she pretended to be doing something else. They laughed at her one day when she referred to *Stat-us Quo* and they all pronounced it *State-us Quo*.

'They're great,' said Catherine. 'Fab even.'

'They're crap. Nobody listens to them any more.'

'Nobody listens to *anything* any more,' Catherine said. 'It's all just noise pollution.'

'Snobby bitch.'

But she was an only child, used to being on her own.

She turned the compact disc over and there she was staring down at herself in the rainbow mirror surface. There was a hole at the centre of her reflection. What was she like? *Something dragged through a hedge backwards* was a phrase her mother liked to use. Her hair was lank and hanging, her eyes swollen with crying. Her mouth was hateful. She pressed the disc back into its tray and snapped the perspex lid shut. She heard the kitchen door open and the volume of the women's voices grew, then it was nipped off as the door shut.

Her mother came into the room with a small half-filled glass in each hand.

'Is this where you are?'

'Yeah.'

'Are you all right?'

'Yeah.'

'Have you been in yet?'

Catherine nodded. Her mother came over and offered her one of the glasses.

'What is it?'

'Brandy. It'll do you no harm.' Catherine took the glass and sniffed at it. 'It's medicinal.'

Her mother sat down and faced her. The older woman kept swallowing – keeping the tears back. She said, 'It's very hard. For the both of us.' Her mother tried a sip of the drink and made a face. Went back to it and sipped again. 'It's supposed to be very good for you.' Catherine nodded. Her mother said, 'We've got a new shower.'

'So I saw.'

'You've been in then.'

'Yeah.'

'It's a good one – gives great power. Electric – it heats the water as it comes out – so you can use as much as you like, without wasting any.'

'That's good.'

'To tell you the truth I didn't think we'd get used to it at our age. I've always preferred a bath.'

'A shower is quicker, uses less water.'

'As long as there's a rubber mat. I'd be a bit afeared of slipping.' Her mother raised her glass a little and looked at the contents. 'The rest of them in there insisted we should have a drink. But you know me.'

'Daddy could have downed the both of them for us.'

'He'll be sorely missed.'

Catherine drank some of hers and her mouth squirmed.

'It tastes worse than it smells.'

'It'll do you good. I always kept a miniature of it in the cupboard. Just in case.'

'Just in case what?'

'Somebody should be taken ill suddenly.' Her mother then took as big a sip as she dared. 'Why don't you have a shower?'

'I'd prefer a sleep. I was up early. To catch the plane.'

'Aye, you look pretty tired. Would you have time to get your hair done before the funeral?'

'I can't be bothered.'

'Suit yourself.'

Catherine drank the rest of her drink.

'Here, you might as well finish mine. If I take it back in there they'll all insist.'

Catherine drank off her mother's glass as well. She said, 'I'm not going back in there.'

'You can sleep in the spare room. Geraldine made up a bed just in case.'

Catherine stood.

'Is there a hot-water bottle?'

'Yes. Your own is still there. Hanging in the kitchen cupboard.'

'Oh my God, I don't believe it.'

'I'll fill it for you.'

'Don't let me sleep too long,' Catherine said. 'I need a drink of water to get rid of the taste of that.' She walked across the landing and filled her empty glass from the tap in the bathroom.

'Tank water's bad for you,' said her mother but Catherine just shrugged.

The spare room was at the back of the house, away from the noise of repair work. Catherine pulled the curtains, against the light rather than to prevent anyone seeing in. She stepped out of her jeans and left them lying on the floor. Beneath the covers she tucked her knees up almost to her chin with the hot-water bottle in between. The alcohol had made her dizzy. The bed began to race backwards out of control and to stop it she had to open her eyes and look at something. This manoeuvre had to be performed many times before she got to sleep. The last things she remembered were the bells from the chapel and the distant hammering of the town's heart being repaired.

She woke, not howling, but with a noise in her throat trying to be howling. As if she was trying to shout Anna's name but no sound was being formed. Her legs and between her breasts were slippery with sweat from the dream. Oh Jesus. Waking doesn't become any easier – sometimes the nightmare is preferable. First thoughts, worst thoughts. The way they come and go – like tides. She felt as if she was locked inside a wheel. It went round and round while she stayed in the same place. Each tread was the same, each thought was the same. Getting nowhere, yet she couldn't stop. She wanted to die. Not to wake again. And the thought made her feel selfish and therefore worse. She was home for her father's funeral, she'd come back to comfort her mother and all she could think of was herself. Lately she'd been so much better – was convinced she was improving. The most recent anti-depressant seemed to be having an effect. Her friend Liz had even commented on how *up* she was for the weeks after the concert. But slipping back was so awful . . . it was the last thing she wanted. Her new doctor had said it might be that way – two steps forward, one step back.

Her period was due. Maybe that was a part of her regression. Two back and full stop. She was now fully awake. The curtains hung in silvery-grey columns, like organ pipes. Her father was dead and little else had changed. A woman was synchronised with the moon and there was nothing she could do about it. Outside in mid-afternoon – sparrows. Cheep cheep cheep cheep cheep cheep. An electric sound. Like a boring electric sound. Cheep cheep cheep cheep. She turned to face the wall. If the moon also affected tides then a woman was in tune with the tides. Water levels rose and fell – a nameless dread. Something had bumped into the wall, a wardrobe or a bedstead and damaged the yellow wallpaper – damaged even the wall beneath. With her fingernail she picked at the flaw, tore a little more of it away to reveal the grey plaster. She stared at the pattern of the paper close to her face. It was a rose which could also be a tiger's head. She ate a fragment of the plaster, chewed it, rendering it down to sand. What the sea does. She made no conscious effort to swallow but eventually it disappeared. It got into her. She used to eat the tar off the roads in summer. Everyone said there was a wee want in her. Chalk in the classroom – touched to the tongue, grasped – it was so dry. Chewed, it made her feel better. Like sand. Like Milk of Magnesia. The hills and hollows of her teeth evened out, became level and slipped over one another. A good feeling.

There was no future. The only things which were real were in the past. The future didn't exist. She was forced to look back because it was impossible to look forward. At school her history teacher had said, *For the next three terms we are going to concentrate on the past.* She had dates like a disease. They also had a fat geography teacher, a Mrs Galbraith, who had very bad skin. She told them gneiss was pronounced nice. The girls called her Pudding-stone. *Not gneiss*, was what one of the girls had written in her geography jotter. Perhaps it ruined her whole life to have a face like that. Buttock skin on her cheeks.

One day Catherine found her in the book cupboard crying. There was a level which was beyond crying. Because crying was the most useless bloody activity on God's earth. Did it change anything? Were they any better off? Mrs Galbraith had shouted at her to get away, then came out of the cupboard and taught a lesson. On the doldrums. With red watery eyes – as if nothing had happened – as if there was nothing wrong in her life. She kept her balled-up hanky in the sleeve of her cardigan. The crying was in her voice the whole period. And they never found out what it was about.

That was scary. You could be going up in a lift with four other people and each one of them had a story as bad as your own to tell. With that kind of weight the lift should be going down. The light at the end of the tunnel was just another dimly lit tunnel.

Catherine turned away from the wall. Work – she must think about her work. That was the most important thing of all. If anything was going to save her it would be that. She must hold on to a sense of herself, of who she was, and how it could be told in terms of sound. In one of her first piano lessons her teacher, Miss Bingham, had said, 'Catherine, clap your name.' Catherine had looked up at her with confusion.

'I said clap your name.' Then she understood. And clapped the rhythm of her name perfectly. Seven little claps in all – spaced out as her name was spoken. That was her.

'Very good. But shouldn't it be six?'

'My music name is my full name, Catherine Anne McKenna. Seven claps are better than six.'

The water in the glass on the bedside table had formed bubbles. In the mornings she liked to drink a mouthful of it at that temperature – neither hot nor cold. Cooler than tepid. As her arm moved to the glass the air trapped beneath the bedclothes exhaled and she smelled the presence of herself. Not bad, but not perfumed either. Herself. It was now mixed with the smell of this house. Cigarette smoke and Guinness from the bar, disinfectant, damp, the dry smell of the pink satin bedspread. Her mouth tasted coppery as she sipped the water. The brandy had dehydrated her and her tongue felt like a dried-out stub. She took a tablet and lay down again. She imagined it dissolving inside her, becoming part of her chemistry.

'Do you compose the music or does the music compose you?'

The first time she saw the Chinese composer Huang Xiao Gang was at a composition workshop in the University. Because the public were to be admitted, it was not in the Music Department but in the lecture theatre overlooking the main quad. Through the window Catherine could see the green of the clipped lawn and the laburnum and cherry trees in full blossom and the cloisters beyond. She thought it would make anybody Chinese feel at home. It was a warm sunny day. The Prof came in with several other men and walked to the rostrum. Huang Xiao Gang was in the middle of the group. The first thing that struck Catherine was his height. She had expected someone small but this man was over six foot – thin and wiry – in his early fifties, although he looked boyish. His hair was black, turning to grey, and short – so short it could not be described as a haircut – more that his head had been shaved some time ago and the hair was growing back. The Prof introduced him to the audience of about thirty. He told them that Huang Xaio Gang had only yesterday flown in from Toronto, where he now lived, so he was still suffering from jet lag. He had been born in a remote province of northern China and the only music he had heard before reaching manhood was ritualistic – funeral music, wedding music. It was only very much later he heard Western music. The University Music Department was more than privileged to have such a man address them.

Left alone on the platform Huang Xiao Gang looked shyly down at his feet and began. He was a beautiful man with an open, immediately likeable face and smile. His English was extremely good. One pronunciation threw her. Peach. She thought he was referring to the fruit but he said it several times and she realised by the context what it was. For him peach and pitch were homophones.

He began by, not dismissing the conservatoire approach, but by putting it in its place. A three- or four-year old child with an innocent ear could produce things every bit as interesting as a Music Professor. There were smiles and nudges and glances at the Prof to see if he'd taken offence. Huang Xiao Gang talked about *pre-hearing* and *inner hearing* and later about categories of sound like peach and rhythm – random or otherwise.

He invited about ten students, including Catherine, on to the platform to do some vocal improvisation. They sat in a half-circle around him, five boys and five girls. He talked about the invisible disciplines of Taoism – the interaction of the two cosmic forces, the *yin* and the *yang* – the feminine and the masculine. Do you compose the music or does the music compose you? Where are the notes between the notes? Graces, grace notes or, as the French would have it, *agréments*. Are you a conduit for the music? Are you the nib or the ink source? He asked the

33

students on the platform to breathe quietly, then to increase the noise of the expiration of each breath. It was astonishing the way the audience were on the edge of their seats listening to the expulsion of breath by ten people as if it was a new sound. Huang Xiao Gang said, 'It is like a class for future mothers.'

Then he interfered with the expelling of the breath, chopping it up into gasps with his hand. He conducted with his hands, diminuendo and crescendo. His gestures were functional but at the same time delicate. Beautiful. The slightest movement of his head to keep time. He asked the students if they could draw the sounds they had heard, put a shape to them. Catherine suggested that if she was to represent the chopping-breath sound it was, 'Out there. The rhythm of the cloisters.' Huang Xiao Gang nodded.

He then talked about *pre-hearing*, asked the students to think about the shape of what they were going to improvise. Each contribution was to have a head, a body and a tail. Silence could be any part of the sound. There were four stages – first they had to, in silence, think about what sound or sounds they were going to make. Then they had to perform it. Having performed it they had to register and remember it. Lastly they had to do it again.

He asked Catherine to do this. She thought, then she gasped. A sigh, belted out sharply. Huang Xiao Gang said he was strangely moved by it, said, 'Ah what a sigh is there.' Called her Lady Macbeth. Catherine knew what he meant. Yet it was perilously close to being laughable. The courage to risk being thought pretentious. But when he said it – it was with a smile and he got away with it.

Later Catherine began improvising with Huang Xiao

34

Gang, alternating 'breath sentences'. Silence was part of hers and there was a mix up. They both waited. And everyone waited. Two chess players, both polite and patient thinking it's the other's move. The silence went on and on and on. For a long time. Then he turned to Catherine and they both smiled, realising their mistake. It was like when she'd pressed the piano keys as a child and no sound had come. Then they did it again, this time correctly, and she was amazed at how complete a thing it was. A series of sounds, formed, swished, swift – the way a series of brush strokes made a Chinese ideogram.

'A composer does not grub around changing this note and trying that note instead. A composer hears the thing in his or her head and writes it down.'

Maybe she *should* have a shower. Being in bed like this in the middle of the day was like being off school with the flu. The pattern was always the same. The resisting it for as long as possible, her mother saying, 'I think you should be in your bed, girl. Your eyes are very heavy looking. I'll make you a jar.' Then the giving in. Her mother pouring near-boiling water into the hot-water bottle, then squeezing any remaining air out so that it wouldn't be tight as a drum and burst. Catherine taking off her clothes and the intense shivering when she felt the cold touch of the sheets. Teeth-chattering. The taste of aspirin. The smell of hot rubber – clutching the jar between her thighs. Sleeping for strange blocks of time, waking in the middle of the night, in the middle of the day. Her mother renewing the hot water in the jar. Meals sliding around on a tray. Then a turning point, an improvement, a feeling that the warm dry nest of the bed was the best and laziest and most beautiful place on earth. Snoozing, warm, hot even, snug. The recognition of being a hypocrite. Asking her mother for the radio, the big transistor that was normally in the kitchen. Her mother bringing it in to her, grumbling and grunting to get at the plug below the bed.

'It's an either-or situation. Bedside light or radio. But not the both.'

Catherine settling down on her pillows and tuning across the air waves listening to the babble of languages and musics and hissing static and wee-oo-ing – the world in sound – a kind of aural atlas. She remembered once coming across something which commanded her attention immediately. A man's voice.

'He strode on without caring, unaware whether the path in front of him rose or fell. He felt full of energy; so much so that sometimes he felt irritated that he could not walk on his head. He couldn't understand why it took him so long to go down a hill or to reach a point in the distance; he felt he should be there in one or two strides.'

She listened to Georg Büchner's story of the poet Lenz and his madness, the hair rising on the back of her neck. Full of a nameless dread, he walks through the mountains to visit his friend Pastor Oberlin. The reading had been accompanied by music from the BBC Radiophonic Workshop – music which had been composed especially for the broadcast. It made her believe totally that Lenz was unhinged. Electronic flutterings, swoops and glissandi that put the fear of God into her. *Doctor Who* stuff. Music could do this, could frighten. Emotional tension came from the music straight into her body. Nights when Lenz's madness was at its worst he would leap into the town fountain — splashing, soothing himself. The townsfolk would stare at him from their bedroom windows.

She recalled it with great vividness, maybe *because* of the flu. Whatever viruses or chemicals were around in her brain had fixed the images and sounds for ever. Now when she felt the flu coming on she needed to write music, to work like a demon, to get things on paper. And no matter what idea she put down it would lead to another idea. She truly worked 'feverishly'. For a few hours at least. Until she took to her bed.

The story of Lenz was inside her head for the rest of her life. Especially the scene where he goes to the house where a dead child is laid out on a table. He falls on his knees and asks God for a sign by bringing the child back to life. The music is tense — shimmers. Faint drums unnerve.

'Then he took the child's hands in his and said in a loud, clear voice. "Stand and walk!" But his words echoed dully back to him as though in mockery and the child remained lifeless. He fell to the floor, half mad, then something drove him to his feet again and he ran fleeing into the mountains.'

The music squeals and slithers. Then gradually it calms, as Lenz runs out of breath, out of energy, out of hope. It becomes cold and rational. The radio voice said,

'Atheism took hold of him, firmly and calmly with a logical certainty.'

It had been in this house, in the room where her father now lay dead, that she'd heard this and been convinced by it.

She had a pumping headache – felt at this minute gutted, empty. Could never again see a creative surge happening to her. The sanctuary lamp was out. All she could hope was that the creative part of herself would not decay. *Neglect your art for one day and it will neglect you for three*, someone had said. Each day she didn't work drove her deeper into panic. Triple time. The accumulation of days which could never be redeemed. She had to believe it was an organism which, if times were bad, would form a spore which would lie dormant until conditions were right. A hard shell at her centre. An iron room. To keep it safe. A tabernacle.

Within a month or so of starting the piano at the age of ten she had begun writing things down, phrases, patterns of notes that she could play. Writing music and playing it were nearly the same thing for her. In a school jotter some pages were unused but the blue horizontal lines were awkwardly far apart. So she turned the page round and drew her own five lines in pencil with a perspex ruler. And she wrote a tune for the right hand and a tune for the left hand. Then she took it to the piano, set the jotter up and played it. Her mother was on the landing and shouted, 'What's that?'

'It's mine. It's my tune.' Her mother leaned against the jamb of the door and asked her to play it again. When it was finished she clapped in a mock fashion, but her face was impressed.

When she played it for her music teacher at the next lesson Miss Bingham said, 'Excellent, wonderful.' When

Catherine grinned Miss Bingham said, 'Not quite as good as young Mozart but certainly up to the standard of Master Crotch.'

'Who was he?'

'The unfortunately named Master Crotch – his father caught him playing "God save the Queen" when he was two. Or was it "God Save the King"? Musically they're not a mile apart. Seventeen seventy seven? Ask your history teacher whether it was a king or a queen. The *God save* part we know.'

The next lesson Miss Bingham brought Catherine a manuscript jotter. It had a blue cover like a school book. The paper was cheap with tiny flecks of wood embedded in it. But the black empty lines made it a colouring-in book for sounds.

'If you dare to write Opus 1 on it, I'll take it back.'

The first thing she did write was a melody for a poem she was doing at school. "The Shell" by James Stephens.

And then I pressed the shell
Close to my ear,
And listened well.

And straightway, like a bell,
Came low and clear
The slow, sad, murmur of far distant seas

Whipped by an icy breeze
Upon a shore
Wind-swept and desolate.

It was a poem which became more and more gloomy until the last line when the mood changed and the shell was taken away from the ear

> *Oh, it was sweet*
> *To hear a cart go jolting down the street.*

Everyone found the piano tune at the end cheeky and most people laughed when they heard it.

She made herself think of what to wear. Going to her father's funeral in jeans would annoy everyone. Her mother would be black affronted. It was simpler to conform when she was at home. This was one of the reasons she'd left – if she'd stayed everything would have been done because it was the line of least resistance. It wasn't so much that she'd left – she just failed to come back after her postgraduate year in Glasgow. One thing led to another. It was a gut reaction and she evolved reasons for it later. She became the prodigal daughter.

This morning she had packed her black graduation skirt, hoping it would still fit her. If it was too big, she could pleat it at the waist. Her cream blouse. Over the lot she could wear her navy raincoat. But the only shoes she had brought were brown. With navy tights. And a black skirt. Oh God – what a combination. She would need to iron everything because she had just thrown these things into her bag the previous night.

She took off her watch and massaged the damp of her wrist. It was after three. She'd slept far too long. And lain far too long. She touched her left hand with her right, held her wrist between finger and thumb as if taking her own pulse. The body's metronome. Fast or slow, friend or foe.

She still wasn't able to gain any weight. The bones radiating in her hand felt like a fan. She closed her eyes. One hand saw the other by touch. She should eat more. Of things which were good. Like bread. Potatoes.

She opened her eyes again. The details of her watch strap, even to the fastening holes, were there in relief on her skin. Beneath the colour was paler than the rest, the blood squeezed out. She set the watch on the bedside table. The second hand clicked slowly round. Today the time mattered. She saw herself chin high at the kitchen table with her mother beating batter with a wooden spoon in the old-fashioned baking bowl. Yellow on the outside, glazed white inside. A piece of equipment dating back generations in the household.

'What time is it, Mammy?'

Without even looking at the clock her mother said, 'About twenty past.'

'How d'you . . .?'

'I wish I had the luxury of *not* knowing the time. A woman with a family *always* knows the time.'

Huang Xaio Gang had talked about time – about how in music it could shrink and expand. Again making small chopping motions with his hand and little movements of his head, he had said that time could be sectioned and moved around. Music was not linear as some people would have us believe. In the two monumental movements of the Beethoven opus III time could stop altogether – like a yoga slowing his heartbeat. The arietta was music from a different planet – a different timescale –

out among the stars, free from the laws of time and space. No matter how many times he heard the 'adagio molto semplice e cantabile' he was forced to accept that the world, and our place within it, was infinitely mysterious.

After the workshop the students took him to the Crown bar for a drink. With pride they showed him the remarkable preserved Victorian interior, with its gas lighting and call bells. About ten of them, including Catherine, squeezed into a snug and they stayed all afternoon drinking bottles of Guinness and hot whiskeys. He seemed much more relaxed when he was away from the University. They were all laughing their heads off. Catherine could only manage two drinks. She hated the feeling of being out of control. Or throwing up. Huang Xaio Gang made a kind of glass harmonica, kneeling on the floor, blowing instead of rubbing the rims of Guinness bottles on the table. Each bottle with its different level produced a different peach. Twelve of them. Serial drinking, he called it. He said he was only following Busoni's dictum of sifting and exploiting all the achievements of previous experiments, and their incorporation into fixed beautiful forms or in this case, beautiful drinks in a beautiful pub with beautiful people. At least that was what Catherine thought he was trying to say. He had another two rounds and then conked out. Catherine and a guy called McGrillen, because they were the only ones still sober, took him back to his Hall of Residence. He fell asleep in the back of a black taxi with his greying head on Catherine's shoulder. My Lady Macbeth, he called her.

Beneath the stream of hot water she relaxed a bit. She

soaped her hands and washed her face. The smell of the Pears. They'd always used the same kind of soap. This bar had worn to an amber oval. Her father would have used this self-same piece of soap. She stood there for a long time allowing the water to pour down on the top of her head, then she turned her face up and drank what hot water sprayed into her mouth. Her headache had begun to ease.

The house was strangely quiet now that all the women had gone. The bar downstairs, which always created a background hum, was shut. When she came out of the bathroom she felt uneasy passing the open door of the room where her Dad was laid out. Her mother called her from the kitchen.

'Yes?'

Catherine went in.

'I made an appointment with Geraldine to do your hair.'

'Is she a hairdresser now?'

'No – but she's good. She told me she wouldn't take a penny for it.'

'I've just washed it.'

'I wouldn't like to let her down.'

'Am I really that bad?'

'It'll give you a bit of a lift.'

'Any aspirin?'

Her mother pointed to the cupboard.

'Where they've always been.'

In Geraldine's kitchen she sat on a wooden chair with a towel tucked into her neck. Geraldine moved around her spraying water from an atomiser, damping her hair. She said, 'Been on any holidays yet?' Catherine laughed.

Geraldine went on combing and shaping, standing back once to get an overall look.

'D'you remember collecting the rain-water in a barrel?' she said. Catherine nodded. 'The softest of water. You did get more lather. And your hair felt so silky afterwards.'

'In the days before conditioners,' said Catherine.

'Give me rain-water any day.' Geraldine began to snip with her scissors. 'I'm not really cutting it – just tidying up your split ends.' Crescents of Catherine's hair began to litter the cream lino floor around her feet.

'What's Glasgow like?'

'Great. Like Belfast without the killing.'

'And what about the island? Which one was it?'

'Islay. It was great in its way. The beaches. The big sky.'

'You get around a bit.'

'One of the travelling people.'

'What made you leave Islay? Was it not idyllic?'

'Oh I dunno . . . maybe the time was right.'

'Any word of a man in Scotland? A kilty?'

'Naw,' Catherine laughed. 'I'm a free agent.'

'Unfortunately so am I. What are we doing wrong Catherine? Eh? You know why I think we'll never get a man?'

'Why?'

'We're too bloody smart. If I was ever with any new male company I used to try and impress – be intelligent. And the men slid away, looking for somebody else. I thought I wasn't smart enough. And then I realised I was TOO smart. In chat-up situations men are looking for an intellectual inferior. They want to feel in charge. All of them are looking for a stereotype to get the leg over. Hey, d'you remember Paul and . . . what was mine called?'

'Fergal.'

'That's right.' Geraldine brandished her scissors and squealed with laughter.

'What a snogathon. We thought they were dead old too. Fourteen or fifteen, at least.'

'City slickers from the Falls Road. Paul Blacker and Fergal McGann. St Mary's Christian Brothers School.'

'Mine was too small for me. I had to genuflect to kiss him. What age were we?'

'Unlucky thirteen.'

'Your Paul had great eyes and the nicest way of smiling.' She stopped laughing. 'We shouldn't be going on like this and your poor Daddy just dead.'

For a while they both kept quiet. Radio Ulster was playing and the news came on. Nobody had been killed. Catherine listened to the snip of the scissors and the tug of the comb.

'I love somebody working with my hair. I could stay here all night.'

At that age kissing a boy she fancied was the greatest thing ever. It was like her whole body was falling through something warm and moist and lovely. When Paul Blacker put his tongue into her mouth she was so startled she didn't know what to do. She knew it was called French kissing. His tongue tasted odd – rough and smooth at the same time – like suede. And all day he kept trying to touch her chest, which she was ashamed of. As well as trying to put his hand up her skirt. She remembered thinking why would anybody want to? What could be more embarrassing? Especially as she knew, after such a long snog that her pants would be wringing. And they were navy schoolers.

'I think it was the first lie I ever told,' said Catherine.

'Oh God – the Inquisition. D'you remember?'

'I'll never forget it.'

'I'll just use some setting lotion. Is that OK?'

'Yeah.'

They'd met up with the two boys late one Saturday afternoon – market day in Cookstown. The boys said they'd be getting a lift back to Belfast at seven and in the meantime did they fancy going for a walk. Catherine phoned home and said that she'd be staying at Geraldine's aunt's in Cookstown for her tea. Geraldine didn't need to phone anybody. And they set off up the fields.

'Of course my bloody mother was so polite she had to phone your aunt and thank her for asking me to stay for tea.'

'Oh Jesus – don't remind me.'

Catherine's parents were waiting for her when she came in. They were both pale.

'Why did you tell the lie?'

'What lie?'

'You weren't where you said you were. Where were you?'

'With Geraldine.'

'Why did you need to tell a lie?'

'I dunno.'

'Where have you been?'

'A walk.'

'Was there anybody else with you?'

'No.'

'Who were you with?' Her mother was now shouting. 'Were there boys involved?'

'They were just friends of Geraldine's.'

'So there *were* boys involved. Where did you go?'

'A walk.'

'Where?'

'I dunno what the place is called. What's all the fuss about?'

At this point her mother smacked her across the face with her open hand. It made Catherine's nose water and she began to cry with anger. Her mother walked to the other side of the room so that she wouldn't hit her again. She rolled her eyes to heaven.

'Jesus Mary and Joseph.'

'The truth – all we want is the truth,' said her father. 'Don't hide behind your hair, girl.'

'What happened?'

'Whatdya think happened?'

'No – I mean *did anything happen?*'

'No . . .'

'What she needs is a good whipping. Brendan, are you just going to stand there?'

'How dare you, Catherine?' he said. 'How dare you tell us a barefaced lie?'

'You girl – go to your room. I'm going to phone Geraldine's mother and get to the bottom of this.'

'Oh no,' Catherine wailed, 'don't phone anybody. Please. Please don't.'

Geraldine scrabbled in a basket of rollers and began to put them in.

'They made me go to confession that very evening.' Catherine said, 'They didn't actually say, but about half-eight my mother shouts across the landing. "There's still time for confession. If you want to go."'

Every Saturday of her childhood she had gone to confession at midday. People queued in a line, one person per pew. When someone came out of the confession box another went in and everybody moved up one. It was like a wave motion as they advanced. Someone always stumbled on a kneeler. Suppressed laughter. The night of the Inquisition grown-ups had looked round at Catherine. Children at evening confessions were frowned upon. Their sins were trivial, assembly-line stuff. Three Hail Marys penance. Chicken feed. Apart from midnight mass, Catherine had never been in church this late. The place was dim – a quarter lit to save electricity. One bulb in four. Sounds were magnified – a candle dropped, high heels on marble, the swing doors whumfing closed. Coughing, with echoes. And old women whispering prayers full of esses. A coin dropped into the box of a candelabra – from the noise it was possible to tell how full it was – click for full, clunk for empty. The sacristy lamp burned steadily in its red glass container – symbol of the real presence in the tabernacle. Jesus in flesh and blood. Not just the appearance – but real flesh and blood. The only time the sacristy lamp was out was on Easter Saturday – when Jesus lay dead in the tomb. At home her father lay dead. She began to cry. Geraldine set down her comb and scissors and held her by the shoulders. Then she stooped and put her arms around her.

'It's OK, love. We all have to go through it. Time's a great healer.'

Catherine went into the bedroom to get ready. She undressed and then remembered the state of her skirt and blouse. A pale blue housecoat of her mother's was hanging on the back of the door. She put it on as a dressing gown. There were no slippers so she put her feet into her shoes. She hated wearing shoes with no stockings or tights – the way her feet stuck to the insides. When she went into the kitchen her mother was sitting in her armchair, not doing anything. She looked up and said, 'The calm before the storm. Oh, your hair looks nice. It gives you a wee boost.'

'I have to iron a blouse.' Catherine put up the ironing board. It screeched and clunked as she unfolded it.

'So everyone's gone?'

'Except for the Maguires – they volunteered to sit with him until tonight. Thanks be to God for good friends.' The ironing board creaked irregularly when Catherine applied pressure to the material of the blouse. Occasionally the steam iron exhaled. When she set it down on its heel there was a metallic click. It scraped when she lifted it, the water in it glugging like a stomach.

'Do you do much ironing?' asked her mother.

'Only when it's pressing.'

'Very funny.'

Catherine arranged the finished blouse and skirt on a hanger and hung the lot on the knob of a cupboard door. The switched-off iron began to tick as it cooled. Her

49

mother said, 'Give your shoes a wee rub.' Catherine looked down. 'Although it's hardly worth your while – the way the street is outside.'

'Where's the shoe things?'

'Where do you think?'

They were always kept in the cupboard beneath the sink. Catherine stooped and opened the door. A raffia basket hung on a hook. She lifted it out. It was brimming with brushes and cloths and spray cans of polish.

'Spread a newspaper.' Catherine did as she was told and cleaned and polished her shoes, kneeling by the sink. Her father did his every day. And then again if he was going out in the evening. Obsessive. Respectable.

As Catherine replaced the raffia basket on the hook she heard the tinkle of tiny bells and knew immediately what it was she had disturbed. Like a rattlesnake.

'The reins,' she said. Her mother laughed. 'They put the fear of God into you when you were wee.'

It was a harness to stop a baby falling when it was learning to walk. There was an array of five tiny bells on a leather breastplate with reins attached. They were made to protect the child from harm but in a strange twist her mother had used them to punish her.

'God, you don't throw much out, do you? My hot-water bottle, now these.' Catherine couldn't actually remember being whipped for doing something wrong but she remembered her mother's threat – *I'll take the reins to you.* And if this didn't work she would threaten her further by opening the cupboard door so that the tiny bells hanging on the back clashed and jingled. That innocent sound, there to amuse the child, had been converted to one which inspired fear. She took the straps out from the back of the shelf and looked at them. The leather had stiffened and become set in the curves it had lain in – all these years. She shook the breastplate with its tiny bells.

'Sounds like a jester.' Catherine said, 'Surely it was a bit over the top to threaten me with these.'

'Every child needs to be chastised. For its own good.' Catherine shrugged and threw the reins back into the darkness at the back of the cupboard.

'Do you remember when we were out? "Just wait till I get you home."'

Her mother smiled and nodded.

'What you were really saying was – not in front of the neighbours. I'll beat you privately. I hated that.'

'But I never did, did I?'

Catherine didn't answer. Her mother cleared her throat. 'Can you stay?'

'For a couple of days.'

'I mean – you're not rushing off tomorrow or anything like that.'

'No.'

'Then things'll keep. One thing at a time. Let's get your poor father buried first.'

From about half-six onwards people started to arrive out of the darkness for the removal of the remains to the church. They came in and shook hands and their hands were ice cold. First with her mother then with Catherine, saying things like *Sorry for your trouble*, or, *It's a sad, sad day for you*. Paddy came and when he saw Catherine had come home, even though he didn't know her, he put his arms round her.

'If you need anything at all, darlin, just give me a shout.' From then on he stayed in the background, pouring drinks, making fresh tea, talking to people who needed to be talked to.

The undertakers were Carlin's from Cookstown and Catherine found the old man and his middle-aged son very sympathetic and sensitive. They both wore black Crombie overcoats which they never took off, even in the house. Beneath, they both had immaculate white cutaway collars and black ties. They had left their hats on the sideboard on the landing. They were the image of one another and Catherine thought they looked like two stages on the way to death – the old man thin, stubble headed and sinewy, the son in fat middle age – the same tune in different keys. Old Carlin seemed not to look people straight in the eye but would listen to everything said, side on, like a priest in confession. And when he spoke it was in the same self-effacing manner. Obliquely. Downwards and to one side of the person he was speaking to. In the kitchen, when Catherine asked him a question, he took her and her mother to one side.

'Yes,' he said. 'In this part of the world Catholic women walk in the funeral – it'd be a different story if you were the other side. But if it starts to pour . . . we have cars.'

'What about tomorrow morning?'

'The same. The women go to the graveside if they so wish.' He cleared his throat and his voice dropped. 'Eh – might I make a suggestion? If you want to take your leave of the deceased before sealing, I suggest you do it now while it's still quiet. In front of a crowd it can be . . . a different gesture. Would you like to go in together or separately?'

Catherine looked at her mother. Her mother said, 'Together. Unless . . .'

'No, that's fine.'

'It's more supportive,' said the old undertaker, gazing down at the stainless-steel draining board.

They both went in. The room was dark, lit only by candles. The sounds of men working had stopped and the room was quiet. Catherine took her mother by the elbow. There were no tears. Her mother whispered a prayer then bent over and brushed Brendan's forehead with her lips. Catherine reached out and touched the back of her father's hand. It was waxy cold and she took her fingers away quickly but not so quickly that her mother would notice. This was not how she wanted to remember him. This was something else, some ritual which had to be gone through. She remembered him saying, 'I don't know how McCormack does it — I defy anyone to listen to his "Il mio tesoro" without astonishment. Without gasping, if you like. His breathing is miraculous. And his singing's good, too.' And for no particular reason his advice to her one day when he caught her cleaning her ear with a matchstick, 'Put nothing smaller than your elbow in your ear.'

Father Desmond, a cousin of her mother's, arrived and hugged them, much to Catherine's surprise. When the undertakers gave them the go ahead, Father Desmond led the prayers. As many as possible crowded into the bedroom. Others knelt on the landing. There were people kneeling all the way down the stairs.

Catherine joined her hands and kept her eyes fixed on the floor.

'In the name of the Father and of the Son and of the Holy Ghost,' Father Desmond started, his voice light and nasal. The people, a deeper more guttural sound, chorused the responses again and again and again. It reminded Catherine of a tape loop. A lead single voice, then the chorus. Again and again and again.

'Holy Mary Mother of God pray for us sinners now and at the hour of our death – Amen.'

Five times for the *Our Father*. Fifty times for the *Hail Mary*. Five times for the *Glory be to the Father*. Like the sparrows earlier in the day. Cheep cheep cheep cheep cheep. A dry sound that needed oil. Rosaries, decades, trimmings. A whole trevally of prayers. Tides, waves, equinoxes, ripples. The man in front of Catherine had a hole beginning in the leather sole of his right shoe. A little map outlined. An island.

'May perpetual light shine upon him and may he rest in peace.'

'Amen,' said the people.

When the prayers were finished Old Carlin and his son rose to their feet. In the silence every noise they made seemed magnified. The hiss of their overcoats as they squeezed past the kneeling figures – the creak of the floorboards, their whispered *excuse me*'s. The coffin lid was set in place and secured. The brass screws tweetered as they were twisted home, setting everyone's teeth on edge.

Old Carlin indicated that the room should be cleared

except for the four men who were to take the first lift. People filed out. Catherine stood on the threshold close to her mother, keeping an eye on her. When they lifted the coffin off the bed by the brass handles the men strained visibly, one even gasped a little at the weight. Her father had not been a particularly big or heavy man – although as a child she had been constantly amazed at the size of his underpants on the washing line. She had heard that coffins were lined with lead, especially if the graveyard was known to be water-logged, although why that should be made no sense to her. She saw the vibrations of the men's arms as they took the strain. Under the guidance of the undertaker's son they manoeuvred the coffin out of the bedroom door. It left an exact indentation where it had rested on the bedspread. There was a hollow wooden thump as the tail end failed to clear the bed. Catherine looked at her mother and reached out and they held hands, a thing they had not done since she was a child. Both women continued to stare at the floor in front of them. In unison they stepped aside to allow the coffin to pass.

'Clear the stairway, please,' said the undertaker's son in a hushed voice. The leading two men held the coffin high, the following two bent over, taking the weight at knee height. There was barely room for them on the creaking stairs.

Catherine and her mother put on their coats and followed. Outside, the cold hit them. They could see each other's breath on the air. Men less well known to the family, or Protestants, who wouldn't be seen dead in a house where the Rosary was being said, stood in the dark waiting. The air was completely still and sounds carried. Footsteps on the road, someone coughing, dishes being clattered in a house on the other side of the street. The chapel bell tolling in the distance.

Old Carlin stood with his hand cradling Mrs McKenna's elbow. He ushered her and Catherine into the roadway behind the men who were carrying the coffin. As the hearse moved away everyone spilled off the pavement and formed a procession. Everyone walked in a strangely formal way, talking quietly, many of the men with their hands joined behind their backs. The funeral moved slowly from street light to street light, towards the church hill.

The crunch of feet on the gravel of the church driveway stopped when they reached the door and the coffin was set down on trestles in the porch. The sound of the tolling bell was strange. Scratchy almost. Thin. Then Catherine realised it was a tape recording, not a real bell at all. Even from this distance she was aware of tape hiss. She looked up in the direction of the bell tower. Now, away from the street lights, the sky was full of stars.

'This is the way it was on the island,' she said to her mother. 'In the city you never see this.' But her mother was now crying. Catherine put her arm around her shoulder.

'Aw Brendan, Brendan, Brendan,' her mother kept repeating. Catherine held her arm tightly, made no attempt to stop her.

A priest, wearing a white alb and purple stole, was

surrounded by six altar boys, each one holding a candle-
stick. He sprinkled the coffin with holy water. He was
young. Catherine had not seen him before. When she'd
last been to church here, the priest had been an old man –
a Father Kerrigan. She hated him because he used a loud
voice in confession – he must have been slightly deaf.
When she told her sins about taking pleasure in touching
herself he would say, 'What? Speak up, boy. I can't hear
you.'

The young priest took the thurible from the altar boy
and moved along the coffin. The metal of the container
chinked against the chains at each flicking movement.
Although the blue smoke disappeared quickly, Catherine
smelled it all around her in the porch. She felt utterly
weary and wanted to sit down. The prayers, spoken aloud
by the priest, seemed like nonsense. And such boring
nonsense. The coffin was carried to the main altar and
placed on purple-covered trestles.

Catherine and her mother knelt in the front row. The
priest began yet another rosary. Five more *Our Fathers*.
Fifty more *Hail Marys*. Five more *Glory be to the Fathers*. It
was as ceaseless as the pounding of the sea. Catherine was
conscious of her elbow touching her mother's. How was
she going to tell her? And when would be the best time?
Maybe it would be better to say nothing. Like Anna, she
had nothing to say for herself.

The main altar was of white marble – an immense
Victorian construction – like a miniature version of Milan
cathedral – full of turrets and traceries, pinnacles, nooks
and flying buttresses. This was decoration obscuring
substance. If, as one of her tutors had once said,

57

architecture was frozen music then she dreaded to think what kind of music this was. In front of panels of green Connemara marble six large candles burned, three on either side of the golden doors of the tabernacle. The altar was an elaborate backdrop to the simple stone slab where mass was said facing the people. Catherine heard her mother answering the prayers with fervour. She was aware that she herself was silent and made an effort to say the responses, which she knew by heart, but had not said in years.

Catherine sat in the corner, blowing on the surface of her tea. Geraldine slid in beside her, eating two sandwiches at once, a double decker of egg and onion with a salmon paste on top.

'How's it going?' Her voice sounded full of food.

'OK,' said Catherine. 'As well as can be expected.'

The kitchen was full of the noise of talk and Catherine had to lean over to hear what Geraldine was saying. People shouted, 'More tea? Anyone for more tea?' Paddy, the barman, moved through the crowd with platefuls of sandwiches. The young priest who had conducted the service turned up and Geraldine introduced him to Catherine.

'This is Father Ferry.'

'So you've been away?' he said.

'Yes. In Scotland.'

'I've been talking to your mother . . . and I was wondering if you would like to play the organ tomorrow? At the requiem mass.' Catherine hesitated. 'Don't feel you have to,' he said.

'Yes. Yes, I would like to do that. It's still the same organ?'

'As far as I know. Well . . . you could come up and have a look.'

'No, it'll be OK. I used to be able to manage it.' Her tea was now cool enough to sip. 'Those bells you have – are they taped?'

'Yes.'

'Taped bells are like dogma. Always the same.' The priest stared at her. 'With five bells you can get a hundred and twenty variations – guess how many with twelve?'

'I've no idea.'

'Four hundred and eighty million.'

'That's probably what new bells would cost.'

'I've heard real bells and they're worth it. It's a truly wonderful sound.'

'Where?'

'In a monastery – in Kiev.'

'You were far from home.'

'I still am.'

It was pitch black. Her stomach sank. The doctor said this was a symptom – waking early. But she didn't know the precise time – just knew it was ridiculously early. She flicked on the bedside light. Half-past four. Then back to blackness again. She lay there feeling as if her body was made of lead. What was the point? What was the point in going on if every waking was to be this plunge into panic? She closed her eyes and tried to get back to sleep, tried to imagine what was happening at home in Glasgow. The microwave, the high chair, Anna's things strewn about, the table speckled with crumbs. As a child she'd imagined empty rooms – not like in children's stories, where dolls in a playroom wake and become human, but in a more sinister, more disturbing way. Catherine imagined an empty room *as it really was* – its furniture, its draperies, its still ornaments. She could imagine these things waiting for a human presence to open the door and break the silence. There was an Irish philosopher, Bishop Berkeley or somebody, who said that things only existed when attention was paid to them. A bit like music. But she knew this to be false. She knew rooms were there when no one was in them. Her bedroom – silent without her, full of an absence. If the room was full of violins, how silent they would be *en masse*, hanging on the wall, side by side with their bows. Would this make the room somehow *more* silent than a room full of shoes or clothes or tennis rackets?

The nearest she had been to witnessing rooms with an absence was when she was alone in a doctor's or dentist's waiting-room. Sitting in a corner to the point of self-effacement she would hear the traffic, see the scattered magazines she did not want to read and the few ornaments cheap enough not to be a temptation to anyone, the walls full of health posters. It was as if the room was empty and she was witnessing it. It was as if she did not exist.

She remembered seeing the word Bechstein on the lid of the piano. Its goldness, its jagged Gothic script and how it could only be seen properly when the lid was open. The rest of the time – which was most of the time – the writing was upside down, facing the keys, in the dark when the lid was shut. She said this to her mother once.

'It only needs to be right when it's on show,' her

mother said. 'Like the man who hangs his smile on the back of the door when he comes in. Your father's a bit inclined to do that.'

Her eyelids were cold. The heating had been off for hours and the air of the room was icy. She put her head beneath the duvet to try to warm her face but it felt, under there, as if she was suffocating. She came up for air. It was going to be a long night. She put her fingertips to her eyes to try and warm the lids. Who could sleep with cold eyelids? Before she'd gone to bed her mother had asked her to escort some people down the stairs. Outside their feet had crackled on the street and their every breath was visible on the still air. The temperature was still falling. Had the grave already been dug? She'd read that in Alaska they left bodies on the roof until spring – like planks. The coldest she had ever been was in Kiev. The hairs in her nose had frozen when she breathed in.

She had won the Moncrieff-Hewitt Award for her Piano Trio – a thousand pounds to be spent exclusively on travel during or after her postgraduate year in Glasgow. She had graduated with a first in composition from Queen's in Belfast and everyone at the Academy expected her to win. The recipient was urged to encounter the music of other countries. At the celebration afterwards Catherine had been introduced to one of the judges – the composer, Helmut Lemberg. He asked her which living composers she liked.

'Apart from yourself . . .' And they both laughed. But she could see that her joke had gone astray. He seemed embarrassed.

'I was not meaning that at all . . .' He held a glass of red wine in one hand and gestured hopelessly with the other. 'I am genuinely interested in who you would like to meet.'

'I'm sorry . . . I mean, I do admire your work,' she said.

'We are not here to talk about me. Tell me who you admire.'

'Melnichuck. Do you know his work?'

'Yes indeed. Anatoli Ivanovich Melnichuck. Interesting.' He nodded and smiled. 'Now that it's possible to go to Kiev you should not waste the opportunity. Ten years ago you couldn't have done it. A good choice. His work is very important. Asian and Western elements.' He set his wine glass down and interlaced the fingers of both hands. 'But, like many of us, he is an old man now. Maybe he will not be around for too long. Where did you come across his work?'

'On Radio Three. A couple of years ago — there was a concert devoted to his stuff.'

'Oh, you heard that?'

'Yes. After that I bought anything of his I could find.'

'Hyperion are going to issue some of his early work on CD.'

'Good — good. I'm glad.' She found it very difficult to talk about music. When she said things out loud it sounded so awful. So phoney. Melnichuck's music had a spareness and an austerity which she loved — like Janáček, with his fragments of melody. And there was also something very spiritual about everything he wrote. And yet he was from the Ukraine. As far east in Europe as it was possible to go. A country which had long ago dispensed with religion and the spirit. How did it spring from an atheist soul and why did it communicate so strongly with her? The wine was beginning to go to her head. She was nervous with somebody as eminent as Lemberg and was drinking too quickly. The old man looked at her glass.

'Can I get you a refill?'

When he came back he presented her with a glass full of red and said, 'I don't usually say this to people but . . .' He looked around to see if anyone else was within earshot, '. . . your trio was wonderful. It reminded me of Fauré's, do you know it?'

Catherine nodded but seemed surprised.

'I don't mean it was *like* Fauré's – the circumstances are completely different – his only trio was at the end of his life. But yours has the same intensity, nothing superfluous. You must continue to write. It must be just the beginning. If there is any way I can help . . . I don't mean to patronise you . . . but y'know. I really loved it. From the first note I knew I was listening to an important musical imagination. You have a sound universe of your own. The other entries were simply good students.'

Catherine didn't know what to say, she could hardly believe her ears. She stammered and blushed.

'Talking of patronising . . .' she said, 'when I was a student in Belfast I asked a producer at the BBC – who shall be nameless – how a composer could get their first work performed. Do you know what he said?' Lemberg shook his head.

' "He should try the Society for Promotion of New Music". Can you imagine?'

'And what was wrong with that?'

' "He's a she. He's me." '

Helmut Lemberg smiled a smile of *what can you expect*. Catherine shrugged so much that the wine in her glass slopped over on to her white linen trousers.

'I'm so bloody clumsy.' She tried to wipe the stain with a tissue but, from past experience, she knew there would be a blue stain. 'Never mind.'

'Ah,' Lemberg said and stepped forward to stop a small balding man with glasses.' Here's somebody to right the wrongs.' He introduced Catherine to Graeme McNicol, Head of Music at BBC Scotland and moved to another group. McNicol congratulated her on the Trio. They talked a bit, then he asked her if he could have it for Radio Three. Catherine was amazed. It was hard to believe but they shook hands on it. He said he was trying to get together a festival of new music for the following year and would be delighted to get something from her. They swapped addresses and telephone numbers.

She turned in the bed and saw a strip of light appear beneath her bedroom door. The toilet flushed and then she heard the rattle of someone in the kitchen. The flush made her want to go to the toilet herself. She switched on the bedside light.

A nail had been driven into the back of the bedroom door. Some metal coat-hangers and the blue housecoat hung on it. The coat was a vague but two-dimensional shape of her mother. Catherine got up and put it on. She went to the lavatory then to the kitchen. Her mother was warming a saucepan of milk.

'Can you not sleep either?'

'I'm just heating up a taste of milk. Would you like some?'

'No. Things'd have to be really bad before I'd resort to that.' Catherine shivered in the thin nylon coat. She went to the bedroom and came back smothered in her duvet. She sat with her knees up to her chin on the old sofa. Her mother had poured the milk into a beaker and was spooning it like soup.

'It forms a skin if you leave it.'

'Did you sleep at all?' asked Catherine.

'For a while. The pill helped.' The spoon chinked against the china. Her mother wore a turquoise dressing gown of thick towelling. In the harsh overhead light she looked exhausted – the colour of the material reflecting up into her face, giving her a sickish pallor. Her grey hair was all over the place. She now made an attempt to tie it back with both hands.

'You were his wee girl.'

Catherine nodded.

'He was very hurt . . .'

'I know, I know. I just feel so bad about it.'

'I don't want to lose you again, Catherine. So I have to watch my tongue.'

'He was such a . . . bossy . . . he wanted to interfere too much.' She stopped abruptly. 'This is the wrong time to be saying this.'

'And him not in the grave yet. Whatever he did, he did it out of love for you.'

'He appeared so different to other people.'

'He'll be sorely missed in this town.' The milk had cooled sufficiently for her to drink it from the mug. 'I

don't know what I'll do without him.' She began to cry a
little. 'Forty years I've known him.' She looked all around
for a hanky. Catherine emerged from the duvet, pulled
tissues from a box on the sideboard and gave them to her
in a crumpled heap.

'Thanks, love.' She blew her nose. 'I'm stunned – just
stunned.'

'Do you think you'll sleep?'

Her mother shook her head.

'Can you not take another tablet?'

'I don't want to take too many of those boys. In case I
get hooked.'

'You've had – what? Two? Three?' Her mother rose to
her feet.

'That's enough to start. I know what. Why don't you
play something for me?'

'Now? At this time of the morning?'

'Yes.'

'What would you like?'

'Nothing sad.'

They went into the living-room. Her mother switched
on a table lamp and sat down in the armchair. Catherine
sat on the piano stool, trying to hold the duvet about her
shoulders but it kept slipping. She opened the piano lid.
The gold lettering *Bechstein* on its underside appeared.

'Oh I hate that,' she gave a little gasp.

'What?'

'The pedals – in bare feet. They're so cold.' She
thought for a moment. 'Do you remember this one?' She
began to play and before she had completed the first
phrase her mother said, 'Oh that one.'

'The Haydn.'

Catherine played with a little tilt of her head, a slight almost imperceptible nodding to the rhythm. Her hands floated lightly above the keyboard, effortlessly fingering. The strutting rhythm to start – a jaunty march almost, which was overtaken by flowing runs, the glittering phrases and trills held in check by the strength of her left hand. Out of the corner of her eye she saw her mother close her eyes and put her head back on the chair. She was smiling – the first time Catherine had seen her do so since she'd come home.

'Glorious,' said her mother. She had her arms folded and her finger was tapping out the rhythm. Not so much tapping, more conducting discreetly.

'I'm not sure of this, it's so long since I played it.'

'It sounds all right to me.'

The duvet had fallen away from her shoulders and covered the piano stool.

'Look,' Catherine shouted above her playing. 'Look at the goose-bumps on my arms.' The sleeves of the housecoat came only to the middle of her upper arm.

When she finished her mother clapped her hands, making no noise – a kind of imitation applause.

'You certainly haven't lost your touch. If anything you've improved. You play so well.'

'That's not the point. It was Haydn who wrote so well.'

'But he's no relation of mine.'

Catherine smiled. She pulled the duvet up around her shoulders again.

'It's so difficult to get enough time to practise.'

'If anybody's walking along that street out there they'll

wonder what in the name of God is going on. Music like that coming out of a dead house at five in the morning.'

Catherine stood and went over to the window trailing the duvet after her like a cope.

'Not a soul,' she said. 'Hey – look. There's frost on the *inside* of these windows.' She reached out her finger and scratched where the pattern had dulled the glass.

'Are you doing any writing?'

'I had a thing on the radio three or four weeks ago.'

'I heard.'

'You heard it?'

'No – I meant I heard it was on.'

'How did you know?'

'People phoned your father afterwards.'

'Who?'

'He didn't say. He was terribly disappointed.'

'Huh?'

'That he missed it.'

'He wouldn't have liked it. He'd have hated it. Especially the drumming.'

'I believe it went out far and wide.'

'Yes – all over.' Catherine shivered again and pulled the duvet tightly about her. She stood and took her mother's cup to the kitchen, rinsed it out and set it on the dish rack. The radio cassette was where it had always been, its bright aluminium finish dulled by the kitchen fumes – like the glass dulled by frost. There was a noticeboard above the fridge with reminders and things pinned to it. A note in her father's writing said *See Dermot – Tues at 4.30*. Whether it was for this Tuesday or a previous one didn't matter. She threw the piece of paper into the waste bin and replaced the drawing pin in the green felt. Her postcard from Kiev was still there – of the golden domes of the monastery at Lavra. It was the last time she'd written home.

She met her mother coming out of the bathroom and kissed her on the cheek.

'Night-night,' she said.

'Night-night,' said her mother. 'I hope you sleep this time.'

But Catherine lay awake. She remembered the clean and basic hotel room in Kiev where she had spent ages waiting for the summons to meet Melnichuck. Two brown single beds, a blue armchair and an empty fridge. The bathroom had oatmeal toilet paper with no perforations – every time she used it, it scourged the behind off her. The only plus point – in the lobbies there was no musak.

Melnichuck was in poor health and Catherine had to wait until his wife, Olga, said that he was well enough to talk to a student. Everything had to be done through her because Melnichuck had little or no English. In the meantime Catherine did the tourist thing. She was amazed at the prostitutes in the bar at night with their mini-skirts and spiked heels. They sat around with a couple of uniformed policemen. Although she was not dressed like the others, Catherine was approached three times in about ten minutes. None of the men spoke English but their intentions were obvious. She thought of complaining but it all seemed so difficult that she just gave up and went to her room. The hotel staff were stone-faced about every-thing – there was not the slightest hint of friendliness. In an effort to compensate Catherine smiled so much her teeth dried. She felt like Sister Immaculata, her old science teacher.

It was several days before the phone rang and Olga's voice said, 'Today is good.'

The Melnichucks were both in their sixties, although she looked better than he did with her grey hair drawn back in a bun. He smoked all the time and had a dark ragged voice. He reminded her of the poet, Hugh McDiarmid, with glasses. His eyes must have been very bad because the lenses were like whirlpools. Olga apologised for her husband being ill and pointed to her heart. 'Too many salt. He eats too many salt. But', she shrugged, 'it's the only thing here cheap.' Catherine had been warned that the average wage in the Ukraine was ten dollars a month. Olga had baked specially for Catherine's coming – like people would do at home.

Catherine asked Melnichuck about the spirit of his music, where its 'soul' came from. He said in English, 'Tomorrow.' She asked him about influences and he repeated the word 'Tomorrow'. He asked her to play something of hers for him. She was very nervous and didn't do herself justice. She played her Piano Studies and he took off his glasses and listened intently. He nodded when she had finished.

Through Olga he said it was 'good'. Then he added another word. Catherine turned from the piano waiting for the translation. Olga said, 'And interesting.'

Later Olga gave them tea and stale white bread, dried to the texture of biscuits in the oven. They dipped it in homemade strawberry jam. All conversation ceased as they crunched their way through a plate of this stuff.

Afterwards Melnichuck said through his wife, 'Let me hear work in progress. If I hear an opus you think is finished and I say do this and do that – you are unhappy. But if an opus is under construction, if you have problem with it and I say do this and do that – you are happy.'

Catherine nodded her head in agreement. She reached into her bag and set up the staff sheets of a piano piece.

'It doesn't have a name yet.' Before she started some jam got from her fingers on to the piano keys and she had to ask Olga for something to wipe both her fingers and the notes. She hated sticky fingers at any time. Olga came in with a damp cloth and said, 'Anatoli says it will be sweet music.' Catherine wiped her fingers and the keys. The piano gave off a rippling, plinking sound.

'Work in Progress,' announced Melnichuck in English, then they all laughed loudly. When she had finished with it Catherine put the cloth on top of the piano. It was an old vest. Whether it belonged to Anatoli or Olga she couldn't tell.

When she began playing it raised their dog, a big black mongrel thing, who came clacking his claws across the wooden floor. By now Olga was lying back in her armchair with her hand masking her eyes, listening. Melnichuck had his glasses off and couldn't see anything anyway. The dog was randy and stood on its hind legs, and she felt it trying to mount her from behind. It put a paw on each of her shoulders and was going hell for leather at her back. She shouted something at it and tried to continue playing. But she had to stop. Olga was mortified. She scolded the dog and threw it out of the room. As it left Catherine saw a little scarlet crayon between its hind legs.

The number of people who turned up for her father's requiem mass made her want to cry. The church car-park was full and cars lined the lanes and side streets of the town. She left her mother with the other members of the family at the front of the church beside the coffin.

'Will you be all right?' Mrs McKenna nodded. Catherine climbed the stairs to the organ loft and slid on to the bench. Her back was to the altar. The organist followed the mass in a mirror tilted above the keyboard. The image she saw mixed up left and right. She glanced down over her shoulder at the altar. Nothing was happening yet. She went through her pockets for the piece of paper on which she'd arranged a programme with her mother and Father Ferry. She set it in front of her.

She played some Bach Chorale Preludes from the *Orgelbüchlein*. Played them as well as the organ would permit. Shuffles and coughs came from the congregation as the church filled. She allowed her musical self to be in charge, so that there would be no tears. Once she'd seen a priest take the funeral service for his own mother and felt there was no chance he would break down – she was confident it was the priest in him saying the mass, not the son.

A small altar boy, in surplice and soutane, came out on to the altar with a burning taper and stood on tiptoe to light the candles. When he went back into the sacristy the door slammed.

At primary school the priest had come in one day and

asked for volunteers for the altar. Catherine put up her hand immediately.

'Altar-*boys* is what we're after, Miss McKenna.' And everybody laughed at his joke. He'd gone on to select six boys to be trained as servers. Catherine ran home on the verge of tears and told her mother.

'I suppose you just sat and played the Silent O'Moyle while all this was going on.' Catherine didn't say anything. Her mother smiled, 'Nothing much changes. When I was your age Master Ryan used to train the boys for the altar. But he would teach the whole class the Latin responses – boys and girls. "Just in case", he said, "some morning no boy turns up." An emergency. Can you imagine?'

The church was now full. People had to stand at the back and lines of men occupied the side aisles. Catherine looked in the mirror and saw the procession of altar boys and priest coming on to the altar. There was a thunderous noise as everyone rose to their feet. Then again as they all knelt.

There was a herd instinct here. People standing and sitting when everybody else did. Like *The Messiah* in the Ulster Hall.

'Lord have mercy,' said Father Ferry. Then the unfocused mumbled roar as the people answered. 'Christ have mercy.'

It sounded so much better in the old form.
Kyrie Eléison.
Christe Eléison.

Seven syllables answered by six syllables. She didn't know what had started her working on the long-term project of a mass but she found the setting of Latin words to music a satisfying experience. Britten had done it beautifully. She had written it for two small choirs braiding the voices but placing them in different parts of the church or concert hall after the manner of Hassler in the sixteenth century. Choirs which were mirror images of each other. If it ever got as far as being recorded then the stereo effect on two speakers would do the same thing. A Latin text used the human voice but put meaning at a distance. As well as the *Kyrie*, she had written a *Sanctus* and *Benedictus*. The *Credo* was in front of her.

During the eulogy she sat with her head down listening. She heard Father Ferry say her father's name – Brendan McKenna – and it brought a lump to her throat. The priest went on to say a lot of things in praise of the family man, the businessman, the father, the husband and all-round good Catholic who had passed away. But nothing touched her more than hearing his name spoken aloud in public by a stranger.

At the Consecration the priest held up the host. Then the chalice of wine. Catherine hated the moments following the silence of the Consecration when everybody coughed and shuffled. It was supposedly the most sacred part of the mass, when bread and wine were turned, literally and not metaphorically, into the body and blood of Christ. Transubstantiation. The people bowed their heads and held their breath and when it was over they exhaled, they made a rumpus. She hated it, not only at mass, but even more so at concerts. Between the movements of a symphony invariably the concert hall would be filled with the noise of hacking coughs and throat-clearings and programme flitterings and leg crossings. Why did people do it?

She'd been in an art gallery once and had seen an exhibit of a tumbler of water on a glass shelf. The artist had called it *Oak Tree*. The programme note had said in outward form it looked like a glass of water but its essence was that of an oak tree. You just had to take the artist's word for it. He was Catholic. Or at least he had been at some stage. His biographical note said he had gone to a Jesuit school.

When the priest drank from the chalice he looked momentarily like a trumpeter. A silent fanfare. During communion she played the remainder of the Chorale Preludes. Being organist meant that she was spared the decision of whether or not to take communion to please her mother.

The graveyard surrounded the church on all sides. Her father's freshly dug grave was on the northern slope. The bearers carried the coffin towards it. Catherine and her mother followed. They took up a position on the path above the grave. Others gathered among the headstones and tried to avoid actually standing on the surrounding graves. Everyone was at an angle to the slope, one leg longer than the other. An old man folded his cap and knelt on it. A breeze had sprung up. The white surplices flapped and ballooned. The altar boys had difficulty keeping their candles lit and cupped their hands around the small flames to shelter them. Catherine heard the priest's voice and the chink of the holy water sprinkler against its bucket. The grumbled responses from the crowd seemed flat and echoless in the open air. There was a frozen margin to the path and she pressed down on the ice with her toe. A white bubble expanded and moved slowly under her weight until her toe snapped through it. Like a wafer.

When the prayers were finished the grave-diggers reached for their spades. One of them spat on his hands. A thin purple mattress had been laid on top of the coffin to minimise the sound of falling earth but she heard the padded thump of each shovelful. The slice of the blade into the heap of soil and the ring of the steel as the dirt left the face of it. Not only did they try to hide the sound, they tried to hide the soil itself. It was freshly dug and heaped beneath a carpet – the sort of awful emerald grass stuff she'd seen in shop windows. The next thing would be to line the grave with tinsel. Catherine bowed her head and tried not to think. But she couldn't stop.

It was Christmas Eve and she was rigid with excitement. Her mother and she – she must have been about eleven – had driven to Belfast to meet her father off the Dublin train. There was a young crowd, a bit drunk, at the platform gates. Some of them wore tinsel round their necks like scarves. Catherine kept looking past them down the empty platform. She hop-hopped on one foot, incessantly talking about her Dad. What kind of presents would he have? Dad this and Dad that. Her mother pretended she was calm.

'Not so loud, Catherine.'

'Why?'

Her mother leaned forward and whispered in her ear, 'Because we're in a crowd. Nobody wants to know our business.' When people whispered like that in her ear she could hear the wet inside their mouths. A pigeon flapped to a different beam beneath the glass roof. Silvery lines curved out into the darkness where a light began to grow slowly. Then the noise of the train chuntering in.

'There he is. There he is,' Catherine yelled so loudly that others in the crowd smiled and nudged one another.

The leading passengers came through the gates handing in their tickets. Then Catherine saw her father again, walking unsteadily. He had a shoulder-bag with gifts wrapped in Christmas paper sticking out of it. Seeing his daughter, he gestured vaguely with his hand. A kind of dismissive wave. The mother held on to Catherine's shoulders with two tight hands. The child had stopped jumping.

'Hey!' he shouted as he came to the gates. He had difficulty finding his ticket but the guard insisted on seeing it. When he came through Catherine ran to him. He hugged and lifted her off her feet, swirled her round unsteadily. For a terrible moment Catherine thought they were going to fall but he set her down and went to her mother. Her mother's face was stiff and turning away from the kiss.

'Brendan, you're drunk.'

'A drink on the train.' He was smiling. Still her mother's face was averted. She jingled her car keys and began pacing away. He shouted, 'A drink on the train at Chrissmus.'

Her mother turned, lowering her voice in the hope that he, too, would lower his.

'Please, don't make things any worse.'

'Christ Almighty. It was an accident.' He was still shouting. His face was red and his hair tousled. 'This is some sort of a bloody welcome.' He was aware that he was holding Catherine's hand and sank to his hunkers to be on a level with her face. She was stiff with embarrassment, smiling but looking round for advice from her mother.

'Wee darlin,' he said to her. Then whatever way he turned to get a parcel from his shoulder-bag he toppled over. He managed to hold himself up off the pigeon shit on the ground with one hand. Her mother walked away. A man, seeing a child involved, gave the drunk a hand up.

'Thanks mate. The condiments of the season to you.' Her father put his arm around Catherine's shoulder and she felt he was steadying himself rather than hugging her. She was frightened of him. Together they followed her mother. The condiments of the season.

As the grave slowly filled, the hollowness of the noise disappeared. The crowd turned away in ones and twos and walked back down towards the church. Catherine and her mother waited by the church doorway and accepted everyone's condolences. Mrs McKenna shook hands with a white-haired woman. Catherine hesitated. It was an instant before she recognised her music teacher. Her mother said, 'It was very good of you to come, Miss Bingham.' She shook hands with Catherine too. She'd become cheekbone thin, her hair had turned white and straw-like, but her skin was sallow – like a faded tan. She wore the same scarlet lipstick and still had the glasses with winged corners.

'Catherine – I'm so sorry.'

'Thank you.' Catherine tried to keep herself under

control. She bit her lower lip to stop herself crying. Miss Bingham's response was to pat her hand.

'How long are you home for?'

'A day or two.'

'You must call – if you feel up to it.'

'Thank you.'

'There is much to talk about,' said Miss Bingham, 'but, sadly, this isn't the time.'

Paddy moved about between the mourners, telling them that the pub would be opening just as soon as they got back and that Mrs McKenna would like to stand everyone a drink. There would also be a bite to eat and tea or coffee, if that was preferred. There were more substantial eats at the hotel for anyone who had travelled from afar.

For the first hour in the bar there was a quiet hum of conversation. Mrs McKenna sat in the corner – she was very rarely in the bar – and drank a glass of lemonade. She talked with whoever approached her. She listened and nodded at what was said, 'He's with his Maker now – there's no call to grieve.'

Townspeople, whiskey travellers, the Gaelic football people, priests, the opera crowd from Belfast, relatives, close and distant.

'Sure, all you can do is look forward to the day you can join him.'

'God bless you,' said Mrs McKenna. Catherine sat beside her and helped where she could, but she was not often called upon to contribute. She noticed that nobody organised anything. People just waited their turn and when her mother was free, they would approach her.

'Let's just be thankful to have had the privilege of knowing him.'

Someone pushed a tray of sausage rolls and sandwiches in front of Catherine. She picked an egg and mayonnaise to be polite. Gradually the place began to fill with cigarette smoke. The cold light from the upper window shone bluely through it. Her throat was becoming irritated and she began to cough. She asked to be excused. On her way out, she met Father Ferry. He said, 'You played extremely well this morning.'

'Thank you.' She choked back the word Father and moved past him, out the door and up the stairs.

There was no one in the kitchen. She discovered she had the egg sandwich still in her hand. She took a bite and chewed it slowly. Whoever had made them had forgotten the salt. She turned and saw the salt cellar on the sideboard. With the crease in its metal top. That probably happened the same Christmas.

The day before the funeral she had managed to blank things out. Today her head was full of him.

It was her Christmas job to help her mother set the table – with pickles and cranberry jelly and mustard – everything that could be thought of. The cutlery was a wedding present, still in its mahogany box. Eight place settings in all, because they had invited aunts and uncles and Father Desmond. There were eight linen napkins which had to be rolled up and slipped into silver rings – just like the seaside boarding house in Portstewart. Another wedding present of a silver salt and pepper – like two gleaming gun shells. Also a silver dish with a blue glass mustard pot inside with the tiniest spoon in the house. Catherine had cleaned all the silver with bits of grey-black wadding till it shone. It left her fingers black.

The crackers had been pulled and everyone had a paper hat. Brendan's was green.

'Ireland for ever,' he shouted and they all laughed.

After the turkey was carved and potatoes and vegetables served, Brendan picked up the salt cellar and shook it over his dinner. 'What's this? Dammit there's no salt.'

'How much have you had to drink, Brendan?'

'Not nearly enough. Where's the bloody salt?' He shook the salt cellar to show that it was light and empty. 'Salt is basic – it's just basic.'

'Did you not fill it, Catherine?'

'I forgot.'

Her mother got the packet of Saxa and brought it to the table. Brendan handed her the salt cellar. Mrs McKenna was annoyed that the whole Christmas dinner was going cold because of an oversight. She tried to unscrew the top half from the bottom but it wouldn't budge.

'Here, you do it.' She handed it to Brendan. He tried but nothing happened. Then he tried harder – until his knuckles where white and his hands trembled.

'Tight as a willick,' he said. 'It rusts from one year till the next.' He put it down between his knees and tried with the leverage of the length of his arm.

'Jesus – it won't budge.' His face had become bright red with the effort. 'Sure, we'll just use the packet.'

'Indeed you will not,' said her mother. 'On Christmas day.'

'Wait – wait a minute.' Brendan got up and went to the kitchen door.

'What are you going to do?'

Brendan opened the door as wide as it would go and put the top half of the salt cellar into the gap at the hinge side of the door.

'Crafty enough,' said Father Desmond.

'The rest of you may start,' said Mrs McKenna. 'The dinner'll be freezing by the time we get it.'

'Like sex without sin,' Brendan said.

'Brendan –'

'Present company, Brendan. Present company.' Father Desmond looked at Catherine and her father.

'An egg without salt.' Brendan laughed. 'Better for me to have a millstone tied around me neck.' He closed the door over, using it as a vice and tried to twist the salt cellar. Then his hat slipped over his eyes.

'Me hat – me hat. Catherine.' Catherine moved it to the back of his head.

The door gave a little jerk.

'Aw Jesus,' said Brendan. Then he looked at the priest. 'Excuse the oul tongue, Father.' He opened the door and took out the salt cellar. He began laughing. The top half had creased in the jaws of the door. 'Would you look at that?'

'My good wedding present. Look what you've done, Brendan.'

'I don't know me own strength.'

'You've had far too much oul booze, that's what.'

He set the silver salt cellar with its crease and its bowed-over head back on the table. Her mother was tight-lipped and didn't see the funny side of it. Brendan sat down to his dinner and lifted the packet of Saxa and sprinkled it on his potatoes. Her mother snapped it out of his hand and went to the kitchen. She poured a little volcano of salt on to a saucer and brought it to the table. She wiped the tiny silver spoon clean of mustard with her serviette and set it on the saucer.

'Anybody wants mustard – use your knife,' she said.

'Anyone wants salt,' said Brendan, 'you can cry your bloody eyes out for it.'

The next day was cloudy and overcast. Catherine and her mother walked towards the grave. There were wreaths piled on the freshly dug clay.

'I didn't get any time to pray,' said Mrs McKenna. 'There was too much going on – too much fuss yesterday.' They were the only people in the graveyard. Her mother stooped to try to read the writing on the cards.

'I don't have my glasses. Maybe, Catherine, you could get somebody to gather the cards and bring them up to the house. There's an awful lot.'

'Yes.' Catherine stood back, not wanting to interfere. Her mother blessed herself and stood praying. Catherine felt she shouldn't be there and walked away. There was a rookery behind the church and crows cawed and clicked as one came and one went, then in an explosive flurry they all rose at once flapping and cawing into the air.

The names of the same families appeared again and again on the headstones – O'Donnell and McPhee and Burns and McKee. There were other McKennas, cousins and second cousins. Graves with white marble chips topped with plastic flowers. She looked over her shoulder and her mother was still absorbed in prayer. There was a republican grave with an Irish tricolour in ceramic.

In Proud and Loving Memory
Of Staff Officer
Patrick Fleck.
Killed on active service

He gave his life for Ireland.

She remembered this boy. He had been in the same year as her at primary school. Fat, with a very big bum. None of the girls liked him. He had lived very close to the school and when his laces became undone in the playground somebody had seen him slip off home. When he came back they were neatly tied. He'd been killed since she'd moved to Scotland.

Janáček had written a piano sonata, *I:X:*1905, From the Street. Four sombre notes started the Adagio, then four more notes followed. Janáček was like that, clusters of short phrases, a feeling of randomness, of aimless exploration, of intense sadness, as if the piece was nosing around looking for a way home. The composer had written the work in response to the death of a youth, killed by Austrian troops on 1 October 1905 for demonstrating in support of the idea of a Czech university. She had played it in front of an audience many times and been shocked by her own intense response to it. The ending. Of chords played at little more than a whisper made her stop breathing – a barely audible passing bell. And if she played it as well as she could the audience stopped breathing too. After the last hushed notes she kept her hands poised above the keys for what seemed an eternity. She knew how well she had played by the reluctance of the audience to applaud. The longer they hesitated, the longer they put off breaking the spell, the better she had played. She dropped her hands to her lap and no one dared break the silence with clapping. It seemed unfinished – it WAS unfinished. Janáček had burned the last movement. After playing what was left he was consumed with self-criticism and, not knowing someone had made a copy, he threw the manuscript into the River Vltava. He must have realised his mistake because he eventually consented to the publication of the remaining two-movement structure.

Someone who knows the end of the work begins to clap – one, two, three hand claps like pistol shots in the silence and everyone else joins in and the volume of the applause grows. She bows her head. It is not for her, it is for Janáček. Maybe it should be for the unknown copyist.

It is only when she plays one of her own pieces that she feels she can accept the applause. She made the work, she played it as it should be played. Something now exists which has never existed before. She remembers the childish awe of stepping on fresh snow, of marking it with her small foot.

She wondered about writing something for Paddy Fleck – what would it be like? The boy who couldn't tie his shoelaces yet died for his country. Was the nationalism Janáček represented different from the kind espoused by the Provisional IRA? She could write a piece for piano and call it *On an Attempt to Burn Down the Linen Hall Library*. She was standing staring at this grave when she heard her mother say, 'The Fleck boy.'

'Yeah.'

'His mother's not been right since.' Mrs McKenna turned. 'Let's walk home the long way.'

'Through the woods?'

'Why not.'

The woods were on a hillside at the edge of the town. Alongside the path was a flat area of grass which stretched for miles. Parts of the path were overgrown with brambles and elder. Janáček had written another piano piece, *On the Overgrown Path*. In nine sections, each one bleaker than the one which went before. Bleak beyond words. But that's what music was – emotion beyond words.

'I meant to say to you – Miss Bingham phoned. She invited you tomorrow – for coffee – at eleven. I said you'd be there. Your flight's not until the afternoon.'

'Yeah.'

There was still a layer of winter leaves on the ground and their feet made scuffling sounds.

'You're very quiet. Is anything wrong?'

'No.'

She knows, Catherine thought. Somehow she senses. She knows about Anna.

'Are you sure?'

Catherine tried to think of an excuse. 'It's just Dad used to take me this way all the time.'

'We did our share of walking out here too.' There were sections of the path which were too narrow and they had to walk in single file but when they came together again Catherine would crook her arm.

'Hook on.'

'That was the airfield during the war.'

'Yes – I know,' said Catherine. 'He told me that every time too.'

'Ohhh – I beg your pardon.'

'I didn't mean it like that.'

'I know you didn't,' her mother said. 'But when they sited the airfield there beside the American camp people were afraid they'd get bombed. Like the Blitz in Belfast. The Germans would try for the airfield and hit the town. But it never happened.' Sparrows cheeped monotonously and their noise echoed through the wood. In the distance they could still hear the crows from behind the church. 'After the IRA bombing your father joked about sleeping in the safe.' She smiled a little. 'To be safe.'

A magpie flew across the airfield and fanned out its blue and white tail before landing. Her mother looked around to try and see another one.

'Don't be so superstitious,' said Catherine.

They came across a waterlogged part of the path.

'What do we do now?'

'Go round it.' They helped one another up the slope, walking almost on the sides of their shoes, putting their knuckles to the ground. They half slithered, half walked on to the path again.

'Terra firma,' said her mother. They linked arms again and walked in silence. Catherine felt her mother gathering herself to ask the difficult question. But she became conversational.

'Where are you teaching now?'

'I'm not. I'm trying to write music.'

'Who or what for?'

'Myself.'

'Lord God. There can't be too much money in that.'

'There isn't. I'm signing on.'

'You gave up a good job teaching?' her mother's voice was incredulous.

'Yes.'

'Is the dole money enough?'

'No.' She smiled and sighed. Then her face straightened and she said, 'Why d'you always think there must be an employer?'

'It's the way the world works.'

Another magpie landed with a flourish in the field. Mrs McKenna smiled but didn't draw Catherine's attention to it. Catherine said, 'What about the bar?'

'I haven't a notion – maybe Paddy will manage it for me.'

'Sell it?'

'Maybe. It's too soon. What made you give up the teaching?'

'I dunno.' Catherine shrugged. 'I wanted to write music.'

'Like the thing on the radio?'

'Yes.'

There was silence. Her mother was tight-lipped.

'There was some who were none too keen on it.'

'That doesn't surprise me.'

'I just don't understand music nowadays. It all sounds the same.'

'That's because you're not listening.'

'Don't talk down to me, Catherine. It used to be that music was aimed at the likes of me.'

'Who's you?'

'People. People with two ears and a toe to tap.'

'If it was in a form you knew – you might cope better.'

'You don't *cope* with music, you listen to it.'

'All I'm saying is that the music might be easier if you knew the form.'

'What's that supposed to mean?'

'I'm trying to write a mass.'

'I thought all that was beneath you.'

'No, it's not . . .' she hesitated.

'Do you still believe in it?'

'Did Dad not tell you? About what was said on the phone?'

'He liked to protect me – sometimes.'

'You were always a great one for telling the truth. The answer is – not really.'

'Not really what?'

'I don't really believe in it.'

'Do you ever go? To pray you'll get it back?'

'No.'

'Then why do it? Why write a mass?'

'It's a great form, a great structure.'

'How dare you?' Her mother detached her arm from Catherine's. 'How dare you, Catherine?'

'What?'

'Talk like that about something your father and I think is . . . You used to be such a nice girl.'

'What do you mean?'

'I don't know what's happened . . . you've changed.'
She shook her head as if to dismiss her.

'If I agree with you, I'm a nice girl. If I disagree, I'm the worst in the world.'

'Don't talk to me.' Her mother's voice was really clipped now. 'It's one thing to do what you like – it's another to mock.' She bustled ahead to walk by herself. Catherine saw the foolishness of the two of them walking home in single file.

'Listen . . .'

'You never came home once in five years.'

'I was told not to.'

'He didn't really mean that. He was always saying things he regretted. And there was too much foolish man in him to take anything back.' Catherine said nothing but sighed loudly enough for her mother to hear.

'This is not the right time.'

'Why didn't you invite us to Glasgow? For your graduation. That hurt him as well, missing that.'

'I was fed up with the whole bloody business of education.'

'And religion, by the sound of it. You'd gone away to that University his talented wee girl and you'd come back a heathen.'

'People must be allowed to make up their own minds. There should be no interference.'

'There's a heck of a difference between interfering and pointing out what's right and what's wrong.' Her mother sighed and there was a kind of shudder with it as well. It was beginning to get dark. 'Would you not think of staying a day or two longer?'

'No – there's people depending on me.'

'Who?'

'I said I'd be back.'

'Fair enough. Ask me no questions and I'll tell you no lies.'

'Can somebody run me to the airport?'

'I'll do it. The more there is to do the less time there is to think.'

They emerged from the woods on to the tarmac road. Her mother began to cry.

'It'll be unbearable when I start to miss him. On top of this.'

'Catherine! Catherine! It's after ten.' She opened her eyes and saw her mother, holding a cup, bending over her. 'I said you'd go to Miss Bingham's at eleven.' Catherine rose up on her elbow. 'That'd say it all if you slept in for an eleven o'clock appointment. With Miss Bingham of all people. The other side are very quick to pounce.'

Catherine reached out for the glass of water. There was a bottle of her tablets beside it.

'There's a cup of tea for you.'

'I don't like tea, first thing.' She drank off some of the tepid water.

'It'll not go to waste in this house.' Her mother began to sip the tea. She made a face. 'I don't know how you drink it without milk. It's that bitter. What time's your flight?'

'Three-thirty. From Aldergrove.'

'What are they?' Her mother pointed to the small bottle

of tablets. Catherine didn't answer. 'I mean what are they for?'

'Anti-depressants.'

'Are you depressed?'

'Naw – the doctor put me on those for my verrucas.'

'I'm serious.'

'I've been feeling very bad about myself lately.' Her mother set down her cup on the bedside table and put a hand on her daughter's bare shoulder. 'Panic attacks, getting uptight about things. The doctor said I was depressed. Clinically. He gave me some tablets to take.'

'Oh dear. You poor thing.' Her mother gave Catherine's shoulder a little squeeze and sat down on the bed beside her. Her hand remained on her shoulder. 'Will they put it away? Will they make you feel better?'

'I don't rightly know. He says it takes them a long time to build up.' Catherine's voice was on the edge of crying. 'I'm feeling – not too bad recently – until this happened with Dad. It kind of knocked me back a bit.'

'How long have you been taking them?'

'Ages.'

'Are they like Valium? Can you get hooked on them?'

'They say no.'

'And how long have you been depressed?'

'A year or so – maybe more.'

'God – why didn't you tell us?'

'When you're like that you don't want to tell anybody anything.'

'Why would someone like you be depressed?' Catherine shrugged and tears filled her eyes. Her mother, now sitting close to her, felt the shrug in her hand rather than saw it. 'One of Brendan's brothers had to get that electric shock treatment. In England. It did him good.'

Catherine was now crying hard – tears streamed down her cheeks and her head was tipped forward. Hair stuck to the damp of her face.

'It would have solved everything if the bloody plane had crashed on the way over.'

'Don't say that.'

'I can't help the way I feel. Have you never woken up and wanted to die?'

'This last couple of mornings I've been close.'

'I'm sorry – I'm not thinking.'

'Faith and prayer will see us both through.'

'You feel bad because a bad thing has happened.' Catherine's voice was raised – she was shouting, trying to make the words distinct despite her crying. 'I feel bad no matter what happens. Practically all the time. I've got ten tons of bad stuff and I can hang it on anything that comes along.' She banged the side of her head with the flat of her hand. 'If the problem is in here – in your brain – then dying seems the only way out.'

'If you're as bad as that I'm going to phone the doctor right away.' Her mother produced a handkerchief and handed it to her. Catherine blew her nose quietly.

'I'm OK. Anyway, I have my own doctor. Tell me about Dad's brother. I didn't know that.'

'He was always religious but then it began to get so that he was going to every mass for miles – and devotions. He'd sit for hours in the church praying. Full of scruples . . . Long ago they'd have made him a saint. Nowadays they said he was mentally ill.'

'But did he get better?' Catherine asked.

'He got better. And so will you.' Her mother smiled and said, 'Then after he got better, he died.' She picked up a hairbrush from the bedside table and began pulling the hair back from the wetness of her daughter's face. Catherine relaxed, put her head back and listened to the hollow swish of the brush.

'It used to be Dad who brushed my hair. He loved working with it when it was long.' Catherine put on a deep voice. '*Sit still − you're like a hen on a hot griddle.*' The brushing had now become rhythmic. Catherine's head moved a little in opposition to each stroke. Her mother said, 'Geraldine made a grand job of it yesterday.'

'Yes.' Catherine stopped and breathed in deeply. 'Mum, it's a kind of post-natal depression.'

'What? What do you mean?'

'The year before . . . I had a baby.'

'Jesus . . .' She set the hairbrush down on the bed and withdrew her hand from Catherine's shoulder.

'You're not joking me − are you? Like the verrucas?'

'No.'

'Oh Jesus − Catherine, Catherine . . .' Her mother slid off the bed and stood, not knowing what to do with her hands.

'I'm sorry − there's no nice way to say these things. There's no right time.'

'I'm just glad your father's dead.'

'What an awful thing to say.'

'Well, it's true,' she was shouting now. She was also beginning to cry. 'If the heart attack hadn't killed him, this certainly would.'

'Is it any wonder I didn't tell you, then?'

Her mother stood facing away from her, transfixed in the centre of the room. Then she went to the dressing table and straightened the doilies under the ornamental glass candlesticks. She covered her face with both hands, making a cage of her fingers.

'Where is . . .? I mean, what have you . . .? Oh you dirty . . . Jesus, Catherine, how awful. How *awful*.'

'This is not getting us anywhere.'

'Where is it now?'

'With a friend of mine. An ex-teacher. In Glasgow.'

'What is it? A boy or a girl?'

'A girl.'

'She'll break her mother's heart – just like you're breaking mine.'

Her mother strode out of the room, crying loudly and slammed the door after her.

Catherine got dressed and sat on the side of the bed and wept. She took one of her tablets and washed it down with the tepid water. She began to pack her things into the hold-all, her face streaming. The best thing would be just to get out. She put her few bits and pieces of dirty washing into a polythene bag. Go visit Miss Bingham. Say nothing. Ask at the Post Office for the bus times.

She looked at herself in the triple mirrors of the dressing table. Three times the reason to stop crying. How could she make a dignified exit? She lifted the cup of tea her mother had left on the bedside table and turned the handle round. She sipped from the far side of the rim. It was no longer hot but it was all she was going to get.

She went out on to the landing and took her raincoat

from the hall stand. It was hard to believe in this day and age. Catherine went down the stairs, past the public bar and out into the street. She tried to cram down the fight that was inside her. She mustn't let it get to her, mustn't get angry. On a slippery slope the only way was down. She must think of something else. Her mother's pain was not her problem. It was the fault of years of conforming. She mustn't think, must for the short time left at home wear blinkers. Protect herself in her fragile state. An earthquake in one department created tidal waves in others. Think of something else. A violin bow is made of pernambuca wood and horsehair. Pernambuca comes only from South America and it is the only wood with the right amount of flexibility. Horsehair is hair from a horse's tail. Beneath a microscope the hair can be seen to be saw-toothed and this is why vibrations occur when the bow is drawn across the strings.

There was a new set of intertwined lines of dog piss running diagonally to the gutter. Tell it slant. It was Emily Dickinson who'd said that. Not about dogs pissing, but about telling it slant. Now *she* was somebody to be admired – working away all her life – doing good work. How unlike our own dear mother. *Don't think of her.* She was full of obliqueness of a different sort. The Northern Ireland art form. Wait till I get you home.

Emily Dickinson was kept in her place by another poet, a man friend of the family – Oliver Wendell Holmes or somebody. Was that his name? Whoever he was, he had three names and said her work wasn't quite up to publishable standard. Too delicate, not strong enough to publish, was what he said. And her, streets ahead of him.

Not even in the same league, God love him. When she died her sister opened a cupboard and hundreds of poems – nine hundred and sixty-two of them, to be precise – tumbled out. In packets tied with twine. In her mother's case it would be nine hundred and sixty mass cards and prayers and relics. *I said stop thinking of her.* Thomas Wentworth Higginson – that was his name, not Oliver Wendell Homes. With names like that you could stand firm. Steady as a three-legged stool. So utterly masculine. The exception to this was Huang Xiao Gang. Somehow his three names suited him. Sir Hamilton bloody Harty was another one. A name like that was a licence to grow a big moustache.

That's all men were really – three-legged stools. Two legs and the other thing. A dick. Prop them up on it, like a shooting stick.

Quinn's shop was owned by two grey-haired sisters neither of whose name was Quinn, Grace and Emily Madden. They had seemed old even when Catherine was a child.

The bell chinked as she pushed the door open. There was some paper wedged into the bell – so that it had a strike note but no hum note. The shop was tiny – a divided front room of a house. The counter was head high with a gap the size of a TV screen out of which Grace or Emily served. The place was crammed with sweets and cheap toys. They also sold small framed copies of the Sacred Heart and Our Lady of Perpetual Succour. A curtained door into the Maddens' living-room gave a swish. Emily's grey head appeared the way a priest's would in confession.

'Yes?'

'A half pound box of Roses, please.'

The head disappeared. Voice only.

'I've no Roses left. Would Dairy Box do?'

'That'll be fine.'

Emily came on screen again with the box of chocolates. Before she passed it over she said, 'Is it you . . . Catherine?'

'Yes.'

'My eyes is going, altogether. Or else you've changed out of all recognition.' She paused and then her voice became a hushed whisper, 'We were all devastated to hear about Brendan.'

Catherine nodded and Emily went on about how good a man her father was. All Catherine could do was agree.

'A wee present for mammy?'

'No. I'm going to see Miss Bingham.'

'She hasn't been keeping well of late. So I believe. Up to the Mid-Ulster Hospital for tests. It doesn't look good.'

'I hadn't heard.'

'Are you still winning prizes for the music?'

'Not so much now,' said Catherine. 'You get to a stage . . .'

'The town was proud of you on graduation day – the big photo in the *Mid-Ulster Mail*. Tell me this and tell me no more – how many in the year would get the first-class honours?'

Catherine shrugged.

'Not many . . . one or two.'

'But how many in your year?'

'One.'

'And you were it. From a wee place like this. You showed them.' Catherine handed her the money. Reaching up made her feel like a child again. Emily gave her the chocolates in a brown paper bag.

There were iron railings by the Old People's Home which, as a child, she had loved to chatter a stick against. Now she touched them gently with her fingers. Without a sound. She was too early and decided to walk the long way round the town, over the back road.

It was her mother who had started the whole music thing. She had asked Miss Bingham, when Catherine was ten, to call and give her piano lessons. Each Wednesday afternoon after school Miss Bingham would arrive at the pub on her breadcart of a bicycle, ringing the bell and dismounting before it came to a halt. She pedalled flat-foot because her saddle was always too low. It was odd to see such a woman riding a bicycle. She claimed she did it because the rheumatism was stiffening her up, even then. It was her interpretation of regular moderate exercise, which the doctor had prescribed to oil her joints.

She taught Catherine things the child seemed to know by instinct. After the first month her mother said at the Sunday dinner table. 'Brendan, we have a very special girl here. She is learning faster than Miss Bingham can teach her. Miss Bingham says it's all inside her head and all she has to do is draw it out.' Catherine had loved her mother saying that. *Think about music.*

When she was writing she always thought in terms of the rhythm first – she could not begin to write anything until she knew that part of it. Like an actor who could never get into a part until they got the walk, or the moustache, or the voice, or the three names. For her it was the rhythm. Everything began to come after that.

She had composed some pieces for the school orchestra on the island. When she joined the school they had a particularly good brass section because the previous music teacher had been in the army, in the band of the Coldstream Guards. As she rehearsed them for the Christmas concert she found them a willing and talented bunch of players.

She told them about Vivaldi in eighteenth-century Venice, a priest who never bothered to say mass – music was enough for him. How he had prepared and drilled an orchestra of orphan girls, dressed handsomely in white, to the point where they were considered the best in Europe. So Handel said when he visited. Vivaldi wrote most of his music, 400 concerti, to be played by them, the girls of the Ospedale della Pieta. In the history of music this orchestra of deprived females seems to have been unique. Girl bastards who until recently would have been thrown into the canals of the city were now addressed as *Maestra*. They were known by their names and instruments – *Maestra Lucretia della Viola, Maestra Cattarin dal Cornetto*.

The first thing she wrote for her school group was a 'Suite for Trumpetists and Tromboners'. At the Christmas concert the Headmaster, a business studies graduate, said that it had been 'very interesting' to hear it. Then he drew her attention to the printed programme.

'Eh . . . should that not be the other way round. Trumpeters and trombonists?' Catherine had smiled and gone off to praise her players again. About this time Graeme McNicol of the BBC had contacted her again for

a strand of programmes to do with music and schools –
he'd heard of their brass reputation. She told him of the
piece she'd just written. This was enough to tempt the
BBC to visit Islay with an outside broadcast unit and
record a rehearsal and interviews with pupils and their
teacher – a sort of master class, she laughingly called it.
They interviewed Catherine by the shore so that the
waves would be in the background. Then they broadcast a
complete performance of the Suite. Again the headmaster
had approached her to correct the title before it went into
the *Radio Times*. He said he was desperately afraid of
wrong things like that, emanating from his school, being
printed in a magazine which went into most of the homes
in Britain.

Miss Bingham lived in a double-fronted stone house across
the road from the Church of Ireland parish church. She
answered the door and shaded her eyes with her hand. She
looked angular and awkward.

'Come in, come in. You know the drill.'

Catherine hung her coat in the cloakroom and followed
Miss Bingham across the parquet hallway. The old woman
wore large black slippers, misshapen by her bunions and
moved with a kind of flat ski-ing motion into the sitting
room.

'Sit yourself down, Cathy.'

Before she sat Catherine handed her the parcel. Miss
Bingham looked inside the brown paper bag.

'Oooh, Dairy Box – it was good of you to remember
my favourites – thank you. How very thoughtful.' She set
the chocolates on the coffee table. There was a tray with

coffee things on it already there. Miss Bingham said, 'I'll just put the kettle on.'

Catherine sat looking around her. After a couple of years of Miss Bingham coming to the McKennas' house Catherine had come here twice a week for lessons. It was also from here they'd set out for the concerts in Belfast. The conductor at the time was Ricardo Cossotto, a man with the glossiest, blackest hair she had ever seen. She imagined him washing it in a barrel of rain-water just before the performance and blow-drying it as the orchestra waited. Then he'd come on-stage with it perfect, his black suit, his stiff butterfly collar and white bow tie immaculate.

Miss Bingham always got the cheap seats in the choir stalls – she said she preferred them. The orchestra was playing outwards, away from them, but they could see the conductor's face, his every gesture. They could read the intimacies between him and his players – a look of praise, a look willing them to play pianissimo – a breath above silence, and at climactic moments a nonchalant look of *well done lads* when they rose to the occasion and the French horns got through without fluffing. He did not use a baton but his hand movements were enough. Miss Bingham told her in whispers between movements the story of Richard Strauss who, when asked how one should conduct, replied 'without perspiring'. It was one of the things she liked about Cossotto, this lack of flamboyance. He seemed to make up for it in intensity and conduct in tiny gestures shielded from the main audience by his body. Both hands cupped and taut – suppressing, suppressing – not yet, not yet, actually pressing down – wait, wait and then letting them go with a flaring of the fingers. Now – yes now. Now you can be your best. It was all in his eyes. By the end of a performance the shine of perspiration was all over his face and a few strands of his perfect black hair hung awry, stuck to his forehead.

'A charlatan of a showman,' Miss Bingham would whisper, unable to take her eyes off him. 'That Richard Strauss – what would he know?'

Catherine heard the click of the kettle in the kitchen as it came to the boil. The room smelled of stale cigarette smoke but there was also the faintest smell of oil of wintergreen and disinfectant. A scallop-shell ashtray had three white cork-tips stuck into it, each marked with a crescent of lipstick. In front of the half-leaded bay window was a concert grand with its shark's fin of a lid open, blocking the light. Catherine walked over to the fire and stood with her back to it, looking down at the Persian rug. She extended her hands behind her to warm them.

Once, they'd driven to Belfast to see Paul Tortelier playing the Elgar Cello Concerto. Catherine had been overwhelmed. That head – tilted back, the eagle-like profile. The white hair. His style of bowing. The involvement of the body in the playing. The precision of a note registered in the raising of an eyebrow. But above all, the sound he made, his phrasing.

Afterwards the drive back took almost an hour. For safety reasons Catherine always travelled in the back and Miss Bingham would talk over her shoulder to her. Gradually Catherine would slide down the leather seat under the tartan car rug. Miss Bingham's voice, the drone of the engine, the hum of the blow heater – the occasional drubbing of wheels on the cat's eyes as she pulled out to pass someone. When she was asked a question Catherine didn't answer because she was warm and almost asleep. To speak would be to break the spell. Both hands between her knees, her cheek on the leather of the back seat which was ribbed like the sand of the seashore.

Miss Bingham came back into the room carrying a steaming kettle. She looked frail as well as awkward.

'I was *so* proud of you.' She sat down and spooned coffee granules into the cups. 'I'm sorry I don't have real coffee, but it just doesn't keep − if you're the only one drinking it.'

'It's OK.'

'As I say, I was as proud as punch. I got settled into this very armchair and I listened to every bar of it.'

'I'm glad.'

'The BBC Scottish Symphony Orchestra.'

'They are *so* good.'

'It was truly splendid. Forgive me, but I said to myself − that is by an ex-pupil of mine.'

'Thank you.' They smiled at each other.

'What was it you called it again?'

'*Vernicle.*'

'I was confusing it with the word votive − knew it began with a Vee − like a votive mass or votive candle. What does it mean?'

'A vernicle is a pilgrim's medal. Chaucer's Pardoner had one sewn on to his hat to show where he'd been.'

'A difficult word for difficult music. It's not the kind of thing I'd listen to doing the dishes. Why did you write it the way you did?'

'It was the way it came.'

'But very powerful. It demanded that you pay attention. Sometimes I have difficulty with the *avant-garde*. There's a gallery in London I've been to and it's difficult to tell what's going on. A bag of nails, a ladder, a hammer – a crisp bag in the corner. Is it an exhibition or are they preparing an exhibition? Is the artist asking me to pay attention to something trivial or important? It's the same with music. Is the orchestra actually getting ready to play something or are they playing it? Are they tuning up or performing? Well, I didn't find that with your piece. It was coherent. I wanted to hear what happened next.' Miss Bingham looked around for her cigarettes and lighter. 'Do you mind?'

'No.'

She lit a cigarette and inhaled it so deeply her cheeks went concave. She coughed a little but made an effort to control it. When her voice was free she said, 'There was some coverage about the concert in the English papers.'

'Oh that . . .'

'A Roman Catholic using Protestant drums. The Lambeg angle.' Miss Bingham rolled her eyes.

'They wanted to make a whole thing of it,' said Catherine. 'I said I just liked the sound.'

'Good for you.'

'But they *are* a great sound – they inspire intense feelings. Really complicated rhythms.'

'That wouldn't interest the press. All they want to get is a story about cementing the divide, or bridging the sectarian gulf.'

'I told them it's the kind of drum a child wants to play.'

Miss Bingham laughed and it started her coughing. There was an upper throat clearing and, deep down, the rumble of disturbed stones. The light from the window made her colour seem worse than at the funeral. Catherine asked the question before she could stop herself.

'How are you?'

'Not so hot. This past year I've been feeling – y'know,' she waved her cigarette hand in a circular motion, 'and the doctor sent me for some tests – the results weren't particularly encouraging. In fact they were downright depressing.'

'Oh . . .'

'But there's chemotherapy and God knows what. There are other options. We're not at the end of the road yet. The Binghams are a hardy lot.' She hesitated. 'Maybe not. It just occurs to me I'm the only one left.' She offered Catherine a Jaffa Cake. 'In fact, let me rephrase that. The Binghams are *not* a hardy lot.' They both laughed.

'But you're looking well.'

'Aye, whatever you say, say nothing.' Miss Bingham stubbed out her longish cigarette among the others in the ashtray. 'They've told me to give these things up. What about yourself?'

'Fine.' Catherine hesitated. 'I was a bit down last year.'

'Any reason? Apart from everything?'

'I'd had a baby . . .'

'Congratulations. I hadn't heard.'

'I only told my mother this morning. Bit of a raised eyebrow.'

'I'd say so. Boy or a girl?'

'A wee girl, Anna. I'm dying to get back. This is the first time I've really been away from her.'

'I suppose it's a bit early to start her on the piano.'

'And beat Master Crotch to it.' They both smiled. 'You were a great teacher.'

'Nonsense, that was only the basics. Anyway lessons are learned, not taught.'

'No, a teacher is for a particular time. I needed to be taught those things then. And in that way.'

'Who else? If a teacher is for a particular time, who else?'

'Huang Xiao Gang.'

Catherine told Miss Bingham about the composer who'd come to do some teaching in her final year at Queen's in Belfast. And about how he had made her think differently about sound.

They talked about everything. About how good the menthol cigarettes were for Miss Bingham's breathing, about John Field's *Nocturnes*, about Cookstown market and how the price of potatoes had soared in recent years, about Britten's choral work, about Catherine's baby, about Miss Bingham's arthritic hands and how she could no longer play. She held them up for Catherine to see. They didn't look too bad – just a little bit like slanted fists.

'If my joints are not moved they cease to be of use. The bike was a way of keeping supple.' She waggled her fingers slowly. 'But now I'm completely inflexible. We're two of a kind – both of us are a bit thran.'

'Me? Thran?'

'Remember you wouldn't stand for the Hallelujah Chorus?'

'I did the first year. Then I found out *why*. All because some bloody King George the First or Second did it three hundred years ago.'

'Can you imagine how I felt? My little charge – sitting – while the whole of Ulster's concert-going public stood.'

'What a piece of nonsense that was.'

'We live in a country where such things matter. Ulster people are far too polite to the other side. Nobody speaks their mind except to their own sort. Do you remember the joke you made?'

Catherine smiled and said, 'Nobody should stand for this.'

Miss Bingham opened the Dairy Box and offered it to Catherine.

'No, you must have first pick – it's your present.'

'Turkish Delight – the mysterious East,' she said. 'What was your man's name again?'

'Huang Xiao Gang.'

'You hear we have a Chinese restaurant now?' Catherine nodded and had a Country Fudge. Miss Bingham rested her cheek against the padded wing of her chair.

'I'll not stay long,' said Catherine.

'What you mean is I look tired.'

'No . . .'

'I'm not too tired to listen. Play me something, preferably of your own.'

Catherine hesitated. 'I can't believe this. But I feel shy – in front of you.'

'Nonsense. I've always been a slight fan of yours.'

'That's maybe what I mean.' Catherine got up and

moved to the bay window. She sat down on the piano stool.

'This is from a suite of piano pieces I'm working on. They're very short.'

'Mercifully,' said Miss Bingham and laughed. 'No, I owe it to the composer to listen to the music with the same intensity as it was composed.'

'They're like *haiku* for piano. And very quiet.' Catherine raised her hands above the keys, then lowered them again. 'There should be about ten of them in all, but I've only completed five. They're about Vermeer's rooms, maybe more about the women in the rooms. The first is *A Girl Asleep*, then *A Girl Reading a Letter*, then *Milkmaid* and . . . and *Young Woman with a Water Jug*. I've forgotten the last one. It'll come to me. I only know the first two by heart.' Again she raised her hands above the keyboard. 'Oh . . . the last one is *Woman Holding Balance*.'

She began to play. Miss Bingham remained where she was. The music seemed tentative. Little clusters of dissonances gave it a random, melancholy feel as if it had never been thought about before. Like a child seeking out a tune but never succeeding. Miss Bingham's eyes were closed. Her clenched hand was to the side of her cheek, bearing the weight of her head. Behind the sleeping girl in the Vermeer, a door was open into another room, empty of furniture. The room and its echo, achieved with subtlety in the piano writing, created an air of mystery. It faded, died softly as if not to wake the girl asleep.

Miss Bingham remained motionless waiting for the second piece. When it began there was something about her absorption in listening which mirrored the absorption of the girl reading the letter. Focused on other. Paying attention to the exclusion of everything else. She does not see the familiar leaded window or her reflection in it. The apple green curtain. The Persian rug. This piece is different in its strength, its simplicity and directness. When it was over Miss Bingham nodded and opened her eyes.

'The mystery of notes in their proper places.'

'Vermeer was a man who could paint women,' said Catherine. 'Do you know the paintings?'

'Only from books. He began by painting religious subjects. Then he turned to the ordinary – elevated it. Made saints of you, me and the likes of us.' Catherine nodded her head, agreeing. 'You play so well. And write so well. As Nadia Boulanger says, one does nothing good without passion; nothing excellent by passion alone. Both of those pieces are great. Very intense.' She made a wigwam of her misshapen fingers and tapped her chest-bone. 'Inner music. I would love to hear them all. They have both passion and pattern.' Catherine stood and made her way back to her chair.

'What started you on Vermeer?'

'Messiaen – he's supposed to see sound as colour and I wondered – what if the reverse happened. People talk about loud colours – you'd come away from a Matisse exhibition deafened.' Miss Bingham laughed, tried not to cough, putting her hand to her throat. The cough did not come. 'Then I asked myself what would Vermeer sound like?'

Catherine accepted an offer of another cup.

'Music hurts us in an allowable, almost palatable way,' said Miss Bingham as she spooned coffee and poured water. 'But nothing works so well as real life. It has no competitors whatsoever.'

Catherine nodded and lifted her coffee.

'Thanks.'

'Are you working on anything else?'

'I'm trying a thing with voices.'

'What?'

'A mass.'

'Phew.' Miss Bingham said the word. Catherine grinned.

'A Latin mass.'

'Even more phew.'

'At the moment it's only bits and pieces.'

'I've always known your Roman Catholicism was very important to you.'

'It was. At one time.'

'And now?' Catherine shook her head. 'Why choose it as a vehicle then?'

'I don't know. I suppose I *am* thran – always the awkward customer. There's not too many masses written by women.' Catherine laughed. 'It's a way of getting my own back because they wouldn't let me serve on the altar.'

There was a long silence as Miss Bingham rearranged herself in the chair.

'My only consolation recently has been religion.'

'I'm sorry I didn't mean to be flippant.'

'But you're right – belief nowadays is so difficult. According to the experts you can't even take the Bible as gospel any more. I believe in you and me and the likes of us. And I believe in my Church. I believe in the trappings every bit as much as I believe in the religion.'

'It's *only* the trappings I believe in,' said Catherine. Miss Bingham considered this.

'The practice of my religion is a great joy to me. It's a way of being human – like music – it is community.' As she said this she made a gesture with her misshapen hands. 'I like its rituals, its support, the ivy on the bricks – everything about it. Even the Reverend Young doesn't put me off. Around here we call him the sinister minister.' She sat forward in her seat and her eyes seemed too wide. 'But all of that is unimportant when it comes to what happens between us. Not you and me – although in this case it *was* you and me. That night I listened to your concert – just before Christmas – the same week the doctor told me things were not as they should be. It was all just beginning to sink in. And when I sat down I was . . . a person can be too much locked up in their own mind – isolated even – then something happens to say no – someone else has been through this. You are not the only one. *I am where you have been.* Your music spoke to me that night.'

Both were quiet. Miss Bingham lit another menthol cigarette, sparking the lighter with her thumb many times before it flared. She said, 'It gave me hope.' The cigarette was still in her mouth and moved up and down as she spoke.

'Thank you.' Catherine's voice was very quiet. The trail of blue smoke hovered and headed for the chimney. At the last moment it swooped up.

'I don't mean for a change in . . . what I have,' said Miss Bingham. 'Our sort doesn't go with that kind of thing –

Lourdes and the like. No – listening to it gave me hope. And joy. The end gave me great joy.'

Catherine looked at the fire when the coals collapsed and the flames flared up.

'Will I put some more on?'

'Yes – it's still chilly.'

Catherine got up and went to the coal scuttle and began building the fire. The claws of the metal tongs clacked together when they slipped off a lump. Miss Bingham watched her as if unable to move. Catherine said, 'I'll go when I've this done.'

'I now have to take a nap in the middle of the day.'

'Oh I'm sorry. I've overstayed.' She stood. Miss Bingham's eyes followed her up. 'Do you want me to wash these cups?'

'No, dear. I have a woman comes in every day. To give a hand.' Miss Bingham made a great effort to get out of her chair. Catherine put out a hand to help her to her feet. She felt too light. They walked into the hall.

'I'll photocopy the rest of the Vermeer pieces and send them to you when they're finished.' Catherine put on her raincoat.

'I'd like that very much. It was very good of you to call. Don't leave it so long the next time.'

'Are you all right?'

'Yes, dear.'

'Goodbye then.'

'Goodbye.'

Catherine wandered about the town, past her primary school where, because it was lunchtime, the children were screaming their heads off in the yard. Then on across the bridge. She stood looking down into the river. At this point it was shallow and stony. There were times of the year when you could see fish facing upstream but not now. Some people she knew stared at her and she nodded to them and moved on. Past the Chinaman's and the police barracks. She stopped to look in Curran's window – a haberdasher's, used all the time by Granny Boyd. She went in and after the required amount of conversation bought a length of red satin ribbon, enough for two bows, which old Mr Curran wound around his fingers and popped into a white paper bag. She considered going for a coffee in the small café on the square but it would be embarrassing. Everybody would want to know why she wasn't drinking coffee at home. Besides, the noise of the pneumatic drills and power saws went on and on. She gave up and went home.

If her mother wanted to say goodbye she could. If not, so be it. Catherine climbed the stairs and went into the bedroom to pick up her things. She didn't bother to take off her raincoat. Her bag was packed and sitting on the bed where she'd left it. She heard the clink of car keys and her mother came out of the kitchen and across the landing with her own coat on.

'I said I'd run you for three-thirty – so I will.' She spoke with her face averted. The way the undertaker had done.

'I can get a bus.' Her mother did not answer but led the way down the stairs, the car keys in her hand. She looked at her watch.

'You have to be there an hour before. And it'll take us

the best part of an hour to get there. So we're all right. There's some more talking to be done.' She spoke in to Paddy who was mopping the floor of the bar.

'We're for the airport.'

'Fair enough. It was good to see you Catherine – don't leave it so long the next time.'

'Goodbye Paddy – thanks for everything.'

The two women got into the car.

'So how did you get on at Miss Bingham's?'

'She'll be dead before the summer.'

'God help and protect her.'

It was a cold day but bright with sunshine and blue sky. When Mrs McKenna had negotiated the lorries and cement mixers littering the street she said, 'So how am I supposed to react to your news?'

'I don't know. That's for you to decide.'

'Does it have a father?'

'It also has a name.'

'What?'

'Anna.'

Having passed through all the dust and debris of the reconstruction the windscreen was dirty. Her mother squirted water on to it and the wipers cleared two overlapping quadrants.

'Are you married?'

'No. Look, things are not the same as in your day.'

'Don't I know it. The young ones nowadays – it would frighten you what they get up to. You only have to look at any women's magazine. It would make your hair stand on end. In my day they'd write in and ask if it was all right to kiss a boy. Now they want to know if it's all right to kiss his what-ya-macallit.'

'Easy Mum. Keep between the ditches. Don't get so agitated.'

'I can't help it. It's the way I was reared. Do you *know* who the father is? Or could it be any one of a dozen?'

'You could drop me here and I could still get a bus.'

'I'm just very angry, very hurt about this.'

'The father is called Dave. He's English. We were in a relationship – we were living together when it happened. By accident.'

'You were living together by accident?'

'We had Anna by accident.'

'Does that mean you use . . .?'

'What is this?' Catherine's voice was close to yelling. 'Another Spanish Inquisition?' The tone put her mother off and she remained quiet for a while. Then she asked, 'What age?'

'Dave or the baby?'

'Don't deliberately annoy me now, Catherine. For God's sake.'

'Eighteen months.'

'Your father would have probably banned you from the house for ever and a day.'

'I know.'

They fell silent again as Mrs McKenna drove through Magherafelt, with its roundabouts and traffic snarl ups. On the open road again she said, 'When am I going to get to see it?' Catherine did not reply but stared ahead at the perspective straight road which led to Toomebridge. 'I mean her. When am I going to get to see her?'

'I don't know.'

'And your husband – will he appear?'

'I'm not married.'

'So you've already boasted. Will he make an appearance?'

'Don't know.'

'Catherine, you're not being much help. Is the baby baptised?'

'No.'

The countryside became flat around Lough Neagh. Road signs warned of low-flying planes. They came to a permanent checkpoint on the road about a mile before the airport. Armed policemen stood about in black flak jackets. They were waved on.

'I haven't thought all this out yet but you must always remember that there's a home for you here. And your baby. And your man if it comes to that. Especially now. That place is too big for the likes of me – by myself. You could swing forty cats in it.'

'It would never work. But thanks.'

'I wouldn't interfere.'

' "Is the baby baptised?" ' Catherine mocked her mother's voice.

'What's right is right. You don't want the wee thing to spend an eternity in limbo. If it died.'

'Nobody in their right mind believes that kind of stuff nowadays . . .'

'I do.'

'We're arguing already . . .'

'We're discussing what's right and what's wrong. And what's the best thing to do.' Catherine sighed and looked out to her right at Lough Neagh glittering in the distance. 'You know, there's one thing that strikes me about all this.'

'What?'

'Your father was a grandfather for eighteen months and he died before he found out. I don't know which is worse. Him knowing or not knowing.'

They stood in front of the shops near the departures gate. Her mother was clicking the car keys in her hand.

'This has been a terrible shock.'

'I'm sorry.'

'Are you going to keep in touch this time?'

'If you want to.'

'Don't say it like that. Of course I want to. It's just so hard for me . . .'

'The baby's father is no longer on the scene.'

'Oh Jesus, Catherine – you're really making a mess of things.'

'I'm not the only single mother in the country.'

'You're the only one in our family.'

Catherine looked round at the clock. Then down at her feet.

'I'm staying with friends in Glasgow. Until I get a place of my own.'

They had to borrow a pen and a piece of paper in one of the gift shops to write down her care-of address and phone number. While Catherine was doing this her mother bought a loaf of wheaten bread.

'If you want to come home,' said her mother. 'I could get used to it. I would hate to lose you a second time.'

'I'll write a piece of music for you someday.' Her mother looked at her and gave a kind of snort.

'The Tune the Oul Cow Died of.'

Catherine smiled and handed her the piece of paper. She was offered the wheaten loaf in return.

'Thanks,' said Catherine.

'It's good bread. Do you for your breakfast.' They stood awkwardly facing one another. 'I'll send you some money.'

'No. I'll be all right.'

'Anna, you say?'

'Yes. I'll phone you.'

'OK. Stay well. And go and see about yourself.'

'I will.'

They hugged each other once, then Catherine was away and through the gate, walking quickly down the carpeted corridor.

In the plane she was in a window seat − not that it mattered because it was almost dark now. She was glad there was no one else in her row. In a couple of hours' time she would see her daughter. She had to control herself. Suppress the emotion rising in her. Occupy herself with something else. Because if she became intense about one thing, it could, without warning, change to another. And she would be swamped. Try not to think about her. She would be asleep − if Liz was being any sort of a responsible sitter. She visualised running downstairs to Anna in the basement. Then pulled herself up short. It was too soon. Something else. A staircase is going up and going down at the same time. Rising and descending.

Beginning and ending. Who is to say that this is a stairway *up* as opposed to this is a stairway *down*. Like polyphony. Ascending voices are indistinguishable from those that are descending.

She took the airline's magazine from the pocket in front of her and flicked through it. The maps portrayed London as the fountain of all red journeys. Kiev still looked like it was in the middle of nowhere – no red strand connected it to London. It would be hard to imagine living that far from the sea. The Black Sea was the nearest. The Black Sea was a blue colour.

The stewardess passed her a tray snack and smiled. She had beautiful teeth. It was a kind of professional smile. One that switched on and off – like Sister Immaculata's. Catherine had asked Melnichuck's wife, Olga, why the people of Kiev who worked in hotels and shops did not smile – the only people she had seen smile were priests and prostitutes. In shops the workers got their salary no matter how much or how little they sold or smiled, said Olga. And, more importantly, it was difficult to smile when they lived in such hard times. Butter now cost 800 times what it did a year ago. Having given her answer she smiled. At that instant she remembered wishing that Olga was her mother.

Catherine opened her tray and ate the contents mechanically. She tore back the foil lid of a plastic tub of water and washed down a tablet. She thought of feeding Anna. Casseroled Vegetables with Turkey, Country Vegetables with Beef, Cauliflower Cheese and Pasta – Catherine had tasted the first spoonful of them all and they all tasted the same. Dipping the spoon into the stuff, taking it out not full enough to spill over, wiping the edge of the spoon against the inside rim of the jar and putting it into the baby's mouth. Sometimes Anna would hold her mouth shut as a game, sometimes they played aeroplanes and Catherine would drone like an engine and deliver the spoon cargo into the open mouth. She remembered the tiny click as the spoon hit her first tooth – she thought it was a piece of broken glass from the jar rim. A bad time. When injury was uppermost. Fear of the worst thing that could happen to a mother. Fear that she would be the cause of it. But things were improving. The thoughts no longer came as frequently as they did. And she could deal with them when they did come. Bibs. She hadn't thought about a bib in four days. Spoons and bibs and jars and cutting things up small with a knife and fork. It was too early to think of all this. She would be up to high doh too soon. It was better than thinking of the other end. Smells and rashes. Soaked and soiled nappies. She had to think of something other than seeing Anna. It was too distant – two hours at least. She'd just be wasting emotional energy. She was like a juggler on a small board balanced on a fulcrum. The slightest carelessness could bring her down on one side or the other. Think of the day Melnichuck said that all would be revealed about the source of his music and its spiritual intensity. The city of Kiev was somewhere else. Other. Half-way between East and West. The weather had been bitterly cold. Melnichuck, Olga and Catherine had walked to the Refectory Church with the other people hurrying along through the light blowing snow. A boy carried an offering of a loaf of bread. Inside, on the monks' table, were last year's apples, brown and white eggs, loaves, one with a burning taper stuck in it, and pickles – all homemade things. Nothing could be further from this packaged airline meal. The choir was magnificent – the men's deep wonderful bass voices and the women's sopranos and altos. Mahogany and teak, gold and silver voices. The Refectory Church was circular, domed. There were no seats and the people stood or walked about. Melnichuck took off his glasses and stood rapt. Olga triple blessed herself. The voices of the priests were different from the choir – louder, with more glissandi – grace notes literally. The only word she recognised was *alleluia*. The choir loved its chords and held them for what seemed an infinity. The congregation was not all old women – although there were many – there were girls and boys, youths, middle-aged men. The priest with a magnificent bass voice sang a text rising in quarter tones that made the hairs on her neck rise. Ezio Pinza or Boris Christoff. There were no microphones or loud-speakers. A simple-minded girl listened to the choir with absolute attention, her eyes wide and smiling – the look of a child listening to a music box. Human pain and suffering were evident everywhere. The people were getting something which satisfied a deep spiritual need. A mother walked her palsied child up and down the floor. An afflicted one brought for healing. How did the mind heal? Was it a chemical process or an adjustment of personality, of soul? The intensity and beauty of the music brought tears to her eyes. The obvious pain and stark poverty of the people made it worse and she found it difficult to stop crying. And she was crying now in the plane over the darkness of the Irish Sea, eating her plastic meal, remembering herself crying in Kiev. And she deflected the reason for her crying – attributing it to the death of her father – the emotional drain of the last few days. Like a prisoner serving two sentences she was crying concurrently. Not wasting anything – doubling up the reasons. The same tears for more miles. She used the dark blue serviette to wipe her face. Before she could turn to the window a stewardess was standing above her.

'Is everything all right?'

Catherine nodded. She had the right to cry – coming from a funeral. She smiled to prove everything was all right. It was an odd device, this rearrangement of muscles of the face which said everything is all right. No need to enquire within. It could be used as a barrier to fend off emotional intruders.

How would Liz have dressed Anna for bed – the night of the homecoming? She could see her baby's face, feel her skin against her cheek. Maybe she could tie her hair in bunches. It had been long enough for ribbons for some time now. But it was too soon. She was anticipating. Be in control – direct the thinking process rather than let it have its head.

At the end of the service Olga and Catherine had gone up the bell tower – Melnichuck couldn't climb the steps because of his heart. It had been four years since the authorities had allowed the bell ringing back without let or hindrance. Two novices took turns to play the great drone bell which set the beat and the treble bells which played the melody. The large bell had a sustain which lasted for what seemed like minutes. Catherine took notes and

123

wrote down some of the phrases. It was bitterly cold and her fingers were numb. But the whole tower reverberated. Tintinnabulation. She said the word aloud stressing each syllable. Tin-tinn-ab-you-la-ish-on. Like a foreign word in a foreign country. She felt the bell ringing in the soles of her feet, she heard it in her sternum – it rang in the bones of her head. She nodded, trying to keep the rhythm. She walked about trying to stay warm in a kind of blundering dance. There was excitement and joy and it was infectious. Visceral music.

Afterwards Melnichuck introduced her to the priest with the deep mahogany voice, Father Theodosius. He was joyous, enthusiastic and open. He looked most impressive in his black soutane and the tall black hat with the veil at the back. Eastern Orthodox. In a safe kind of way she quite fancied him – despite his auburn beard which almost stood out straight with energy. His white hands, against the black of his garment, were restless – constantly touching the gold cross which hung from his neck. He was a monk, part of the monastery, rather than a secular priest. The churches were opening again, he said through Olga – the government had closed them and thought they would stay closed for ever. For many years their monastery was nothing but a shell. The government was waiting for the old people to die and, with them, religion – it was banned in the schools. The communists thought it would die of neglect. In spite of all, the church was alive and the candle still burned there. Nothing could extinguish it. Since the Middle Ages this monastery had had its own music – its own music school. 'Nowhere else do they sing and ring bells as we do here.' Father Theodosius smiled.

'Too bloody right,' said Catherine.

He took them to a huge room which was being converted. The floor was covered in dust and plaster, wires hung out of holes in walls above wooden trestles. He talked rapidly to Melnichuck and showed him what was being planned. There were six monks – lovely men, clowning a little – standing in the middle of the floor waiting to be introduced to the Westerner. They seemed shy of Catherine. They gave off a kind of gentleness. Suddenly with no warning they burst into song. It was not sacred singing – there was a lightness to it. It was like a round or catch, full of repetition, sung for fun and beautifully done. In an instant she was right back with Granny Boyd singing 'The Bell Doth Toll'. The fathers sang something which was very close to 'Silent Night'. Outside the window the snow swirled. Some sang countertenor, some tenor, some bass. The acoustic of the empty room with its slight echo fitted around the music perfectly. Someone hit a wrong note and they laughed and stopped.

After they had been introduced to Catherine they sang a hymn, glorifying Jesus, thanking Him for the gift of music. They walked away, the hems of their black soutanes grey with the dust of the place, singing until gradually the air returned to silence. Again Melnichuck took off his glasses. He said through Olga, 'I can see music as the grace of God. Through all the communist times they did not allow religion. For us music was a way of praying, music was a way of receiving God's grace.'

125

They went back to the Melnichucks' house and Olga cooked breakfast. Afterwards Anatoli played Catherine a tape of a work he had recently recorded.

'A Hymn to the Mother of God Seated on the Throne of Heaven,' said Olga. The tape machine was ancient, totally unable to reproduce the sounds he had given to the choir. But still the magnificence came through. It was spare and structured and utterly memorable. When the last notes died away the tape hiss continued and the dog's tail thumped on the rug. Olga said, 'Since the political changes he can give his work the names he has inside his head. Ten years ago he would call it Chronos Four or something. Shostakovich said to him once, "Your head is a safe. Only you know the numbers to open it." '

'You knew Shostakovich?'

'Yes. Dmitri Dmitriyevich came here to Kiev with his wife number three, Irina Supinskaya. To discuss his Babi Yar symphony. It was very brave music to write at the time.'

'Why?'

'You know Babi Yar?'

'No, not . . .'

'Maybe you are too young. Babi Yar is a place of death. In 1941 the Nazis made all the Jews of Kiev come together and they took them to Babi Yar — thirty-five thousand — men, women, children — and they shot them and put them down in a ravine to be buried. Evtushenko wrote a poem and Shostakovich put it in a symphony. But the anti-Semites said not all the dead are Jews. There is Russians and other prisoners.'

Hearing the words Babi Yar and Shostakovich Anatoli became agitated. He spoke to Olga.

'He says they were all Jews who were killed. Dmitri Dmitriyevich was right – we must all fight anti-Semitism. The beginning of anti-Semitism is talk, is hatred – the end is Babi Yar. But, of course, in 1962 the State said there is no anti-Semitism in the USSR.'

The stewardess came and stacked the empty meal trays, crowded them one on top of the other and pushed them into her trolley. Catherine thought of the geography of the places of death in her own country – it was a map which would not exist if women made the decisions – Cornmarket, Claudy, Teebane Crossroads, Six Mile Water, the Bogside, Greysteel, the Shankill Road, Long Kesh, Dublin, Darkley, Enniskillen, Loughinisland, Armagh, Monaghan town. And of places of multiple deaths further to the east – Birmingham, Guildford, Warrington. It was like the Litany. Horse Guards Parade. Pray for us. Tower of London. Pray for us. Alone or with others. For the dead it didn't matter how many companions they had or where it happened. It was awful to think that if she wrote the most profound music in the history of the world it would have no effect on this litany – it would go on and on adding place names. Once in the University library looking through the *Encyclopedia Britannica* of 1911 for something on the sonata form – the eleventh edition had been recommended for its excellent philosophical and musical contributions – she came across *Somme*. It was described as a department of northern France – great rolling plains generally well cultivated and fertile etcetera etcetera. And that was all. Yet somehow she knew that her act of creation, whether it was making another person or a symphonic work, defined her as human, defined her as an individual. And defined all individuals as important.

The pilot announced they would soon be landing. Again she had to choke back the anticipation. She was as liable to cry as she was to laugh. Her feeling was of an excess of emotion but she could never be sure which way it would go. She thought about how she would get home from the airport. Taxi was the quickest but it was too expensive – about ten times dearer than public transport. The bus was slow – there was only one every half-hour. And that would only leave her as far as the Underground. Which would take her another ten or fifteen minutes. Then there would be the walking after that – she just knew she would half run, half walk. Nonsense, she knew she would run the whole way. And arrive at the door out of breath.

There was an urgency. Not *an* urgency. *Urgency*. Then out of nowhere she heard a rhythm. *Its* rhythm – the rhythm of urgency. Driving – like Stravinsky's *Rite of Spring. Scenes of Pagan Russia.* Somewhere between that and a rant – a sort of jig time. Like that pounding rhythm at the start of Mussorgsky's *The Great Gate of Kiev.* A Courante. That was a crazy phrase they used at home – a speedy courante – where or how did Irish speech pick up a word for a French dance? *I kicked the dog and he took a brave speedy courante out the door.* She laughed. Whatever it was, it was fast. Pounding. It was a mistake according to Stravinsky to talk about 'fast rhythm'. Rhythm was intervals of a certain duration. Beats, accents, measures. This was a gathering momentum. Insistent. The grouping of notes into beats, the grouping of beats into measures, the grouping of measures into phrases. Waves, tides, ripples. Hail Marys, decades, rosaries, novenas. She was hearing inside her head the opening movement of something. Music was being conceived. Something tantalising. Something spiky with urgency. Like in primary school when she'd had that infection. Needing the toilet. *Please, Miss, please, Miss. Just this once, Catherine.* Down the stairs, tippy steps, very fast, holding everything in. A needle pain. A bursting. A wrestling with the toilet door. Have I time to lock it? Before an accident?

The memory made her want to go to the toilet. But the seat-belt sign was lit so she would have to wait until the terminal.

She was going home. To her baby. To her friend Liz. When they'd shared a flat as students she'd brought her a present – a Rose of Jericho. Just a wee something from a street market in Kiev. From a hippy capitalist – selling them for dollars only. It was a dried-up fern. Like a nest of All-Bran. There was a sheet of instructions in four currency-rich languages which they followed with some incredulity the night she came back.

'It says to pour boiling water on to it.' Liz and she had made tea and poured the remaining water on to the thing. The sheet said it was a desert plant first brought back from the Holy Land by the Crusaders. Sometimes known as the Resurrection plant, it was brought out to astound the children at Christmas.

'Are you astounded?'

'Only slightly,' said Liz.

Then gradually over the next ten minutes they did

become astounded. The plant flattened and unfurled, turned from brown to a dark, sage green radiating throughout the white porcelain dish.

'It's just great that something can lie around for so long and still be alive,' said Catherine. 'Like spores. TB can lie around for years. Until one fine day a draught blows it up your nose. Then everything gets moist and you've got TB.'

'I've always heard that draughts were dangerous,' said Liz. 'And I never knew why. What a wondrous thing.'

'Transubstantiation.'

'It's changing colour and shape, Kate, not substance.'

'Listen to the resident theologian.'

They had allowed the plant to lie in the water for a week. Then Liz drained it and set it on the bookshelf, where it reverted to a dried-up nest.

The plane tilted and she looked out of the window. The sight took her breath away. It was a clear night and the city lights glittered on the ground beneath her. Yellow sodium lights in chains and necklaces, loops and patterns – the whole city was like a flattened chandelier – stretched as far as she could see. Like gleaming prinkles – hundreds and thousands. The lights became more crowded the further away they were. One light for every person.

There was a black wedge of darkness beneath her which she could not, at first, understand. Then she knew it was the River Clyde – a black river – putting out the lights – as if the water had flowed like carbon dioxide and winked out every light in its path – the darkness widening as it moved out to sea behind her – towards the west and Ireland – black and heavy as the soil of Babi Yar.

* * *

She has no baggage to collect so she moves quickly past the carousel, while others have to stand and wait. She is in such a hurry that she forgets to go to the toilet. Not so much forgets but sees it as a minor problem. It might be a bad time for taxis and by going to the toilet she might miss the only one for ages. But she is wrong. There is a line of thirty or forty of them. There is also a bus at the stance, going into the city centre. She doesn't hesitate but moves towards the taxi rank. The first one in line has a NO SMOKING symbol on the windscreen. The driver is smoking with the window down and his arm outside. She knows the car will stink of smoke and it'll go for her throat but she hasn't time to endure the hassle of choosing the second car, in which the driver sits not smoking. She gets into the taxi and has to shout her address from the back seat because Radio One music is pounding loudly from the speakers in the back window – kind of techno stuff. The driver flicks away his cigarette and edges out into the stream of traffic. When the cigarette hits the dark roadway there is a shower of sparks. What if she's not there? What if Peter looks up at her when she comes in the door and says Liz has gone to her mother's for the night. And she took Anna with her. Oh Jesus, that was too awful to contemplate. Negative thinking. *There's more where that came from. And a lot worse.* Liz is crying when Catherine goes in and can't find the words to tell her that it was an incredibly simple accident. A peanut going down the wrong way. *Stop this nonsense right now! Think of something else.* Alasdair Kirkpatrick in a tutorial said that in Hieronymus Bosch's *Garden of Earthly Delights* there was a naked figure with music written on its bare arse and it was difficult to tell if it was a man's or a woman's. Catherine had asked, 'Music or arse?' and everyone in the class had laughed. She turns her head. She concentrates on what is outside the taxi. They are driving fast on the motorway. The night is full of red tail lights. For a moment she is part of an American movie and the pounding music on the radio is the soundtrack. Then they drive even faster, accelerating into the fast lane. Good. The sooner the better. She can see the driver's eyes in the mirror as he stares ahead. She knows his eyes are flicking between her in the back seat and the road behind. But she wants him always to look forward. The driver says something to her which she can't make out. She leans forward from the back seat. She tells him she can't hear properly and asks him if he can do without the radio. He snaps the beat off and doesn't repeat what he said in the first place. The only sound now is the high whine of their own tyres and the whoosh as they pass huge trucks. In the relative silence the rhythm she heard in the plane bounces into her head again. But now it is more agitato. Driving forward. In the fast lane. The first section of something. Leading the way. A symphony. Called Symphony. You couldn't call it your first Symphony until you had written your second Symphony. Then she knows with certainty what it is. The *Credo*. Her *Credo*. The linchpin of the mass she is writing. *Credo in unum* ... Voices barking one sound at a time – single syllables. Nonsense syllables.

Cre
Do
In
Un

Um
De
Um

Seven in all. That was her. A mythic number. Seven little claps in all. Catherine Anne McKenna. Mysterious. The first voice like a precentor. Followed by others, each of whom is a precentor to the rest. Grace notes – notes which were neither one thing nor the other. A note between the notes. Notes that occurred outside time. Ornaments dictating the character of the music, the slur and slide of it. This is decoration becoming substance. Like a round in Granny Boyd's kitchen. Or Purcell's Songs of the Tavern. Soarings. Voices slipping. Joining folk music and art music. East and West. Male and female. A female precentor is a precentatrix, God help her. Later the joined voices will become layered when the line lengthens – like the singing of the monks at Lavra. The thread of the single voice meshes with the next voice and its neighbours to become a skein which weaves with other skeins of basses and tenors and altos and sopranos to make a rope of sound, a cincture which will girdle the earth so that there is neither East nor West. She is getting carried away. No, she isn't – she is being carried home. *Credo.* I believe. The chords of voices stack vertically. Chords becoming cords, unravelling. She feels good about this. And suddenly she feels good about herself. Someday she will be better. Wellness was inside her, waiting, on the edge of its seat. Like the Rose of Jericho. Ready to flower however long it has been dormant. She has to believe it. She will see her daughter again and together they will advance. It is never the form which is important but what is said within it. Sonnets were still being written. She feels she is carrying this rhythm within her, she is pregnant with it – the way she sometimes carries her creativity with such care – like a brimming beaker, determined not to spill a drop. She hoards what little juices she has.

She now thinks it was a mistake not to have gone to the toilet in the airport. Bladder pressure. She crosses her legs and leans slightly forward. The driver thinks she wants to say something and half turns. But she has nothing to say to him so rather than disappoint him she says that it is the next turn off. He says he knows. He calls her darlin. The traffic in the town is bad. The car stops and starts. The price on the meter rises. Red lights. Flashing orange. Green. They drive past the Museum of Religion. The first of its kind in the world. But why build one? Why not just designate all churches as Museums of Religion? The driver watches her in the mirror and tells her to sit back, to take it easy. This time he calls her Missus. Catherine does as she's told but fiddles with the buckle of the back seat-belt. She is close enough now to allow herself to visualise what is about to happen. The front-door steps, the leaded glass door, up the hallway, on through the door to the basement, down the staircase, into the room to the right at the bottom. The door would be wedged open for Liz to hear if Anna was crying. Also the door at the top of the stairs would have been wedged open with a little slice of wood so she wouldn't have had to open that. Maybe as a treat Liz would have kept her up late – and she would see her the minute she went in the front door. The taxi turns right into a side street. Getting close. The childish game

134

when everyone shouted. Warm. Getting warmer. Then a turn to the left. Warmer still. Lit windows of houses showing life going on. Hot. Outside the house the driver stops in the middle of the roadway so that nothing can pass. Hotter. A car sits behind in the darkness and flashes its lights. Catherine asks the price of the journey. She takes a ten from her purse. There is not much light in the back of the taxi. She is due two pounds change but the driver is fiddling. He's looking in his wallet and she can hear him poking in a tray of coins with his finger. He's taking too long. The man behind flashes his lights again and for good measure parps his horn once. Shit – Catherine opens the door and runs to the front-door steps of the house. She looks over her shoulder and sees the taxi driver getting out, walking around his cab and closing the back door properly. Clunk. The motorist behind waves his arms as if in despair.

Catherine doesn't know where her key is and presses the bell. Keeps her finger on it. She looks this way and that through the leaded panes of the door. She makes a shade of her hand trying to see up the hallway. A light comes on and Liz's shape appears and walks towards the door. Walks. When she could run. Liz pulls the door open, her face full of sympathy for someone returning from a funeral.

'Hi, Kate.'

'Hi, Liz.' They touch cheeks. 'Where is she?'

'Anna?'

'Yes.'

'Downstairs.'

Liz begins a question about the trip to Ireland standing

between Catherine and the staircase. Catherine puts out her arms and turns her, in a dance movement so that she is the one nearest the basement stairs. The toilet is to her left. She ignores it and runs. She is running downstairs, tippy steps, very fast, holding everything in. A pain in the heart. A bursting. The bedroom door is open. The room dark. Four days' absence — five including the hours of the night she didn't see her. There is a head on the pillow. Catherine looks, bends over the cot. But she can't see well enough. Anna. She whispers so as not to wake her. Then louder. She speaks her baby's name. She wants her to wake. She looks at the face on the pillow. A spasm of fright rips through her. It can't be. It can't be true. Jesus . . . aw Jesus. It is not her baby. A changeling. This baby is not Anna. She switches on the bedside lamp. A bye-child. Someone has substituted a different baby. Liz has done something to her. She reaches down into the cot and lifts the baby lying there. Holds it up in front of her at arm's length. The baby's eyes cringe into wrinkles against the light. Its dummy falls out of its mouth on to the floor. It begins to cry. And yet it looks a bit like Anna. Catherine yells for Liz, who has followed her down the stairs anyway. Liz leans against the jamb of the door and snaps on the overhead light. The baby is like a cousin of Anna's. Then Catherine realises that the baby has changed in five days — it *IS* Anna. To the extent a seedling changes over five days. She has grown, has filled out, her features have lengthened. Now she knows the baby she holds in her arms is her own. She holds her close, hugs her. She was trying to place a guitar tune first heard on a viola. Plucked not bowed. Anna. She smells her powder perfume, feels her warm skin against her own, which is cold coming from outside. Her wee pet. Catherine tells her that she hardly knew her. There are now tears in her eyes. She turns to Liz and laughs and admits that she didn't recognise her own baby. She'd changed *so* much in five days. But oh, she was gorgeous. Her hen of gold. She tells her baby that she has a present for her. The baby looks at the woman holding her and her lip drops, turns down and wobbles and she begins to howl. Liz laughs and says that the baby doesn't know its own mother. Catherine hugs her close so that her tiny face is looking over her shoulder at Liz. A mother hiding her face from her own child. Liz backs out of the room and switches off the light. She says now that she's wakened her why doesn't she bring her upstairs. Catherine says that she needs the toilet anyway. Liz offers to take the baby from her but Catherine refuses and climbs the stairs behind her, up into the light. She holds her baby close.

Liz says, 'You have a surprise coming.'

'What?'

'She spoke.'

'What? Who did?'

'This one.'

'Who's a clever girl then?' Catherine turns Anna to face her. 'Who's a clever girl? What did she say?'

'It was mostly a tirade against the Tory government . . .'

'Naw – come on . . .'

'She said Mama, clear as a bell. Twice.'

Catherine stares at her child's face, then she kisses the top of her head.

'To you?'

137

'I'm afraid so.'

'How many times have I told you not to speak to strangers,' Catherine says. She puts on her own mother's voice, 'Just you wait till I get you home.'

'Give her to me,' says Liz.

'I'm not letting go of her until she says it to me.'

Liz laughs. Catherine takes Anna, who has stopped crying, into the bathroom with her and says, 'Silent O'Moyle no longer.'

Inside Catherine bolts the door and goes to the toilet with the baby clinging round her neck.

Getting her clothes back the way they were is awkward but she succeeds without disturbing Anna too much. On the way out Catherine pauses in front of the mirror, cheek to cheek with her baby. They look at themselves and each other. The child smiles at what it sees. So does Catherine.

Credo.

Part Two

DAY CROW. *Taglied.* Morning song. A rooster making a racket from the Muirs' place. In Kiev, Olga had a different name for the sound. Ko-ko-reek-o. A homophone of sorts. Certainly more accurate than the English cock-a-doodle-doo. Dave was gone. Catherine lurched into a sitting position and rocked herself off the bed. In the mirror on the wardrobe door she swung herself into view. It was as if she'd been fitted with a Lambeg drum. Even when she rapped her belly with her finger it sounded like a drum. Or one of those ripe fruit, a watermelon or cantaloupe – a hollow bump each time she tapped. She felt huge despite the baby's head having dropped in the last couple of days. Even though this was her first baby she had deep violet stretch marks. Through the material of her nightdress she could feel her navel – *big enough to hang your hat on*, as Dave said.

She opened the curtains, hung just on a string and looked out at the early summer's day. The sun was bright. On the one side, down by the rocks and the diving board, the sea was an intense mussel-shell blue. On the other was the green grass of a fenced field where now and again there was a horse to look at. The bungalow, at the edge of the town, overlooked the shore which was made up of stones and, nearer the sea, shingle. When the wind was in the right direction she could hear the waves. Dave had taken the van, leaving an oily patch on the cement path. Metal air bottles stood by the wall. A navy and yellow wet suit hung on the line, its arms and legs aslant, jerking occasionally in the breeze. It looked odd – like a skin, the man having been extracted. A shell of a thing – just as she was an envelope for this baby. That was her only function and when it was born she would be hung out on the line. That would be her finished.

She washed and dressed and went across to the kitchen where she sat at the table eating cereal. In order not to read the packet with its *Fibre for Life* recipes she looked elsewhere. On the windowsill were some of the shells and sea urchins she had collected – periwinkles, limpets, needle shells like spires or minarets, top shells like churches, scallop ashtrays, mussel shells of the exact blue beneath chipped enamel. Razor shells. It was only incomers to the island who bothered with things like gathering shells. Islay people didn't collect city things when they went there – bin lids, or lollipop sticks or Underground tickets. She thought it odd to collect the remains of something, the shell, once the life had gone from it. But they were beautiful.

Throughout the summer, when the water was not as cold, Dave dived for scallops and sold them to the fish factory. This fine warm spell, unexpected so early in the summer, meant that he could dive for longer periods. And the price of scallops at the fish factory was good at the moment. Running a one-man diving operation like this and hiring the equipment meant that he could get to inshore beds which the boats with their raking and trawling equipment couldn't get near. So the money was good but the work was dangerous and very tiring. Taxing on the body.

She felt good when Dave got up and left the house early. There was something positive about him going to work. She hated him lying in bed, the hangover, the aimlessness of the winter weeks when she was teaching at school. When he had to sign on, when there was nothing to do.

The table wobbled and milk spilled over the rim of her dish. It was an old spindly legged thing they'd bought for next to nothing at an auction. For many people a sale was the best of island entertainment – livestock in the morning, furniture in the evening. People went with no intention of buying. It was a way of prying, a kind of nosiness to see the possessions of the recently dead. Catherine loved the rhythm of the auctioneer's voice, machine-gunning on with its meaningless noises filling up between words. Like a foreign language – like Latin. When the sale was complete he banged the rostrum, not with a gavel, but a stick for driving cattle.

When she'd first rented this place it was unfurnished and she'd filled it from the auctions – a bed, a drop-leaf table, cutlery, a half dinner set, lamps with bruised shades, a real oil lamp, floor rugs worn through to the hessian back, a three-piece suite. All for a few quid. The thing she had paid dearest for was the piano. Five fishermen and Dave had manoeuvred it off the trailer up to the bungalow. Later in the pub she'd paid them with pints and whiskies. She had to discipline herself not to lift the lid until the next time the school piano tuner visited the island. He reckoned she'd got a real bargain.

She made tea and toast and took it into the front room where the sunlight was. Her papers were on the desk where she had left them the night before. On the windowsill Dave's empty half bottle of vodka and some lager cans. Drowning his tomorrows, she called it.

She sat down at the desk and read over what she had done the previous day. Some crumbs scattered on her pages as she bit into her toast. She was working on a set of variations for string orchestra on a Catch of Purcell's. Stitching small segments together the way Granny Boyd had made quilts. She held the pages steady with one finger and blew the crumbs away.

> *'Tis women makes us love,*
> *'Tis love that makes us sad,*
> *'Tis sadness makes us drink,*
> *And drinking makes us mad.*

It was a form Purcell seemed to like – he'd written at least fifty. To be performed in the pub. Out of the Chapel Royal after a hard day's hymn singing, straight over to the pub to sing dirty songs with his mates. But this one wasn't dirty – it was stately with a kind of intense sadness to it.

She'd learned catches from her Granny Boyd. The old woman had a sewing machine which she worked with a treadle footplate. Sometimes she sang along to the rhythm of what she was doing.

'That's why they call it a Singer Sewing machine. Cause you have to sing when you work it.'

144

She taught Catherine 'Three Blind Mice'. And once the girl had learned it – after a matter of minutes – it could break out at any time, whatever they were doing. The grandmother could be boiling a kettle and start,

Three blind mice, three blind mice . . .

And Catherine knew to chime in on the beat as her Granny started the second line. Or Catherine could start when the grandmother was doing the dishes and the old woman would have to take the second line,

They all ran after the farmer's wife
Who cut off their tails with a carving knife.
Did you ever see such a thing in your life
As three blind mice
As three blind mice.

Granny Boyd called these 'the rounds of the kitchen'. Catherine loved the way the rhythms clashed – like a wave coming into the harbour wall. Once it struck, lots of wavelets jigged and bounced back and jostled the next big wave coming in. Granny Boyd taught her others, 'Frère Jacques' and 'The Bell Doth Toll'. They sang them just whenever they felt like it.

The bell doth toll
The echoes roll
I know that sound so well.
For I love its ringing
When it calls to singing

After the sound of their voices died away Granny Boyd said, 'It must be a terrible affliction not to be able to hear.'

'What?'

'It's even worse not to be able to listen. There's a difference, ye wee head-in-the-clouds.' She said that her own father was deaf towards the end of his life. Loyalists had shot at him as he came out of St Patrick's Church in Clifton Street and the bullet had smacked the wall just by his right ear. Whether it was the sound or the shock, but from that day forward he never heard another thing – as deaf as a post. When she told this story she always shook her head in disbelief at such misfortune.

The unfinished quilt was kept in a cardboard box. When she was shown it Catherine would say, 'Hey, that's mine – that used to be my dress.'

'Aye, I mind that – right enough. Your mammy gave it over.'

'It was the zip,' said Catherine.

'Any garment is only as good as its zip. That's what I always say.'

Sometimes Granny Boyd would scold her and she hated that.

'Sit properly. You're eight years of age now – the world isn't interested in the colour of your pants.' Then seeing the hurt on her face her Granny would call her. 'Come here, darlin. Sure you know I didn't mean it.' The old woman would put her arms round her. 'Snuggle in,' she would say. 'My granddaughter. Grand by name and grand by nature. Did I ever tell you – on the day you were born

I said — SHE is mine. She's *my* hen of gold. I thought you'd be the first of many — but it wasn't to be. The Lord works in mysterious ways. Careful with that needle — don't jag yourself.' Her grandmother would stroke her hair and hold her close. 'Did I ever tell you that before?'

'Yes,' Catherine would say and run home, up the stairs, past the smell of cigarette smoke and Guinness.

She decided to play over what she had written of the Purcell Catch Variations the previous evening. She squeezed herself between the stool and the piano. She should write a *How To* manual — *How To Play the Piano When Pregnant*. In the same vein as *Comfortable Sex Positions in Late Pregnancy*. With drawings. With illustrations would be better. Withdrawings in this context meant something different. Middle C — the most difficult note to reach because of her bump. Yesterday's work was good — had a good feel to it. Then she felt a pain in her lower back. Posture, her posture at the piano had always been poor. She straightened.

The High School had given her twelve weeks' maternity leave. She had hoped to use it for her work but mood swings caught her unawares. One day she'd be hyper and excited and looking forward to the baby enough to ache — then the next she'd be down, couldn't give a toss, worried about her parents and how she was going to tell them. Other days she got a lot done — forgetting to feed herself until two and three o'clock. Scolding herself for neglecting the child within her. Since leaving school it had become a very active baby. Away from the bells of school it thought it was in the playground. Elbows and knees, head and heels butted her. And when she played music she was sure it knew. She improvised to calm the baby within her.

Again she felt a pain. Again she straightened. Could she be starting? Maybe she should phone the doctor. It happened twice in the space of a hour – a belt of pain under her belly and round her back – a clamping sensation. She phoned the doctor and he came within the hour. He tapped and poked and listened and looked and pronounced her 'ready for the road'. He ordered the ambulance plane. She scrawled a note for Dave with a big marker pen

AWAY TO HAVE YOUR BABY

and put it in front of the mirror. The doctor drove her and her little navy hold-all to the airport.

'The hospital is called Rotten Row,' he said, 'but it's nowhere near as bad as that.'

The plane was a Bandereike and looked very small sitting on the tarmac. When she got on and the engines were started it was loud enough to prevent any conversation between her and the nurse. Catherine pointed to her ears and smiled. On take-off the engines rose to screaming pitch. She thought the acceleration pressed the baby back to her spine. In the air she leaned forward to look out the window. Beneath, the island was yellow except for the black lines of peat cuttings. The seat-belt had been lengthened as far as it would go but it was still taut across her bump.

The plane in its long slow turn passed over the school and its playing fields. From this height the goal posts looked like white staples. Everything had its shadow.

What was she doing here? Thousands of feet in the air above such a place?

When she'd been offered a job as a music teacher on Islay she thought of Peter Maxwell Davies living on the island of Hoy and promptly said yes. It was a crazy reason to base any decision on but it seemed a better idea than a city school. Her thinking was that if she didn't like it she could move back to the mainland without too much difficulty. Many people had pulled faces and said that she was putting herself outside the music networks necessary for her at such an important stage – Maxwell Davies had gone to Hoy *after* he had established himself. Catherine shrugged and said it could all be done by phone.

As the coastline came into view she felt a pain in her lower back. It was enough to make her catch her breath but it disappeared almost immediately. The nurse looked at her. Catherine shouted close to the nurse's ear, 'What happens if I have . . .'

The nurse shook her head vigorously.

'No chance – no way,' she said and reached out and grinned, squeezing the back of Catherine's clenched fist. 'I know it has happened. Born at five thousand feet. But not to the likes of you.' The nurse then smoothed the backs of both Catherine's hands, indicated that she should relax. They reminded Catherine of Miss Bingham's first piano manual on which there were two outlines of spread hands.

She leaned her head against the wall and felt the engine drone soothingly in the bones of her head. She must try not to think of what lay ahead. Think of work.

She had begun to convince herself that it would be reasonable for her to write a mass. Janáček wrote his

Glagolitic Mass but denied that he was a believer. She had also heard Poulenc's *Gloria* in the concert hall and been swept away by it. Now she had begun to sketch her own *Kyrie* and *Gloria* for two choirs. It would be an antiphon, two blocks of voices singing at and with each other in turn. Like question and answer. Sometimes like question and no answer.

The opening seven syllables of the Kyrie

Kee
Ree
Eh
Ell
Eh
Ee
Son

One choir sings a rhythm, which forms steps down which the voices of the other choir descend in a cascade. One after the other, tripping down the steps, hard on each other's heels. She had split the school choir and asked them to practise it.

'Chewing gum in the bin before we start. And today let your consonants be one degree louder than your vowels.' Catherine would conduct and encourage and shout above their singing, 'Keep it light, like glass. Stop. One of the problems of being a singer is that what we hear on the outside is not what you're hearing on the inside. This group – give it more. Make it more mezzo-y. It is difficult, I know, but you will learn it because you're smart.' And they did learn it and their performance of it on the night was magical. It was so great when the sound made by human beings was as good as the music created in her head.

Suddenly the note of the engine changed and Catherine looked to the nurse for reassurance. The speed of the plane seemed to have dropped and it was turning on its side. They broke through the white racing cloud and Glasgow appeared beneath them. Catherine felt she was going deaf. All the sounds around her were suddenly distanced and she thought of the great-grandfather she had never known who had to live for part of his life in silence. When the plane came to a halt and the engine had been switched off, there was quiet. Catherine mock-yawned and felt her ears crack. The real world of sounds rushed back. She thanked the nurse for her kindness. The nurse smiled and helped her down on to the tarmac, telling her that everything was going to be all right.

She had another pain in the ambulance as she sat straight-backed and stiff, clutching her hold-all. When they were stopped at traffic lights she heard the whooping squeal of an ambulance siren – like one from New York. For a moment she wondered if it was theirs. Then the speeding ambulance broke the lights and its sound dwindled into the traffic. She thought of death, the everlastingness of it. Of a life coming and a life going. People had died from something as simple as going to the dentist's.

In Rotten Row everyone spoke to her in the same soft way. She thought she would have objected to this, making a child of her, but instead she relaxed and enjoyed it.

People called her pet, dearie, hen, love – took her bag from her, helped her off with her coat. Dressed her as if for bed, did all but kiss her. When she was asked for her Christian name she said, 'Catherine. A plain Jane of a name.' But the nurse who was writing down the details failed to see the joke.

When a midwife came to examine her she lay on the bed. Her cotton nightie was rucked up over the full moon of her stomach and from where she lay it almost blocked out the midwife and her own knees. The midwife had glasses on and squinted up her eyes, wrinkling the bridge of her nose to hold the glasses in position as she stooped forward. She disappeared behind Catherine's dome of flesh and Catherine winced at the poking up into her.

'Hm-hm,' said the midwife. 'I think you've started.'

Another Sister checked for the baby's heart and took Catherine's temperature, pulse and blood pressure. Were they as they should be? Catherine watched the Sister's face trying to interpret her look. The Sister smiled back at her, then walked away rustling with starch. But then everything stopped. She had no more contractions. She was put in a room with magnolia walls and told to walk about – gravity would help to get her going again.

She thought about her own mother in the same situation. Catherine had been born in Belfast in a nursing home called Malone Place. Going in, her mother had noticed that the M had fallen off the sign so that it read – alone Place.

'It was well named,' her mother had said. 'Lying waiting for you was the loneliest I've ever been. Hours on end by myself. Knowing your father couldn't get in to see me – in those days it was frowned upon.'

Now Catherine felt that same feeling of isolation. The father of her child was on an island. She had cut herself off from her parents. There was just herself and the child fish-breathing inside her. Head down, feet in the air, waiting for opening time.

How would she tell her parents? There'd been a big falling out on the phone after her postgraduate year in Glasgow but she knew that somehow, sooner or later, contact would have to be made again. She hadn't gone home that summer but stayed on in Glasgow and worked as a waitress in the Tron Theatre bar. She graduated *in absentia* because she was fed up with the whole academic thing. She waitressed right up until Christmas and in all that time only rang home once or twice. On 8 December she phoned and it was her father who answered. She told him she wouldn't be home for Christmas – she'd won a travel scholarship and the only time it suited the people she was going to visit was January and to make the trip worthwhile etcetera she had to prepare herself blah blah blah. Her father was silent at his end of the line. She knew he was disappointed and angry, could sense the bristling in the earpiece. He asked her if she knew what day it was and when she said no he asked her if she had been to mass. He said a good Catholic would *know* it was the Feast of the Immaculate Conception, one of the Church's most important Holidays of Obligation. Catherine had laughed out loud. Then he said he was glad that she wasn't coming home for Christmas, the house would be a better place without her. As a matter of fact he wouldn't care if she never came home again. She could stay in heathen England. Scotland, Catherine had said and the line went dead.

The Victorian radiator was painted magnolia as well – its panels like fat uncooked sausages. She sat on the bed in a kind of daze, staring. Paint had run and formed hardened drips at the bottom of each section of the radiator. Over the years a hook had inscribed a white arc beneath itself into the paint. She wet her finger and touched it to the scored plaster. Grey crumbs which she brought to her tongue. Chew them – like when she was a child. Her watch said five past. The last pain had been over an hour ago.

The year she was eleven she passed her qualifying exam and as a reward her parents bought her the New Marian Missal. The gilt edging to the pages was so shiny that she could almost see her reflection in the side of the book when it was shut. And six silk ribbons of different colours as bookmarks. Catherine loved the thinness of the paper, loved wetting her finger with the tip of her tongue and turning the pages. The first thing she looked up was the patron saint of music.

22 *November*
ST CECILIA, Virgin, Martyr
3*cl.* – *Red*

St Cecilia (or Cecily) of an illustrious Roman family, converted her husband, Valerianus, and her brother-in-law, Tiburtius, conserved her virginity, and was beheaded during the pontificate of St Urban I (AD 230).

She asked her mother what *conserved her virginity* meant but her mother just turned away and read something out of the paper to Brendan which had amused her.

The story of Cecilia was a complete fabrication, Catherine had found out years later reading a dictionary of saints. It seems she refused to engage in an act of idolatry and was sentenced to death. The method of execution was odd, to say the least. She was to be stifled in her own bathroom. More like the patron saint of saunas. But the method failed and a Roman soldier was sent to behead her. He had three goes at it and it took her three days to die. The story made her shudder. But worse was to come. Her connection with music was non-existent. She was portrayed in early art playing the organ but this notion arose from a misreading of a Latin text which said that pipes were played on her wedding day. The whole edifice of her reputation as patron saint of music had sprung from a duff translation.

And yet there was another part of Catherine which continued to believe in this fiction and to be thankful for all the music which had been composed in honour of St Cecilia – Handel, Purcell, Britten – in much the same way as children with armfuls of presents are grateful to St Nicholas at Christmas.

When she told Dave the *conserved her virginity* story he said it probably meant she put jam on it.

She walked to the window and leaned her elbows on the sill. There were no curtains. Outside it had begun to get dark. Steam, yellow in the sodium light, drifted from somewhere and melted into nothing. She heard the repeated cry of a seagull and it reminded her of the island.

She tried to think of something pleasant to take her mind off things but it kept slipping back to her family. It was she, the daughter, who should have enough sense to mend fences. Her parents were set in their ways. She should forgive *them*. Maybe she should write, tell them the news that they soon would be grandparents. She tried to imagine the scene at the breakfast table. Because her father always worked late in the bar, her mother got up first and opened any post that was addressed to her or to both of them. Half an hour, sometimes an hour, later her father would get up. Her mother would go into the bedroom and make the warm bed while he ate his breakfast and read the paper. If she read the letter first she'd have to go and wake him and tell him the news. He would go into one of his black silent rages.

Her baby was still only an idea. A physical part of her but not yet a person – something easily dispensed with. If it was stillborn, she wouldn't have to write the letter. Her parents would be spared. But there was still the matter of not having made contact. In all that time. The longer it went on the harder it became to think of writing. Or simply picking up the phone.

The nurse came in to check on her.

'Everything OK?'

'Why have I stopped? First, the midwife tells me I've started then . . .'

'It happens.' Suddenly a belter of a pain went around beneath her stomach. She held her breath and her eyes widened. She gasped out the air. 'You see,' said the nurse. 'Plenty of pain – no need to worry.' This set of contractions seemed more severe and there was less time between them. They were seismic – massive internal cosmic events. The pain was not at the point of exit – it came from a place you couldn't get at. If she believed in the soul, that was where it was hurting.

Another event made her moan and clench her teeth together. The nurses came and went, monitoring her.

'Remember your breathing,' they said. Huang Xiao Gang would have been proud of her. *Pre-hearing.* What she was about to produce had a head, a body and a tail. If it had a tail then it would be a boy. But she wanted a girl. *Inner hearing.* She tried to imagine what it would be like but couldn't. They moved her to a different ward. Her bare feet arched against the cold of the terrazzo floor. It was a small ward with four beds. One other woman lay asleep. The two remaining beds were empty, their bedclothes like geometry. She had two more pains of increasing intensity before anyone came near her. Her hands were wet with nervous sweat.

It occurred to her that she should pray – a thing she hadn't thought about in ages. When she started to lose her belief she had prefaced her prayers with 'If you exist, God . . .' but even this had disappeared. She was sure there was nothing. And even if there was a Supreme Being, could she get him to change his mind about something by praying to him? If the All-Powerful One had decided that today it was curtains for Catherine Anne McKenna would whispering to Him make Him reverse His decision?

There had been a time when she had believed absolutely. The May altars. They always had one at school and a few girls would be selected to go to the woods and gather flowers – bluebells, primroses – daffodils if there were any left. At the weekend she would gather flowers for her own altar at home which she set up on a chest of drawers. She would move the statue of Our Blessed Lady from her normal place and take down the picture of Our Lady of Perpetual Succour and set them both together. Then surround them with flowers and say prayers more fervently than at any other time. It had something to do with the smell of the flowers. Unseeable, untouchable, beautiful. She closed her eyes when she prayed and in the darkness of her eyelids the smell of the woods seemed more intense. And therefore the prayers seemed more intense.

When they had the school altar set up Master Collins would make them sing,

> *Bring flowers of the fairest*
> *And blossoms the rarest . . .*
> *O Mary we crown thee with blossoms today*
> *Queen of the Angels and Queen of the May.*

She liked things that came around every year. The fireworks at Hallowe'en, the hollowed-out turnips with a candle inside, Christmas, the May altars, the marble season (for some reason she could never understand girls weren't supposed to be interested in marbles). Time passing, always looking forward to the next thing. She even liked going back to school after the holidays. Backing the new books with wallpaper.

The dark-haired nurse who checked on her now and again made her move around and asked a lot of questions, small-talk. Catherine small-talked back to her. Yes, she wanted a girl – more than anyone could imagine. Someone to buy dresses for, to plait her hair, to tie it in bunches with red satin ribbons.

When the nurse gave her an injection for the pain, Catherine said, 'I should have this nightie fitted with cords – like a venetian blind.' The needle pierced her hip and deposited a lead weight in her. She lay back and felt the drug begin to relax her. A dreamy sensation, a levitation above the level of the bed, a pleasantness cloaking her like drunkenness.

'Your travail will soon be over.'

She wondered if the nurse said it or she had made it up herself. Her watch said ten o'clock. The pains when they came now were more distant and between them she floated and closed her eyes.

Islay was good – digging peats, the earth vibrating beneath their feet like a sprung floor. A communication. Like sound.

The young nurse came back with an air of having tidied up everything.

'How's the injection working?'

'Fine,' she laughed.

'How long ago was your last pain?'

'About ten minutes now.'

'Everything's going to be all right.' The nurse reached over and touched her hand.

'You're just saying that. I bet you say that to everybody.'

'Well it's true – in most cases. Ninety-nine per cent. We have no reason to suspect you'll be any different.' The nurse's eyes slid away from her patient's gaze. Catherine squinted at the nurse's name-tag.

'Janet?'

'Yes.'

'Janet's nice. Did you ever get anybody calling the baby after you?'

'A couple of times.'

As they talked Catherine was aware that the nurse was just trying to keep her mind off what was to come. She let her think she was succeeding. Yes, she did have a job. In the island school – a music teacher.

'What do you play?'

'Piano.'

'Oh, I'd love to be able to do that,' said the nurse. 'And write my own songs.'

'Why don't you? There's nothing to stop you.' The nurse stared past her at the wall and shrugged. 'Except I can't play the piano.'

'You can learn.'

A pain made her stop and catch her breath. It was coming to the surface again. She gripped the rail of the bed behind her head until it passed.

The nurse said, 'What's it like living on an island?'

'Oh fine. But there's very little work around . . .'

She was talking like a drunk now but could not stop herself. Last year, around about February, Dave had been working for a farmer and he nearly burned half the island. They were setting fire to the heather to bring on the new grass but he had misjudged the wind. It was out of control for three days and they had to move beasts and everything. The island was black for months and when . . . Another pain erupted above the surface of the drug and she cried out.

'Remember your breathing,' said the nurse. Catherine gasped like the Lady Macbeth sigh she'd performed for Huang Xiao Gang.

'I don't want to talk,' she said.

'It's better this way.'

'What about yourself?'

The nurse told her that she was going with a medical student. He had taken her out . . . Another pain.

'I want to push,' Catherine gasped out. 'I feel like pushing.'

'Well, don't,' said the nurse. She got up and left as if everything was normal but ran the last few steps out of the ward. The clear plastic door slapped shut.

After a quick examination the midwife shifted her from the bed to a trolley. Catherine felt awkward. The baby inside her seemed to have increased by stones in the last hour. Some part of her flopped and gonged loudly against the trolley. The midwife tidied her leg on to it as they began to move.

The corridor clock swivelled past her and then she was in the bright lights of the delivery room full of bustle and starched nurses who fitted her with a pair of white wool socks and she tried to say anyone for tennis but nobody heard or else she didn't say it properly because they put her legs into slings, one to each side of the table, to abduct her hips, they said – it was a bit like composing music, really, parading the personal as they all stood at the bottom looking at the pain which was now cracking her open and which was responsible for her yelling so that a nurse who seemed to be orchestrating the whole thing came to her to hold her hand and dab the moisture from her forehead because there were too many lights and the place was too hot, stifling.

'Push now. That's the girl, push.'

She made it sound as if it was a voluntary thing, whereas Catherine felt it as a force sweeping through the lower half of her body and she was trying to hold on, trying not to get left behind as the midwife at the bottom end shouted, 'Come on, we can see it. Push now.'

And when the contractions did come her teeth were together and she made a weird whinnying sound because now the effect of the drug seemed to have left her completely and the pain was naked and razor-like – maybe they *were* making an incision – anything was possible – maybe they had no instruments and they were ripping her open, pulling her apart because their instruments had no cutting edge, were too blunt what with cut-backs and the like as the nurse wiped the sweat from her eyelids and forehead she wanted to ask why did they keep this place so fucking hot, they could save money that way, instead of not sharpening their instruments. And it was not the pain which was the worst – the ache was deeper than that – at the very core of her. The patron saint of childbirth was St Gerard Majella – how like the Catholic Church to appoint a man to the role – but she swore she would believe in him if only all this would stop. The nightmare to end all nightmares. The cloth was so cool. What if it should be deformed?

'Everything's going to be all right. One last big push?'

They kept praising her – good girl, good girl, they

shouted over and over again. What were they talking about? She tried to remember her breathing but everything that she knew was scattered by the next pain. She wanted to climb out of her body and help from the bedside.

'Here comes the head,' shouted the midwife. 'Push. *Push.*'

At the next contraction it all slithered out. She wailed a long aaahh of relief, this time with her teeth open. The release of the pressure was . . . She tried to look but the nurse put her head back and wiped the perspiration from her face. All the voices she could hear were singing her praises. Alleluia, alleluia from church. Hallelujah, hallelujah from the concert hall. The midwife said, 'Congratulations – you have a little girl.'

'The afterbirth – just one more push,' said the nearest nurse and began pressing down on her stomach, her arm straight, putting her shoulder behind it. She heard the baby cry – at first like a small cat cry with bubbles in it – then like a baby. Her baby. Her baby girl. She closed her eyes. She wanted to laugh, now that the pain had been pulled out of her. To laugh and sing, to make music. They handed the baby to her in a loose cellular blanket and she laid it against her breast.

'Is it all right?'

'She's fine,' said the midwife. She was cleaning her glasses.

'All its fingers and toes?'

'Yes, perfect.'

It was as if the fluids which had flooded her body in the effort of giving birth were fixing everything, making every impression, every sensation indelible. Everything was heightened. Everything was intense. She wanted to squeal and dance. She knew she would not forget one iota of this till the day she died.

Immediately she was aware of its femininity, this tiny wizened red girl. She was very fine, her hair Brylcreemed and flat and wet to her head. The wings of her tiny nostrils flared as she tried to breathe, her eyelids clenched against the harsh lights of the theatre. Its pores were clean white pin-points. The mother probed into the blanket and took out a fist to check for herself. The fingers tiny, ending in the most perfect crescent nails. She put the baby to her face and touched their cheeks together. It opened its mouth and gave a gummy yawn. Catherine realised that she was crying and heard herself saying – she's lovely, she's lovely, she's lovely. A vow welled up in her that this creature she had given birth to must never, never come to any harm. She must be protected with all her strength and love and care. She must surround and envelop her. She kissed her and the baby's eyes opened fractionally to reveal grape-purple pupils at east and west and the mother laughed, still crying.

As the nurse took the baby away for tests Catherine saw the perfection of her daughter's ear, whorled and tiny and precise as a shore shell. There was so much of her they hadn't allowed her to see.

They cleaned Catherine up and wheeled her back to a different ward and gave her a cup of tea and toast. The tea was hot and strong. She felt she could fly – she felt light with love. For her girl, for herself. For all the other women in the world who had ever given birth. Especially for her own mother – the feeling was totally unexpected, came from nowhere into her. She wanted to be with her mother, they had both shared an experience which should unite them in love. She wanted to tell her as another mother, as an equal about her girl child who would some day, maybe, give birth to her own girl.

She forgave her mother for some of her anxieties which grew out of concern, grew out of love and resolved *never* to do to her daughter what her mother had done to her. Turn her against her. She would trust her and her trust would be repaid.

The nurse came and took away her cup and checked that everything was all right. She said that a Dave Dewhurst had phoned and offered his congratulations. Catherine wondered what his reaction would be. They had discussed names at some length – if it was a boy he wanted to call it Simon, if a girl, she wanted her to be Anna. It was definitely an Anna she had held in her arms.

'Anna.' She tried saying it out loud. It felt right.

The nurse came with Catherine's baby and put the cot snug beside the bed. Catherine lifted her immediately and held her close to her cheek. The baby opened its mouth and began nudging her face.

'It's not there,' she said. 'Nurse, can you stand by?' The nurse came over. 'I've never done this before.'

'Fix her on well,' said the nurse. She grinned. 'Let her get a good grip of you.'

Catherine put the baby to her breast and felt the mouth clamp like a limpet on her. The nurse smiled and said, 'She may not get anything for a while . . .'

It was a strange sensation. She could actually feel her

breasts heating up. Tingling. The baby's jaws were working and her little fist was balled up close to her face. The clear plastic bracelet said Baby McKenna and her date of birth. Catherine looked down on its fontanelle – she could see her baby's pulse in this diamond of thin skin. Not a heartbeat, more a head beat – a head throb, not a heart throb. The rest of the women in the ward were asleep or trying to sleep. After a while the sucking at her breast stopped. Catherine looked down at her baby's sleeping head but didn't dare wake her. She put her back in the cot, covered her with the blanket.

'Is that OK?' she asked the nurse. The nurse bent over and tucked in the blanket, more to her liking. It was well after three in the morning. Catherine heard the deep breathing from the woman in the next bed and tried to synchronise with it. For ages she couldn't sleep. She was so close to the woman she felt they were in the same bed. She couldn't wait until the next time she could hold her baby. Her daughter, Anna. Even though her own eyes were closed she smiled. Eventually, as the sky became white, she fell into an exhausted sleep.

The noise of the ward wakened her at six o'clock and her first thought was of her baby. She closed her eyes against the glare of the uncurtained window. The ward was full of bustling and the sound of babies crying. A nurse with rubber-soled shoes squidged around the bed and helped her up, rearranging her pillows from horizontal to upright. Catherine leaned over and looked at her baby. She was still asleep. It seemed strange to be able to bend in the middle again. Her hands went beneath the bedclothes to feel the absence of her bump. She got out of bed to go to the bathroom.

'Will she be all right?' The nurse smiled and nodded. It felt strange to be moving about. Five of the six beds in the ward were occupied. She went to the toilet and a girl called Alison was head and shoulders out of the lavatory window smoking a cigarette.

Breakfast was in a small room off the corridor. Everybody said good morning like it was a small hotel except that they were all in their nighties. Catherine was given tea and toast and a boiled egg. She sat by herself and chewed the toast which had gone slightly tuggy. The egg was solid, the yolk dry and crumbly.

In a Portstewart guest house her father liked to play tricks when he had eaten his egg. He would put the shell upside down in someone else's eggcup. The McKennas would sit and watch the next person lift a spoon and cave in the top of the hollow egg. It was all for seven-year-old Catherine's benefit because they watched her delighted reaction more than the person who was fooled. Whoever was the victim would shout, 'Brendan!' and look all around. Laughter and much thigh slapping. How would he react when he found out his wee girl had had a baby?

Catherine left her crusts. When the auxiliary came and cleared away the breakfast things on to a trolley she said, 'I see you haven't grown up yet.'

Catherine was joined by an older woman called Marge and they were just chatting when Marge stiffened and half screamed out. Catherine was concerned for her but Marge said that she was still suffering contractions, even though she had had her baby two days ago. Having a ghost baby, she called it. Pain for fuck all. She patted Catherine's hand and assured her it never happened to women with their first baby.

When the mothers went back Anna was the only one who was crying. Catherine picked her up and began feeding her. She looked at the crown of her wee head. The hair, now that it was dry, was *so* fine. The fontanelle fascinated her as it pulsed. She thought again of her father and the empty eggshell. The fragility of this creature in her arms made her innards quake.

She felt the same quaking feeling later when she was bathing and changing her. The baby howled in the tiniest and tinniest of cries and Catherine talked to her and tried to comfort her as best she could. The nurse supervised and praised her. Catherine covered the bed and laid her baby in its hospital gown on the cover. The nurse brought a basin with warm water and set it on a stand beside the bed.

'Test it for temperature,' said the nurse. It still felt odd for Catherine to be able to bend over.

The sight of the inside of the baby's nappy made Catherine feel ill. Black treacle.

'Did they not tell you about that?' said the nurse.

'They did. What's it called?'

'Meconium.'

'I'd no idea it was like that.'

'It's a one off. You'll never see the like of that again — unless, of course, you have another baby.'

'It's a bit soon.'

As she lowered the baby into the water Catherine's foot

hit the tubular stand for the bath and the baby leapt and flung its arms out.

'Oh Jesus . . .'

'A good startle reflex,' said the nurse.

'Her or me?'

Catherine lifted her baby out of the water and held her close.

'I'm sorry, I'm sorry, pet. How could I do such a thing.' She was half crying, half laughing. She turned to the nurse. 'I thought it was a conducting reflex. We are all born conductors and gradually lose the ability over the rest of our lives. Discuss.' The nurse looked at her. Catherine said, 'I'm a music teacher.' The baby's legs were wide open and her knees were bent. 'Do you know who the greatest musical child prodigy was?' At first the nurse shook her head, then guessed Mozart.

'No. It was Master Crotch. A little Englishman. With a very strange name. He could play the organ at two years of age.' The nurse raised an eyebrow and they both smiled. When the nurse went away Catherine stooped over her baby and said, 'You'll be better than that. Little Miss Crotch.'

When she was clean and clothed Baby McKenna was put down to sleep. And as she slept her mother watched her, as if through a magnifying glass. *My soul doth magnify the Lord.* It was funny how the word meant 'to enlarge' and 'to praise' at the same time. Catherine laid herself down on the bed parallel to her baby, saw the eyelids move, the eyes flitter behind the lids. Rapid Eye Movement. Her baby, dreaming. She said this to the nurse when she came back and asked, 'What is there to dream about? Yesterday?'

'Maybe womb memories,' said the nurse.

'I played the piano for her when she was in there. She waltzed with me.'

She walked painfully to the phone in the middle of the afternoon to phone Dave and listened to the ringing tone purr-purring. She visualised the empty room, the rectangles of sunlight falling on the board floor. Vermeer. She knew where the phone was, could hear its bell echoing and not being answered. The weather was still good and Dave would be making the most of it. She hung up after a minute or so. Then looked up a number in her diary and dialled it.

'Hi, Liz?'

'Kate?'

'Yeah – I had a baby girl. Yesterday.'

'Oh my God – out of the blue – is it congratulations?'

'Seven pounds three ounces.'

'I didn't know. I didn't even know you were married.'

'I'm not.'

'Where – where are you?'

'Rotten Row.' Catherine told her the best time to visit. 'I just had to talk to someone.'

When she came back from the phone she lay down on her bed and watched Anna again. It was like the lover and the beloved. She could not get enough of her, this tiny person who had grown out of her body. Half her, half Dave. Nothing had prepared her for it. Yes, she had gone to pre-natal classes on the island. She knew what to expect. Everybody she knew, or ever would know, had gone through this process of being born. She saw her own family nested like Russian dolls. She'd had this baby inside her, while she had come from inside her mother, who had in her turn been inside Granny Boyd.

It was so utterly common and ordinary. And yet when it happened, it was a miracle. That her baby should be here, that she should be who she was, was a profound mystery. And if it wasn't a profound mystery, then her child was a burden to her, a mere nuisance. Her child was so much more than Catherine's eyes could take in. Although what she saw astonished her. The fingernails, the dark fluffy hair of the head, the whorl of the ear, they were all part of her and yet they belonged to someone else. Somebody totally other. It was like attending musical theory classes all her life, learning to sight-read, being shown the instruments and handling them, seeing photographs of composers, reading books about harmony and counterpoint but at no time *ever* hearing a single note of music. Then on a particular day, at a particular time after all the preparation, after all the theory and the rules and the speculation, she is led blindfold into a hall and an orchestra explodes into the celebratory sounds of, say, the voices' entry in Handel's *Zadok the Priest* or the final section of Beethoven's *Ode to Joy* or the closing section of Messiaen's *Turangalîla* symphony.

And the voice of her teacher leans close to her blindfolded ear and says quietly, 'That's what it is. *Now* do you understand?'

This is what it was. Anna. Her baby lying in front of her, an arm's length away. There was the baby she had carried inside her head and there was the baby she had carried inside her body. They were not the same. The one in front of her was better by far.

It occurred to her that there was no form of music to celebrate or mark this momentous event. If someone died a Requiem was written, if someone married an Epithalamium, why then was there not a piece of music to celebrate birth? Because the history of music was all male, that's why. Composers were men and they were usually barred from the birthing room. It was something that happened off-stage and was not worthy of their manly attention. However it was, no form existed for it. Yes, there was plenty of music, carols and Christmas masses by the ton to celebrate the birth of one particular infant, his nibs, Jesus Christ, but that was more a celebration for the God-part rather than the man-part arriving on earth. She wanted a celebration for the birth of her ordinary but exquisite girl-child. From nowhere a breathing rhythm came to her and a three-note sequence. She heard it in her head. A moment later it added two notes and became better, a five-note phrase. She turned to the bedside locker and picked up her biro pen and sketched down the idea. Janáček wrote down the notes and speech rhythms for things he heard – it was even said that, at the death bed of a friend, he wrote down the musical notation for his last gasp. God, how awful. She began developing the birth idea in her head. A hymn of welcome, maybe.

Dave rang and they brought the phone to the bed.

'Hi,' she said. 'Seven pounds three ounces. What do you think of me? And a girl.' He said he'd phoned from the bar late last night and the hospital had told him. After that they'd had one hell of a fuckin night. The place didn't close to four. She entwined her index finger in the slack spiral of the telephone cable. 'So are you going to make it out here to see her?'

Her face went solemn as she listened to him explaining about how expensive it would be for him to take a couple of days off – all for a half-hour visit to the hospital on the mainland. Not only the time lost working but the cost of the airfare and the bed and breakfast.

'You've no idea what it's like. Come out, Dave. You'll just love her. Believe me. You can make the money another time.'

But he wouldn't budge. The weather was still holding. The prices were still high. It would be madness to lose two days, going there and back, when there was such money to be made. Anyway it would only be a day or two before she was home. He said they were people with responsibilities now. And he was the provider. Last night some joker had asked him if he had put her name down for Eton. And he'd said, 'Aye, and for drinkin as well.' He didn't remember the half of it. Neither did half the island. Every bastard was buying him drink. And the singing. And the jokes. People slapping him on the back. But he was really looking forward to seeing them both.

'On Friday – two o'clock,' she said. 'If there are no complications. No – really, everything is fine. It'll not be the ambulance plane. Just the regular afternoon flight. Gets in at two forty-five.'

Catherine was the only one in a ward of six who was breastfeeding. Anna wakened at three in the morning looking for a feed. One of the women snorted in her dreams and made wet eating noises. Another turned in the bed with a slither of sheets. When she heard her baby's cries Catherine would sit bolt upright in the bed, both breasts already seeping milk. In a kind of trance she'd open the nursing bra and attach the baby – then maybe nod off. Not sleeping exactly but the kind of thing that used to happen in the crowded church at home during a sermon. Boredom, heat, shoulder to shoulder with her neighbours, the world would begin to disappear, her eyelids would droop, sounds would become distorted like a radio drifting off the station – still audible but the words making no sense – the incomprehensible voice was a comforter – it droned – if it stopped suddenly she'd probably wake. But she'd wake anyway her chin jerking up, her head back. No longer in church, she felt the tug and suck and swallow of the baby at her breast. And then the whole process would be repeated.

'Other side,' she'd say and change her from one breast to the other. The ward was in darkness except for the tent of light over her own bed. Outside the dawn would just be beginning. The navy sky lightening, stars still obvious.

During these night feeds her baby cried and Catherine tried to shush her. The sleeping mothers would wake and it made Catherine feel worse. The more women wakened the worse she felt. She would get up and put the baby over her shoulder and walk and jig her up and down. She tried to sing to her. One of her teachers at the Royal Scottish Academy of Music and Drama – Alasdair Kirkpatrick – giving a talk about Scottish and Irish song made the observation that all songs about children could be divided into lullabys or songs of infanticide.

'Nae half measures,' he said. 'We'll get ye quiet one way or anither.'

She hated one song – hated it more now that she'd had her own baby. *A weela weela wall-ya.*

I stuck the penknife in the babby's head.

She thought of the fontanelle. The penknife. She must try and think of other things. She shouldn't distress herself. The lullaby was a strange thing – music with an extra-musical purpose. But it would never have worked for her – the idea that music could be soothing. She would have wanted to stay wide awake to listen to every note, every nuance. On edge to hear what came next. It would have been better to read to her from the newspaper. Paragraphs of endless human folly. She'd have been over in a trice. Warmth and the security of the human voice saying incredibly boring things. Snore, snore. ZZZZZZzzzzzzz. Like the comics. At pre-natal classes she'd been told that the baby was not just sucking milk out of her but was in some way making the milk for itself – stimulating the reflex which manufactured the milk. If the baby ceased to suck then the reflex would die.

What if it was like that with writing music? If, in all the tumult of the baby being brought into the world, the pattern of her music writing was interrupted. If she ceased to call on it, would the flow of it cease? Would her musical reflex just die? And never come back? Isak Dinesen said that she wrote a little every day without hope and without despair. It was hard to believe that such a profound change could happen because of a biological

175

event. But at the moment she did not care. All she wanted to do was to put her baby down and get back to sleep.

The thought of the fontanelle and the penknife came to her again. She must stop thinking of that, of hurting a child. This child of hers she would protect with all her will, all her strength. She would give her life for her, if someone tried to harm her.

At home in Ireland they'd had a small play park. There was a man there sometimes, Jack Bolton. He came over to the slide to make sure that none of the little girls got hurt. He would stand with his protective hands out looking up at them on the top of the slide. Catherine had loved the slide. *Ding dang dung ding dong.* Ascending notes as she'd run up the iron steps – *sleeth* – she'd slide down the shute and then race back to climb the steps. *Ding dang dung ding dong* running up, *sleeth*, down again. She must have been the only child in the town who liked running up the steps better than sliding down the shute. The shute was just a quicker way of getting her back to hear the ringing of her shoes on the iron steps.

Then one day something happened and the police came and took Jack Bolton away from the swing park. When Catherine asked why, her mother said, 'Just don't speak to strangers.'

'He's not a stranger. He's Jack Bolton.'

Her mother sniffed. Catherine said, 'But what would a stranger *do*?' Her mother looked over her shoulder to see that no one was listening.

'They could hurt you.'

'Why – why would they want to hurt you?'

'Because there are some bad men. Men who want to hurt you.'

Eventually the baby would be fed and winded and falling asleep on her shoulder. Catherine would return her to the cot – delicate as eggs so as not to wake her. Despite her exhaustion Catherine would lie awake with her eyes closed, her mind repeating and repeating. Monotonous as the dawn sparrows outside. Cheep cheep cheep cheep cheep.

They let Catherine have a bath. Anna had been fed and put down for the afternoon and the nurse ran Catherine's bath for her and threw a handful of coarse salt splishing on to the surface of the water.

'It's plain saline from here on in,' she said. Catherine laughed for her. 'It's a great healing fluid. The oul salt water.' The bath was much fuller than she would have had it at home – there was a kind of extravagance of hot water here. She got into it uttering little noises of pleasure. Immediately in the hot water she got goose-flesh and the hairs stood on her arms. She was still bleeding enough to tinge the water. She lay back and relaxed – the bath so full she was almost floating. The nurse left her on her own. Catherine closed her eyes. The soap was Pears – a smell that reminded her of childhood. She soaped her hands and began to wash herself. Her tummy looked strange and felt even stranger – like blancmange. Loose, deflated, blubbery. The stretch marks had not disappeared. If the nurse was to be believed they would never disappear. The most she could hope for was that they would lose their raw liver colour and turn silvery white. Would Dave still find her sexy? He was always wanting to get in the bath with her.

He was mad for soaping her and her soaping him. But after a while she didn't enjoy this kind of thing. A bath was a private experience – nothing whatsoever to do with sex or lovemaking. She started locking the bathroom door, telling Dave it was an invasion of her privacy for him to come in and want to write his own agenda in her bathtime. He laughed and sarcastically quoted her own phrase back to her often.

They had met in a bar at the other side of the island. She had been with her friend Liz – over for the weekend to plan a geography trip for her students. The island was full of interesting deposits of pudding-stone and gneiss and shale and God knows what. They had aimed to tour the whole place but they didn't see much of it because of the head-high cloud. It was the insides of pubs they had seen. And she'd met Dave.

Catherine had gone to the counter to buy her round. As she stood waiting for the drinks to be set up she heard a voice beside her ordering a large round. The accent was English but she couldn't place the region. She turned and looked at the speaker. He was a guy about the same age as herself. When she met men the first things she took account of were the negative things. Wimpishness, a bully, shiftiness, recklessness, elaborate facial hair. She saw none of these things. He just looked good. And he was friendly.

'How're you doing? All right?' he said. She nodded to him and his face lit up with the smile. He looked at her and she at him. He swirled the ice which remained in his glass. 'Ever swallow an ice cube?' She shook her head. He drunk one off with a gulp and rolled his eyes a little. 'Have you any idea what it's like?'

'No.'

'A cold feeling in the pit of your stomach.'

Catherine laughed. She took her two glasses and carried them back to where Liz was sitting. She told her of the encounter and Liz raised her eyebrows.

'Where's he sitting?' Catherine tried to indicate without pointing. 'Is he on his own?' asked Liz.

'He's with a crowd.'

'Thank God for that – lone drunks are just pests.'

'He's not drunk.'

Catherine turned to look at him again. Black hair, tanned face – an outdoor kind of guy. Lots of denim. He caught her looking at him and grinned back at her.

Later in the evening they happened to coincide at the bar again. He listened to her accent when she spoke to the barman. He said, 'Whatcha doing here then?'

'Ordering drink.'

'But have you the money to pay for it?' Catherine held up a five pound note between two fingers.

'Naw – come on. Whatcha doing on the island?'

'Just over for the weekend.'

'From Ireland?'

'From Glasgow.'

'How does a girl with an accent like that get to be in Glasgow?'

'The same way a guy like you ends up here.'

'And what's that?'

'Luck.' She looked at him hard. 'Or lack of it.'

'You're smart enough to be a student in Glasgow.'

'Do I look like one?' He nodded and lifted his wobbling tin tray of drinks. 'What particular branch of study are you

179

engaged in?' Catherine hesitated. 'I mean what do they think they're leading you out of.'

'I don't understand.'

'E – duco. To lead out. They mustn't like the darkness you're in.'

'Silence. I'm studying music.'

'That's why I left London,' he said. 'I was trying to teach community singing on the tube. When I was part of the rat race – but did they want to know – on their way to work in the mornings?' Catherine smiled. 'What dead people – they've had their souls removed at birth.' Later he walked past their table on his way to the Gents and said, 'A word in your shell-like.' He had to shout to make himself heard above the noise of the pub. 'I tried to simplify it to community whistling but they didn't want to know about that either. City gents – preoccupied with Mammon. No room in their souls for anything else. Hyperventilating exhaust fumes.'

When he was in the toilet Liz said, 'I think he's cute.'

'As a bag of weasels.'

And as he made his way back he stopped at their table again.

'Let me tell you something . . .' Before they could say anything he was sliding into an empty seat opposite. His jeans rubbed against the mock leather and there was a distinct farting noise. He looked surprised and said, 'That was me – it wasn't the seat.' Then he laughed his head off. 'What's your names then girls?' Liz introduced herself and then Catherine.

'McKenna?' He laughed. 'Jesus, there's not much doubt

about where you're from. Is McKenna with or without a Y?'

'Eh – without.'

'Good. If there was a Y in it I couldn't see where the hell it was going to be.' They shook hands and his handshake was firm and warm. In Catherine's case he even covered her hand with his other hand.

'What are you doing over here?'

Liz told him about her geography trip.

'Oh, there's no geography here – just rocks and mountains and alluvial plains.'

'What about pudding-stone?'

'Enough pudding-stone to sicken you.'

'And what do you do?' asked Liz.

'Precious fucking little.' Then he put his hands up in apology. 'I'm sorry – I'm overstepping the mark. You might both be daughters of the Manse.' They shook their heads – definitely not. 'My main work is signing on. Right now I'm doing a bit of diving. The one doesn't interfere with the other. I figured when I was in Nottingham that if I was going to be on the dole then I might as well be on the dole somewhere nice.'

She massaged the flesh of her stomach and thought of Dave's fingertips. The nurse came in.

'You'll be going all wrinkly, Mrs McKenna.' She held the towel for her to step into, then allowed her to dry herself.

'I'd like to become a skin donor,' said Catherine rubbing herself with the towel. 'Can you arrange that for me?'

'Certainly mam. How many metres?'

★　★　★

Liz came to visit her and brought a thin bunch of irises. The stems were still wet when she took them from her so she must have bought them at the stall downstairs. They hugged each other hard.

'You're looking great,' said Liz.

'You too.'

'Your hair's all different. It suits you.'

'Thanks.'

Catherine lay on top of the bed against her pillows, Liz stood by the visiting chair.

'Where is . . .?' She moved quickly to the other side of the bed to the baby's cot and stooped over it. 'Aww . . . she's gorgeous.' She looked round at Catherine.' Does she take after you or its father – whoever he is?' Liz came away from the cot and sat down on the chair. Her eyes were lit up. 'Who is he?'

'You'll never guess.'

'No, you're right, I won't – there's a lot of them about.'

'Remember the English guy we met in the pub . . .'

'Him! He's dishy enough. Very Liam Neesonish. But then I was very drunk that night.' Liz reached out and held Catherine's hand. 'Do you intend to get married or not?'

Catherine shook her head. 'Naw – maybe some-time . . .'

'So she wasn't planned for?'

'What do you think? You're beginning to sound like my mother.'

'I'm just getting the picture. You're not exactly the best person in the world at keeping in touch. Tell me the story so far.'

Catherine looked towards the cot.

'Her name is Anna and the father's name is Dave . . .'

At night, what with the breastfeeding and the crowded ward and the close proximity of the other women, she was sleeping badly and the night before she went home she did not sleep at all. She just lay in the bed thinking with her eyes closed. There would have to be changes. Dave's drinking was moving rapidly from heavy drinking to problem drinking. Drink was involved in every single thing he did. Work was for having a drink after. Barbecues on the beach were for drinking. Going down the pub was a seven-night-a-week activity. On one or two nights Catherine would go with him – mostly at the weekend. God knows what he drank at the pub when she wasn't there but when he came home he'd have a half-bottle of vodka swinging in his pocket to get him off to sleep.

'You're damaging yourself, Dave.'

'I don't get hangovers. Have I ever missed a day's work because of drink?'

'No.'

'Have you ever seen me drunk – staggering about?'

'Yes.'

'When?'

'At the McKenzies' barbecue. And that night you threw up all night . . .'

'That was a bug.'

'The weekend on the mainland you kept bumping into walls. At Hilary's christening in broad daylight. And at Donald's wedding . . .'

'Bloody hell. That's crap and you know it.'

'I see known alcoholics in the pub who drink *less* than you.'

'Fuck off.' Doors slamming. His retreat to the pub yet again.

She had heard arguments like this before, coming from other rooms – between her mother and father. And she had put her hands over her ears to try and stop the sounds.

'Brendan – you are your own best customer.'

'Have a titter of wit, woman. What's wrong with having a drink to keep a customer happy? What's wrong with having a drink when things are slack?'

'Everything. Everything's wrong with it.'

'Grumpy bitch.' Doors slamming. A retreat downstairs once again. Catherine would run to Granny Boyd's. Nine time out of ten the old woman would be sewing.

'I can whistle,'

'Now that IS something,' said the old woman. 'Let me hear.' Catherine pursed her lips and made a blowing noise. A whistle came into it but it disappeared again. 'Very good. It's a bit of a dry land sailor's whistle. But it'll get better. It's all that can happen to it. Our Lady never whistled, so they say.'

'Did she have a dog?'

'Not that I know of.'

The inside of the lid of Granny Boyd's sewing basket was a pincushion made of plush, red velvet. Needles were slanted into it with wisps of different coloured threads hanging from them. Sometimes the old woman asked Catherine to thread needles for her. Her own eyes, she said, were away with it. Sometimes she asked her to cut out paper hexagons from a cardboard template for the quilts she was making. As she cut out, her grandmother would tease her.

'It's all in the way you hold your tongue.'

Catherine's tongue would disappear and she would listen to the whisper of her grandmother's thread being drawn through the material and to her own scissor noise as she cut the papers.

In the hospital shop Catherine bought a box of Roses chocolates to be shared among the nurses on her floor. She said she would miss the pampering, the banter, the other women. The ward was like an exclusive female club. She associated her time there not with pain, but with sunshine on the floor, white sheets and bright colours, women's voices, the smell of bouquets of flowers, leaking breasts, the slap of perspex doors, the sound of curtains being pulled around beds. Before she left she began to feel anxious for no reason. She attributed it to the lack of sleep – a couple of hours in three days. The weather was still good but, now inside, it seemed stifling. The nurses brought a fan into the ward. Her anxieties were mostly about herself and how she wasn't feeling the same way about her baby. She worried about . . . she didn't know what she worried about. All she knew was that she felt tense and uneasy. The slack muscles of her gut felt taut all the time even though she could take a handful of them. When she woke after a fifteen-minute sleep she did not want to move, did not want to believe that she was awake. In her last day in the ward the hospital routine proceeded as if she was still dreaming. Everything seemed unreal and she felt isolated. Apart from the sound, it was as if there was a pane of glass between her and everything going on around her. The rattle of instruments against a stainless-steel kidney dish – the flushing of Victorian plumbing – the medicine trolley with its squeak from one wheel – all these things seemed distant and yet at the same time hateful. The smiles of nurses. The very name of the place. They made her feel that something awful was about to happen and she had to tense herself against it. Most frightening of all was the sound of her baby crying. But now, waiting for the taxi, Anna lay beside her quiet, wrapped in a cellular blanket. She was like a white lozenge with a pink face at one end.

'She's a gorgeous little madam,' said the nurse, who was run off her feet. She helped Catherine on with her navy raincoat. Sand. Catherine's pockets were always gritty because she carried home shells. She dusted her fingers and indicated the chocolates on the bedside locker.

'There was no need,' said the nurse. 'But they'll not last long round here.'

'Just a token. Thanks for everything.' They both moved towards the ward door.

'Don't forget the baby,' said Catherine. The nurse banged her forehead with the heel of her hand and laughed. Then picked Anna up from her cot.

Outside the main door Catherine stepped up into the black taxi with her bag. The nurse set the baby on her mother's knee.

'Sit well back there, Missus,' the driver shouted over the noise of the engine. 'You're in safe hands now.' Things looked further away than they actually were. Inaccessible beyond the taxi window with its little instruction picture of a red hand opening it.

She knew some of the people going on the plane. They crowded around her in the airport lounge. Peter, the young postman, who was reputed to travel to the mainland for his haircuts, bent over and said, 'She's an armful.' Catherine sat beside Mrs Shaw from the Co-op.

'She's a wee dote.' She asked for a carry of her and walked up and down the carpet, shushing her and grinning down at the face in the white blanket. Catherine said she wanted to go to the toilet. She sat for ages in the cubicle long after she had finished, reluctant to rejoin the others. When she came back Mrs Shaw handed the baby back to her.

'A future customer,' she said. Catherine indicated that she could have her for a while longer. Mrs Shaw cuddled the bundle. 'I suppose Dave's meeting you at the other side?'

'Aye.'

'I've the car in the car park over there and I'd be going your way.'

'No – I'm fine. Thanks all the same.'

Donald, one of the barmen in the Seaview Hotel predicted that he would see a lot more of Dave, now that they had brought a screamer into the house. He poked his big stubby finger, with hair above the knuckle, into the blankets and chucked the baby under the chin. Catherine felt a strange detachment from the whole thing. She was beginning to feel things no mother should admit to feeling.

Her baby got the same kind of reception when they

landed on the island. Catherine couldn't see Dave at the window. The terminal was a pre-fab which was crowded with people waiting for the outgoing flight and those who were meeting the incoming one.

'Isn't she lovely.'

'A wee darlin, God bless her.'

'Can I give you and the screamer a lift?' said Donald, the barman.

'No – Dave's meeting me.'

The passengers for the flight out sat near the door to the airfield. The papers came off the plane and were loaded on to the bus. Several of the island's postmen sorted through sacks of mail before heading out to their red post vans. Catherine, with her baby held stiffly, sat down to wait. The air hostess, Ingrid, whom she knew, came from behind the check-in desk to the centre of the floor and made an announcement, 'Ladies and gentlemen – your flight is now ready for boarding.' Catherine watched the whole procedure. Ingrid checked their tickets, which she had just issued at the desk then led the little line of passengers out to the plane sitting on the tarmac. She indicated the steps with a gesture. When everyone was aboard the propellers started up and she had to hold on to her red pill-box hat with one hand and give a company wave with the other. With an incredible roaring the plane taxied off towards the runway. Ingrid continued to wave.

Catherine sat facing the swing doors at the entrance into the car park. They needed a squirt of what her dad called 'Father, Son and Holy Ghost', because every time anyone came in or out the doors gave a screech followed by a diminishing flopping sound until they were still. The incoming passengers had nearly all gone now. Somewhere a radio was playing pop music. The baby was asleep. Catherine looked down at her. If anything, her appearance had improved. In the first couple of days her face had a clenched fist kind of appearance. Now it was relaxed, it had blossomed and unfurled, the rawness gone. When she was born Catherine could hardly wait to show her to Dave. To get him to take photographs of her. But now the urgency seemed to have disappeared. He would see her when he saw her. She heard the door screech open again and looked up. One of the postmen had forgotten something. When he went out again the door screeched again. Again the diminishing flopping sound until the doors were still. At the end of the runway the note of the plane's engines rose to a hornet sound as it raced to take off. Ingrid came back into the terminal, taking off her hat, her high heels clicking. Catherine and her baby were the only ones left.

'Hi, Catherine. Nobody come yet?'

'He said he'd be here.'

Ingrid disappeared into the office behind the check-in desk. The noise of the departing plane faded into a drone, then into silence. The radio in the office was switched off. Out over the flat landscape of the airport curlews tumbled and chased each other in the air. Their calls were just audible inside the terminal. Ingrid appeared, now in flat shoes. She still had her grey and scarlet uniform on, except for the hat.

'I'm going back right now, if you want a lift.'

'This is so bloody typical.' Catherine stood and Ingrid took her bag.

'Let's have a look at her now that I have time to breathe.' She bent in close to the sleeping baby.

'Och would you look at her, the wee lamb. Is she good?'

'Yes.'

'Are you getting enough sleep?'

'None at all.'

Ingrid locked the building and they walked to the solitary car in the car park. She got mother and daughter settled in the front seat. Catherine put the seat belt on, tried somehow to lengthen it and loop it around the baby.

'If we crash it'll be strangled,' she said. 'And I'll know who to blame.'

'I'll go very canny.'

'No, not you – Dave.'

They drove out on to the road. Even within the space of a week Catherine had forgotten how big the sky was on the island. From sea horizon to land horizon it arched overhead clouded and blue and huge.

'So how was it?'

'It was fine.'

'Were you long in labour?'

'About twelve hours.'

'What weight was she?'

'Seven pounds three ounces.' Ingrid whistled. 'She's put on almost a pound this week.'

'Very good.'

Ingrid caught up with a distillery lorry and she kept edging out over the white line to see if she could pass but there always seemed to be a bend or oncoming cars. She tucked in again behind the lorry.

'Thanks very much for this,' said Catherine. 'I don't know what has happened.'

'I saw him earlier – when I was coming in.'

'Where?'

'In town – outside the Seaview.'

'Jesus . . .'

'I don't mean . . . I'm not telling tales . . . he wasn't going in or anything. I mean he was just there. Talking to Tam Campbell and The Bruce.'

Catherine adjusted her hand beneath the baby's back. She was still sleeping.

'Come on you big thug,' said Ingrid and edged out a little, then quickly back in again to avoid a blue van. 'Is that him now?' Catherine turned and saw their blue van racing towards the airport.

'That's him.'

'Do you want me to go after him?'

'No – no point.'

'He'll see the place locked up and put two and two together.'

'Aye.'

The car turned the bend at the top of the hill and the jumbled houses of the town, the river, the school, the churches lay beneath them. It seemed like a postcard – remote, untouchable. Catherine felt as if a trap was closing.

Ingrid dropped her at the bungalow and helped her as far as the door with her hold-all.

'Good luck with the wee darlin,' she said. 'I'll see you around.' The front door was open – they never locked it – and Catherine pushed in. The place was tidy. He had done that much at least but, after the hospital, the place smelled of cigarettes.

'Here we are. Home at last,' she said to the baby. She put her down in the cot they had bought. Dave had painted the room white and stencilled some animal shapes in bright poster colours. A fox, a kangaroo, a puffin, an elephant. But he hadn't got around to finishing it – one wall remained matt white.

She took off her coat and hung it up. She walked into the living-room. There, where she had left them, were her papers for the Purcell. She went over to the desk and turned the top one to face her.

'Tis women makes us love,
'Tis love that makes us sad,
'Tis sadness makes us drink,
And drinking makes us mad.

On the windowsill behind the shells was the stapled booklet of the island phone numbers. She rang the district nurse to say that she and her baby were home. Then looked up another number, McKechnie's Garage, which she dialled. When someone answered she said, 'I would like to learn to drive.'

The man at the other end said, 'There's nothing to it, missus, now that they've put the white lines in the middle of the road.'

It took the best part of a year. Dave refused to teach her in the van because he said it could only lead to fights and a fucked up gear-box. Forty lessons and two test failures before she finally passed. And still she hadn't seen a traffic light or a roundabout. The examiner from the mainland showed her pictures of a roundabout in a laminated file and asked her questions about how she would approach it. She showed him with her shaking fingernail. Afterwards he told her that she had passed. Third time lucky, she said. McKechnie sold her a car for next to nothing – said it had *a good strong engine in her* – although the bodywork left a lot to be desired. *There's more miles left in her than a ball of string*, he said, whatever that meant. On an island a mother with a young baby found a car was an absolute necessity. It was not a question of a luxury. She had to be independent of Dave. He needed his van for work. In the evenings he was too drunk to drive it, although most of the time this didn't stop him. During the day Catherine needed to get to the shops, to travel to other places on the island, to take her night class, to run a babysitter home.

She woke at five-thirty. Became conscious. Oh Jesus. The realisation that nothing had gone away. Everything was still there. She could hear Dave snoring and occasionally gagging from the sofa in the living-room. Think of something else. It would be her baby's first birthday next week. She wasn't one of those mothers who wanted to hold a party for a group of screaming infants whose centrepiece was a cake with a single candle. She wasn't one of those mothers full stop. Think of something else. Sister Immaculata taught them chemistry and biology. She had a round solemn face with her two front teeth hung out to dry. She had a strange switched-on smile. Her face would flick from solemn to smile and back again in an instant. There were no intermediate positions.

The possibility existed that if the person who was wide awake did nothing she, he or it would drift back to sleep. If she, he or it stirred up muck from the bottom of their brain it would keep them awake. Be still. Breathe simply and regularly. Think of something different.

'The experiment we are engaged in today is to show two things.' Solemn. Smile. Solemn. 'That a gas can be heavier than air and that carbon dioxide will not sustain combustion.' The girls sat around laboratory benches. Their uniform was earth-brown and sky-blue. Our Lady's blue, Sister Immaculata called it. She took from the cupboard a small flight of darkly stained stairs, blew some dust away and set the apparatus in front of the class. It is all right to think of this. This is quite a good thing to think of. It stops the awful thoughts – like what was happening to her and her baby. It wasn't as a result of any kind of mental illness – it was just that she was a bad mother. Devoid of all the right emotions. Oh Jesus, she was at it again. Doing it before she knew she was doing it. Thinking it again. Back, back to something else. Sister Immaculata dived into her raffia basket and produced handfuls of candle stubs. Her heartbeat was in the pillow. Pounding in her ear. Too fast. Last night – she could not believe what had happened. Last night. How could he? When she was feeling as bad as she was? Stop it.

'I saved these candle stubs from our little oratory. Waste not, want not.' She began setting them on the steps of the apparatus. 'This is a rare case of the Church being the handmaid of science.' Three on each shelf, seven shelves in all.

The previous lesson they had made carbon dioxide and it had wallowed invisibly in a square glass jar in the fume cupboard over the weekend. Sister Immaculata produced a cheap cigarette lighter. The girls nudged each other and imagined her smoking. The nun lit a taper and faced the class.

'Observe.'

She dipped the lit taper into the jar. It went out. Then she solemnly lit each candle stub on the little staircase. It became a small altar with its twenty-one pinpoints of light flickering in the draughts of the classroom. On a real altar so many candles meant it was a special occasion – a High Mass or the Exposition of the Blessed Sacrament. A girl's hand went up.

'Miss – miss, I mean Sister . . .'

Damn – now she needed the toilet. At this time of the morning the slightest noise would waken the baby.

'Observe,' said Sister Immaculata. She lifted a glass container and slowly up-ended it as if she was pouring water down the staircase. Nothing happened. The candles flickered and burned as brightly as ever. A girl in the front row coughed and the candle flames momentarily shrank, blew to one side and back again.

'Well, what have you observed?'

'You picked up the wrong container, Sister.'

'Thank you, Catherine.' She rounded on the rest of the class. 'I told you to *observe*, 1A.' Some girls turned to look at Catherine and her face burned a bit. The two girls she hated most, Sarah and Ann-Marie, sneered at her. But she did not care.

'The blinds, please, girls.' Whoever was nearest pulled the black blinds. Lit from underneath by candle light, Sister Immaculata's face looked scary.

'Now the CO_2.' She lifted the container from the fume-cupboard and very slowly and dramatically began to pour what looked like emptiness down the flight of stairs. The first three candles snuffed out. There was no smoke. A murmur of awe came from the girls. Then the next three winked out as the invisible stuff flowed down. The Black Sea. Then the next three. And the next – so on down the stairs, extinguishing every candle to the bottom. It gave Catherine a strange feeling, this invisible cascade of darkness. She felt suffocated by it quilting downwards – whatever it was. This diminuendo of light brought about by something intangible – odourless – invisible. The classroom was dark and silent, it even felt cold, until someone began to applaud in a way that was both mocking and full of admiration. Then the blinds were snapped up and sunlight flooded the place.

'Wasn't that something?' Solemn. Smile. Solemn. 'Get out your writing-up books.'

Another thing Sister Immaculata had told them was about the Golden Mean and the Fibonacci series – how God's favourite ratio was 1 to 1.62 and how almost all growing things corresponded to this. The Fibonacci series was made by adding any two consecutive numbers to get the next one.

0 1 1 2 3 5 8 13 21 34 55 89 and so on.

She made them measure the spirals of chrysanthemum

heads and the chambers of shells and the points where twigs emerged from branches. She shepherded their calculations and the class was amazed to discover the ratio was always the same. Then she asked them to measure where the horizon was in famous paintings. Catherine and some others, who did music, were volunteered to look at the climaxes in a Mozart piano sonata. The ratio was the same in every case – 1 to 1.62. How could this be?

'It's just that it's God's favourite number. A work of art is a prayer – and when artists create they instinctively offer back to their Maker things which are constructed in his favourite ratio. Mister Fibonacci lived in the Renaissance, although he didn't know it at the time, because nobody called it that then – the only things we should pigeonhole, girls, are pigeons. Mister Fibonacci was also largely responsible for introducing the zero into Western culture. Stolen from the much-maligned Arabs.'

She definitely did need the toilet. Her bladder was nipping. *Vexations*. It would be nice to be a baby again. Just go where she lay. Let somebody else clean up. Take the yellowed nappy off her, dispose of it, wash her, powder her – maybe some zinc ointment in her crease to prevent the rash – a clean white dry nappy. Then the plastic pants. Then the Babygro. Above all not having to think. Not giving a toss about anything. Just lying there. If only. If only so many things. Her eyes were closed – she was unable to get back to sleep. After a certain amount of time she knew she'd lost it – sleep would not take over. For a time the snoring stopped. Dave's heavy breathing from the other room was long and slow as if nothing had happened. Once the thoughts were active she had no chance. First thoughts, worst thoughts. It was as if they strode in, slammed the door and said, 'Pay attention, when I'm around nothing, but nothing else happens. Nothing moves in or out. And as for anything to do with music – forget it.' And now a new one had been added. How dare he, how *dare* he, do a thing like that to her? Blackness. Unremitting blackness. Zero. Thank you for the concept, Mister Fibonacci.

She slid out of bed as quietly as she could and went to the toilet, keeping her eyes half closed. Pretending she was still asleep. She daren't look at herself in a mirror – not even a glimpse as she passed it by. When she finished she did not flush it for fear of waking the baby. Or Dave. She didn't know which was worse. If he found she hadn't used the flush he'd ask her if she was keeping this stale piss and paper for a particular reason. Or should he just dispose of it by the normal means? She got back into the bed and settled down. The house once again reverberated to snoring. And the bedroom was light and made her clench her eyes to increase the darkness. No one could sleep with clenched eyes. No one could sleep with that pig noise. To sleep you had to be relaxed. If she relaxed her eyes then it was too bright. Still her heartbeat pounded in the pillow. Look for positive things. The weather was good. She nearly laughed – what the hell did that matter? What good was that to anybody? She had a few strategies which didn't help but which made things less bad. She was able to do things inside her head to lessen the hurt. Throughout the day other windows would be opened, artificial light shone into corners until, at night, she slept. In the morning she awakened in blackness again. Day after day. Morning after morning it went on. Repeating. Erik Satie indicated in his piano piece *Vexations* that it was to be played 840 times. An eccentric joke until some modern musicians took him seriously and gave it a relay performance lasting eighteen hours. It was like that inside her head. Except that her thoughts were unpleasant to start with. And they came again and again and again. And again. Miss Bingham had arthritis, an auto-immune disease – the body attacking itself. In Catherine's case, the mind was attacking itself. Steps, flowing down the days. Take off the nappy – a quick squint at the contents, wash between and around the kicking legs with a facecloth in a basin, zinc ointment, baby talc, dry nappy, plastic pants, a Babygro. Her heartbeat muffled between her ear and her pillow. Telling her she was alive whether she liked it or not. Repeating. Sparrows below the window. Repeating. Cheep cheep cheep cheep. Not only the days repeating but the everyday thoughts repeating. Endless loops. Like a refrain. Over and over again. Her mind flagellating itself. A crown of thorns worn on the inside. An attempt to reach the eight hundred and fortieth time. The same thing. A chorus. A refrain. Recapitulation. The same thing. From the outside, people in her state were supposed to look catatonic. Just sitting there. Glum. Dumb. Down. But it was far from the truth. The outside light was turned off to allow the brain more time to screw itself up. Full of scorpions – that said it all. Pain for fuck all, as Marge in the hospital had said. Endless repetition. Remove the nappy – review the contents, sluice it out down the toilet, making sure not to let it go and bugger the plumbing for the foreseeable future, wash baby's undercarriage with facecloth, slap on zinc ointment, baby talc, fresh nappy, those horrible plastic pants – like a shower cap with leg holes, a pink Babygro. Her heart-beat muffled between her ear and her pillow. Think of something else. Get away from this repetitive stuff. Leave repeats behind. Like a shoelace threaded through the eyelets, zig-zag, this way and that but always due to end up in the last hole no matter what way it goes. Think of something else. Her baby. Oh no – that *was* it. That was what she did *not want to think about. Weela, weela, wall-ya.* Inside a boiled egg there was a skin. Thin as tracing paper. If you cracked and crazy-paved the shell and peeled it off then beneath that was the skin. You could tear it. A membrane. Like the fontanelle. *She stuck the penknife in the babby's head.* Think of something else. Huang Xaio Gang. But he had called her Lady Macbeth, someone who did awful things to children. Leave yourself alone. You're worrying about worrying. I am thinking about what I do not want to think about. Day after every day. Morning after every morning it goes on. Repeating. Repeat marks. Da capo means return to the beginning. Literally – from the head. The babby's head. Where she stuck the penknife. Or dashed the brains out. Think of other things. Something else. Bis means perform the passage twice. Repeat it. A recap. Sparrows below the window. Repeating. Cheep cheep cheep cheep. Not only the days repeating but the everyday thoughts repeating. Endless loops. Like a refrain. Over and over again. The same thing. A chorus. Ritornello – a little repeat, a recurring musical passage. A refrain. The same thing. *Kindertotenlieder* was by Mahler. She had it in a version by Kathleen Ferrier which could break her heart. She didn't like a voice full of emotion but this was different. This was a voice full of pure music which broke the heart. It was a long time after first hearing it before she knew it translated as 'Songs on the Death of Children'. And she was back thinking about what she did *not want to think about*. She felt the darkness of the bright days descending on her step by step. A cascade winking out hope.

In the beginning she'd gone to the island doctor a lot – the baby had a cold – a bubbly nose – it was crying too much – it wasn't feeding properly. She wasn't getting enough sleep. Somehow she hoped he would spot the way she was feeling and help her. Did all babies cry as much as hers did? She broke down and cried in his surgery when she asked this. She said she found it difficult to cope. That she never knew how hard it was to be a mother. If she'd known . . . The doctor assured her that everyone felt this – it was normal. She was too tense. If only she would take it easy, everything would improve. He recommended that she buy a tape to help her relax. Set time aside for it. It would make her feel so much better. The first time she tried it she stretched out on the floor and heard a man's dreamy voice say, 'Imagine yourself on an island.' She struggled up but before she could switch off the tape there was a cascade of syrupy violins and the voice said, 'Listen to the music and let your mind go limp . . .'

Her baby was going to wake. Her stomach was clenched waiting for it. Just as her eyes were clenched against the light. The window was open a bit and the curtain moved in the slight breeze of the opening. Bright sunshine again. Day after day, since the beginning of June, it had been like this. For the second year in a row. And each day seemed to get warmer as the summer settled in. The land gradually warmed, the sea gradually warmed. So much so that she was almost becoming tired of it. Day after day. Repeating. Too much of a good thing – like her baby. How could she still think these things? Women in the shop, with tanned and red faces confided, 'It's too hot, I can't stick it.' Another said, 'It might be OK in France or Spain but we're not used to it here. Three bloody weeks . . . Day after day.' If Catherine didn't dare complain about the weather, how could she say anything about her child? She should get away for the day. Be on her own and avoid this man snoring in the room next to hers. She did not know how she could face him. Or the curious eyes she would meet in the town.

She put her hand to her mouth and felt her lip. It was fat and tender to the touch.

Sometimes Catherine did not trust herself. She never visualised what she dreaded most, had not the courage to, but sometimes she imagined the baby dead, buried after a short illness or an accident and people sympathising with her and her nodding sadly – although beneath it all was a sense of relief that the whole bizarre experience was at last over. There was a Heaney poem – 'Limbo' – about a girl drowning her illegitimate child – 'ducking him tenderly'.

As if on cue from the baby's room she heard the plastic balls on the cot click and bounce and her stomach sank. She heaved herself out of bed and went towards the noise. Anna had pulled herself up and stood hitting the coloured balls. They were spring loaded and filled with tiny beads like maracas. Her hand pressed one down and when she released it, it jumped and rattled its contents. The room smelled of dirty nappy.

'Shhh or you'll waken him.'

On the kitchen radio, turned low, the six o'clock weather man said that today would again be warm and sunny – the high pressure seemed static over the British Isles. Afterwards, on the news she heard of the death of a British soldier in Northern Ireland. Responsibility had been claimed by the Provisional IRA. *Mea culpa, mea culpa, mea maxima culpa.* He'd been killed on a street in Belfast, thirty-five miles from her home town. Dying yesterday in that hot camouflage uniform – everybody else in shorts, standing behind police tapes trying to get a glimpse. She opened a tin of baby rice, emptied it into Anna's dish and put a spoon into the baby's hand. The doctor, as well as prescribing pills said she should talk to her baby more.

'There you are,' she said.

Catherine ate some Bran Flakes and made a cup of tea with a tea-bag in a mug, making sure not to chink the spoon against the side. Even though she felt they were utterly useless she took one of her anti-depressants, washed it down with water. She made a large cheese and tomato sandwich with the two heels of the loaf – on the island they called them *outsiders* – and wrapped it in tin-foil. She took an apple and a can of juice from the fridge and put them in a Co-op polythene bag along with the baby's stuff, a spoon and some high-factor sun cream. She did everything with stealth and stopped to listen every so often.

'You and I are going for a long walk.'

* * *

The baby was on her back. Below where she had parked her car the beach was stony and difficult. The oval stones shifted under her feet, avalanching with a hollow sound. Broad strips of brown leathery seaweed lay here and there. She looked down at her feet walking over the stones. Other seaweeds had washed up – bright green, translucent lettuce stuff – occasionally fronds of purple red, very delicate. Further up the beach at the high-tide mark was a brown line of weed and flotsam containing fragments of bright blue nylon net, plastic bottles, light bulbs, bird feathers. Whatever way the currents ran, the debris seemed to collect at this end. Further on, when the stones gave way to sand, the beach was clean.

She heeled off her sandals and carried them for a while, the heel strap hooked on her fingers. Then she couldn't be bothered and left them high above the water mark. Here they were the only interruption to the sand for as far as the eye could see. From a distance they looked like two small animals side by side. Then she was so far from them that she could not make them out. She walked along the firm sand in bare feet. To her left-hand side, the west, was the open ocean – to her right the beach, backed by tall sand-dunes with grey grass hissing in the dry wind, nothing else. The air was so clear that Ireland looked close, like a further headland rather than a different island. The Land of Saints and Scholars and Murderers. In the sand at her feet were some tracks of a bird walking along parallel to the sea – the marks were like tiny arrows, all pointing in one direction. It was a paradox because the arrows pointed, not the way the bird was going but *in the direction the bird had come from.* It was cheating. She'd played a chasing game as a child, getting a start to a hundred with a bit of chalk and running, making arrows — three quick strokes for the others to follow, always trying to keep ahead. Thinking of cheating, an arrow pointing round the wrong corner, but always unable to do it.

She decided to try to walk to the point, she'd never been that far before. She did not stroll but walked fast, setting herself a good pace. Step by step. One foot after the other. Repetition. But not like the repetition of the morning, her first waking. Not like the cascade of blackness. Left heel, right heel into the stiff sand. From this low position by the water's edge the sea looked shelved, like a series of shallow steps as each wave followed the next, in its long slow run to the beach. When she looked up she could see the emptiness from one horizon to the other. The wind was coming from the south and it was warm. She was wind-bathing. She held her arms out from her body so that the air moved beneath her arms. It buffeted her, blowing her hair around her face, but she didn't bother. She narrowed her eyes against the brightness and the breeze. Her eyes watered salty tears — nothing to do with emotion, just a reaction to the glare and the warm wind. She swung her arms at each step, stretched out her neck, shook her hair, made herself conscious of the air blowing around her. For a game she put herself to the test by closing her eyes and keeping them shut and continuing to walk. Testing her bravery, her faith. The way before her had no hazard as far as she could see. She would not slacken her pace, but stride along as if she was blind. Even then she could not keep it up for anything more than a minute. She had to open her eyes to check if there was any danger in front of her. As if suddenly the wind could turn to rock.

Occasionally she saw a blemish – a cluster of stones, a washed-up jellyfish, a razor shell which she could have stepped on. Walking quickly like this, purely on the hard sand was difficult, almost painful. It hurt her heels each time she made contact. After a time it felt like concrete. The contact was increased by the weight of the baby in its sling on her back. But the fast walking would do her good. And the addition of the baby would be better for her – she would be like an athlete who trained with weights in order to compete better without them. So to make things easier she walked the shallows of the incoming waves – not so much waves as broad slow-moving ripples. Pacing through the water. It seemed to cushion the impact – each heel breaking the skin of the tepid water before touching the sand a millimetre beneath. Repetitively. Splashing. The tail of her skirt was becoming soaked and for a time she held it up away from the splashes her feet made. Then she gave up and just let it get soaked. She became aware that if she looked over her shoulder the splash patterns looked as if like someone was behind her, following her. Apart from Anna. Some ghostly presence was pacing after her making identical splashes in her wake. The water was warm, sluicing in over the hot sand – the tide was on its way in – and she felt beneath the arches of her feet the pattern, the rhythm of mackerel clouds gone hard.

She had tried to find different ways to discuss patterns and rhythms with her pupils.

'What are the rhythms of the sea?' And they had all looked at her. 'What time intervals are there?' One boy looked like he was on the verge of an idea. He raised his shoulder but not his hand. She pointed at him anyway.

'The ferry, miss?'

'That's not what I mean.' The boy looked disappointed.

'Tides?' said a girl.

'Yes – very good,' said Catherine and chalked the word TIDES on the board. 'Anything else?'

'High and low tide, miss.'

'Yes.'

'Eventide?' The class sniggered. 'The Eventide Home, miss.'

'No thank you, Alex.' Catherine looked from face to face, waiting. 'What do you notice walking along the edge of the sea?'

'Toilet paper.' This time everyone giggled.

'I'm talking about rhythm, about intervals of time.'

'Moon-rags, miss.' It was Alex again.

'He means STs, miss.' said a girl's voice. One of the boys said, 'Sanitary towels.' Everybody was grinning.

'Almost there – the moon and tides again, Alex.'

'Waves,' said someone.

'Yes.' Catherine chalked the word below TIDES. 'In intervals of the clock – what's a unit of time?'

'A minute, miss.'

'Yes.'

'A day.'

'Well . . .'

'An hour.'

'Yes.'

'Seconds, sir – I mean, miss.'

'Yes – now what about the sea? We have TIDES and

WAVES . . .' Again the blank faces returned. A girl put up
her hand.

'Yes, Kathy?'

'Miss, I have a dental appointment.'

Catherine let her go then said, 'Neap tides, ripples,
every seventh wave, equinoxes, storms – all of them
intervals of different duration. A slow swell, choppiness.
It's like music. Complex. There's a wave machine at
Butlin's. The same wave all the time. That's like techno.
The same beat. Boring – like listening to a machine.'

The children stared blankly back at her. Some of them
nodded. Coming to an island Catherine had expected
better pupils than in her teaching practice in the city. But
it was not the case. The island kids had TV, radio. Their
remote surroundings were seen as a deprivation, not
something to be enjoyed. They felt cut off from the
mainstream. To be on an island was a source of discontent,
not as good as the mainland. As soon as they were out of
school the bright ones would leave and go on to higher
education of some sort. Some girls would get pregnant and
stay.

She paused and crouched and lifted a handful of salt
water to her mouth, washed the tenderness. If it had been
term-time she would have had to give an account of
herself to her pupils.

'Miss, miss – what happened your lip?'

Out of term the check-out girls at the Co-op, only
recently left school themselves, would be the first to
notice.

'So what have you been doing with yourself?'

It stung a little, then was soothing – salty to the taste.

Plain saline, as the nurse said. Anything but. Crouching, she was aware how wet the hem of her cotton sarong was. Then suddenly she was drenched by a wave larger than the others. One in seven. She unwrapped the skirt from around her waist and carried it until she came across a stone. The dry part of the skirt fluttered in the warm breeze where she left it high on the beach weighted with the rock. She could pick it up on the way back, then her sandals – if she ever came back. Then it would be dry. She returned barelegged to the water's edge. The wind on her white legs was lovely. She thought of the soldier yesterday, lying dead on a street in Belfast, his face in death the colour of her legs. His mates running, taking cover in small gardens, scared shitless waiting for the sniper to have another go at them. Hiding. Fleeing. Hoping he would have another go so's they could nail the bastard.

She wondered if Anna was asleep. She was very quiet. What she really needed was a mirror. To see behind her.

'Are you all right back there?' she said. Like a taxi driver. Or like when she played the organ as a teenager in the church at home. Watching the proceedings back to front.

Later when she stopped for something to eat she swung the baby off her back.

'Jesus, you're a ton weight.' Anna, in her sun bonnet, sat still in her harness. Looking at her mother, waiting to be fed. Catherine took her out and set her down on the sand. The child had developed a way of moving around on her backside. She preferred it to crawling. Her legs hinged and she dug her heels in and inched herself forward. *Bumming around*, Dave called it. Sand got into her plastic pants. Catherine felt it would chafe her so she took them off altogether and let her go bare-bummed. The discarded nappy was clean. Just like the thing. So many times she had put on a clean nappy to see, within minutes, the child sitting there, her face going red with the strain of destroying the good work. Filling her crease. Catherine covered her own pale legs with sunblock.

The worst thing was the crying. As Mrs Shaw from the Co-op said, 'A colicky baby's enough to drive you round the twist.' After a feed Anna would roar and pull her little knees up. In the beginning Catherine felt sorry for her but then she became angry and depressed. She thought it couldn't happen if the baby was being breastfed. Walking the floor, patting her on the back helped but as soon as she was put back in her cot she would start again. At first Catherine tried cottonwool in her ears but could still hear her cries through it. She thought it was her fault. That she was an incompetent mother who picked the child up too soon. Had spoiled her. And could think of no way to unspoil her. No one had told her of the regularity of a baby's crying. The repetitiveness of it. Again and again. Every feed. No one had told her of the interminable duration of a baby's crying. Catherine lay stiff on her bed, her fists tight, willing the child to stop. If Dave was not in, as was nearly always the case, she would go into the kitchen and turn on Radio Three loud enough to drown the sound. But when she did this she wondered if the child had choked itself to death and would turn the radio down to hear if she was still crying. Invariably she was. She hated the music which submerged the anguish of this baby whether it was Mozart or Bartók or once, memorably,

Percy Grainger. She hated the baby because she couldn't listen with any attention to the music.

She had no excuse to fall back on – she couldn't say she was trying to train the child. Not to be lifted every time she cried – a little loving discipline. She simply hated the child crying – she had given birth to a car alarm that shat and pissed. And when the colic began to go away it was replaced by teething. Sometimes she did not trust herself, terrified that she would harm her baby in some way.

It was so warm. She took off Anna's top and carried her down to the water's edge. After the initial shock of being sat down in the wet the baby began to splash with her hands. She wore only her sun hat.

'Do you like that?'

Suddenly from nowhere Catherine felt good. Were her tablets beginning to work – after all this time? Was it the weather? Or her hormones? Whatever it was she hadn't felt like this since the baby was born.

'This is nice. I could get used to this.' She looked all around. 'This is really, really nice.' The landscape was empty. She stepped out of the rest of her clothes – T-shirt, bra, pants, the lot and pinioned them beneath the square of foil and her apple in the sandwich bag. She ran back to the sea and set her baby down in the shallows again. Without her clothes she was even more aware of the warm wind across and through her. Making tangents to her, playing across her, forming a windbreak for her baby. She waded out, the water now up to her thighs. At this depth there were currents of noticeably cold water. She dandled Anna between her legs. The water came up to the baby's chest.

She seemed not to notice that it was cold. Then Catherine got down into the water.

'Jesus Christ.'

She gasped with the iciness of it. She held her baby close to her chest. The water made both their skins seem slippery. The baby's knees were between her mother's breasts. But once she was down it didn't seem as cold. What had she been making such a fuss about? Catherine crawled back in towards the water frilling at the edge, her hands careful to keep Anna's chin out of the water.

'It's warmer here.'

The baby sat four-square and grinned. Made noises with her mouth. Pre-speech, the books called it. She splashed flat hands down. Catherine laughed and hugged her. Then she sat back with her legs straight out to sea, her baby on her lap. She leaned back, propped on her arms with her fingers wedged firmly in the sand. Each wave that ran in clunked beneath Anna, making the baby squeal with delight. It sounded almost like singing.

'The infant Crotch,' said Catherine and laughed. And she felt so good at this moment that she was overcome by a fierce joy and tears sprang into her eyes. They brimmed over and she was aware of weeping salt into the sea.

When they came back up the beach the wind dried them. This summer was hard to believe so far. It was as if the weather was going to be this way for ever. Her shadow was at its shortest. She had to be careful with her baby's skin, her own skin. She renewed their sunblock then fed Anna, spooning another jar of apple and baby rice into her. She made a makeshift sun shield from her T-shirt and bits of a washed-up bamboo stick. The baby slept in its shade.

Catherine sat beside her, cross-legged, in a yoga position eating her sandwich. A slice of tomato fell out into the sand but she just ate it scratchily, pretending the sand grains were pepper. She lifted her apple and, without thinking, was going to rub it clean on her lapel when she realised she was naked. She smiled and bit into it. *Cranching* was a Scots word she'd come across for eating hard fruit. So exact, so descriptive – no English word could get near it. She flung the core away down towards the water. Bio-degradable. Her eyes wandered over the landscape of beach and sand-dune. On a distant headland the white smoke of a whin fire could be seen. All was quiet except for the sliding in of the sea, the rhythmic unfurling of small waves and sometimes the metallic screeching of a gull. Did sea birds eat fruit? Or did this one just snatch it up out of sheer greed? Gannets.

She thought back to the school yard at break-time. Kids stuffing their faces – the silence of the class ripped by the bell, followed by the charge of feet and the yelling and the banging of doors and the thump of bags being thrown and the cumulative effect of screaming and shouting. I yell because you yell and you yell louder because I yell and the whole school yells to make themselves heard above the yelling of the school. Here there was such silence. Not silence, but appropriate noise. Catherine sat there by the sea, lost in her ears. *Pre-hearing*.

Suddenly she heard a sound. A gentle tremolo of strings of different tones. She chose to listen to only the main tone. But joined to it were a higher and lower octave building to a chord. These sounds led to a brass idea. Trombones, tuba, trumpets. What a mysterious process it was. *Inner-hearing*. Her heart began to beat faster as she took hold of the idea and she felt the excitement rising in her. Within her head she heard a performance of the first notes of it – all that remained was to write down what she heard. *Committing to memory*. In this place, at this moment, sounds were shaping themselves. She had no pen, but she would remember it. And she would add to it. The idea was growing in size. What began as strings was now a full orchestra. It was becoming textured. There would have to be bells – chimes at any rate. She heard the music in the silence of her head. It was far too early but she wondered about a name to identify it – Metamorphoses. Reconciliation. She hated these Latinate words that thrust into her head. By the sea. At the water's edge. By the sea's edge. Yes, that was simple and good. By the Sea's Edge. But it was clumsy. Four words like that. The trend was to give musical works a single word title. Neat. Enigmatic. Just an identifier. Whatever it was to be called she vowed it would be dedicated to Anna.

The child stirred and looked at her, then turned away and sucked her thumb harder.

'Hello, you. I think we'd better be getting back.' She shook sand from her underwear and got dressed. Then started to dress Anna. 'I need to get to a pen and paper.' Some food slop had spilled on Anna's top. Catherine scraped it with a spoon and flicked the blob into the sand. Then she ran to the water's edge to rinse it off. She turned and came back up the beach. Anna was standing waiting for her. Bow leggéd and wavering, but standing none the less. Catherine didn't know what to say. She dropped the baby's top into the sand and extended both her hands.

'Come on.'

Anna stepped shakily forward with her hands up – one, two steps and clamped on to Catherine's fingers.

All packed up and nowhere to go. She lay listening to the boom and rattle of the wind about the bungalow. Great heaves of it had shaken the house all night – one of the worst storms since she'd come to the island. But that was not what was keeping her awake – it was the excitement of finally leaving the place. She turned in the bed – tried to bunch up her pillows to be more comfortable. Tried to stop worrying. The repetition of thoughts which caused her pain amazed her. Why did she continually do it? Like picking at a scab on her knee. Or her tongue probing at the socket of a recently pulled tooth. It prevented healing and she knew it prevented healing. Yet she did it. The best way to stop doing it was to invite other things into her head. But then there was always the underlying knowledge that she was thinking of this thing to stop thinking about what she didn't want to think about. Now she concentrated on the people in the next house along the road towards the town. The Muirs. That summer they had invited an old and blind relative for a holiday and the Muir boy, who could not swim, was given the job of taking him down to the rock pool just below Catherine's place where a springboard and an iron ladder had been anchored to the rock. Catherine would watch them as they passed. The old man had the kind of blindness which gave him dark olive skin around his eye sockets. His right eye was permanently shut, his left was slightly open showing just some white in the shape of a crescent moon. Under his left arm he carried red bathing trunks wrapped in a white towel. Like a jam roll. In his right hand, a thin white cane, held as if it was a pen. The Muir boy was a pale and spindly nine year old. One day, when she'd finally got Anna settled in the pram for her afternoon sleep, Catherine had gone down to the rocks to sunbathe. She knew she shouldn't, even though she was well within earshot. She spread her towel and lay down on her front facing the sea. On the rocks below her, barnacles and limpets and winkles clung on waiting for the next tide. On hot days they could dry up or cook, on stormy days they could be ripped from the rock and washed away. But somehow they stayed on. What if her baby choked silently? Was unable to cry out? Then things would be simplified. Jesus – how awful. It didn't happen – and if it didn't happen it was not a problem. The blind man and the boy came along and she watched the old man undress. He surrounded his waist with a tucked-in towel and, leaning on the boy for balance, angled his thin legs into his bathing trunks. He had a large belly for such a thin man. The boy led him down the cement path and on to the diving board, then returned to the little pile of clothes and the white cane. The old man walked the matting of the board, four confident steps before he stopped. Then his toes moved like antennae to find the end. He raised his arms and sprung up and down on the board. On the third bounce he launched himself, diving head-first into the icy water. He surfaced and lay on his back, blowing and breathing, his toes held up as if for inspection. Then he turned and swam for the iron ladder, listening for the voice of the boy, feeling for his outstretched hand. Catherine turned and tried to focus her hearing on the pram. Anna was still asleep. Or worse. Would it be worse? Oh Jesus, we're away again. When the blind man came out he swept the water from his pallid chest with the palms of his hands. Then he took the towel from the boy and began drying his face. How could he know, how could he be absolutely sure that the water was there? What if everyone had conspired to lie?

It was like religion – what if everyone had conspired to lie? People she respected – her teachers, both at school and at University – the clergy, of course – people she loved, her mother and father. Some friends. All of them believed and supported one another in their belief. If she was to begin to argue that religion was a deceit, that it was nothing more than organised superstition, then they would point to books, mighty tomes written over the space of two thousand years by the most intellectual, most well-meaning, respectable men on earth. Libraries backed the whole thing up. There were a thousand buildings with spires and onion domes and cupolas – and each one of them contained crosses and crucifixes and transepts – and they existed in every city on earth. And they were put there, not by accident, but by the hard work and skill of craftsmen. They could point to these things, not as proof but as evidence as to why she, a convent schoolgirl from a small town in the British part of Ireland, should believe the same thing as everybody else. How could she, insignificant as she was, turn around and say that they were all wrong – that religion was a trick? That the tide had gone out and there were only rocks beneath the diving board? She would be the worst in the world to express such an idea. Indeed such an idea, if expressed to her parents, would cause them immense grief. They would rather endure the pain of seeing her dead. At least then they would think of her as in heaven. In the arms of the Lord.

She turned on her opposite side and put the pillow between her shoulder and her ear. She had to get *some* sleep – she had to flit tomorrow, for God's sake. Although the wind would have to drop a bit first. But maybe it was doing that now. The bumps and buffets were less frequent and now and again she heard the wind whistle and tweeter like a thin blade. Like the storm was dying.

After another fifteen minutes of going around and around the same thought circuit she cursed and got up. It was cold and draughty. She thought about putting on a raincoat of Dave's which hung in the hallway but felt so revolted by the idea that she sorted through one of the black plastic bags for an overcoat of her own. She made a cup of hot milk and tiptoed through the chaos to the hearth. It was a trick of her mother's – to take hot milk when she couldn't sleep. For Catherine it rarely made any difference. The peat was still warm beneath its white ash and it reddened sometimes when the wind roared above the chimney. She sat close to the hearth and watched the steam from her cup waver, then head straight for the opening of the fireplace. The milk was too hot to drink.

The room was full of labelled cardboard cartons and tea-chests. The records, in three Blue Band margarine boxes – packed spine up from Bach to Zemlinsky belonged to her. Dave's, in a separate carton, were badly scratched, mostly of Irish and Scottish folk groups – Runrig, Capercaille, the Chieftains, Van Morrison played to death before she even met him. He also had some embarrassingly out-of-date pop records which he was always threatening to give to a charity shop because he knew nobody would buy them. She had arranged with the removal firm that Dave's stuff could go into storage on the island until he picked it up.

The books were mostly hers – hardbacks on the history of music, dictionaries of twentieth-century music, Tovey's volumes of *Musical Analysis*, *The Story of the Blues*, the Norton/Grove *Dictionary of Women Composers*. There was also some fiction, mostly paperbacks – on top, a copy of Georg Büchner's *Lenz*. The removal man had said on the phone that, as far as books were concerned, she should only fill the tea-chests about a third full. 'Otherwise the boys'll bust their guts lifting them.'

The only books which belonged to Dave were some sci-fi novels, a couple of car manuals and the *Reader's Digest Book of Strange and Amazing Facts*.

She hated to throw things away. She had kept all her notes from her University days in Belfast. And her post-graduate year at the Royal Scottish Academy of Music and Drama in Glasgow. Black cardboard ring-binders with the institution's crest on the front. She had written the name of the subject in white correcting fluid on the spine. COMPOSITION, STRICT COUNTERPOINT, CHORAL, MODERN. She flicked open the Modern file. She saw an essay she had done – *A Mirror on Which to Dwell: An examination of Elliot Carter's Song Cycle to Poems by Elizabeth Bishop*. She turned the pages.

Aleatory music – Indeterminacy. A cul-de-sac or the way forward? In your discussion keep in mind Joseph Byrd's statement, 'Art is simply that which is perceived aesthetically'.

Her writing looked strange, like it was done by someone else. An awkward backhand. She wrote in a completely different style now. She had hand-written the title and begun her answer by setting out the *Credo*.

1 Any sound or no sound at all is valid, as 'good' as any other sound.

2 Each sound is a separate event. It is not related to any other sound by any hierarchy. It need carry no implication of what has preceded it or will follow it. It is important for itself, not for what it contributes to a musical line or development.

3 Any assemblage of sounds is as valid as any other.

4 Any means of generating an assemblage of sounds is as valid as any other.

5 Any piece of music is as 'good' as any other, any composer as 'good' as any other.

6 Traditional concepts of value, expertise and authority are meaningless.

She was amazed that she could have discussed this Pol Pot–Year Zero approach to music at such length. There were eight and a half closely written pages. Her tutor, Malcolm Black, had given her a C++ for it, whereas she would normally have expected an A. It maddened her that a tutor would give good marks to those who agreed with him – invariably it was a him – whereas those people who argued, however logically, that they disagreed with the tutor's view always ended up with a poor mark. If you took notes at Black's lecture and wove them into your written answer then Black would underline his own views and write *Good!* in the margin. Maybe she was marked down because she had characterised the music which resulted from these principles as stuff which was listened to only by people who were teaching twentieth-century music in University music departments.

It was such an amazingly small audience. People voted with their ears. She had written, 'To write music for University music departments and Radio Three music producers, who are themselves straight out of university music departments, is a thing which does not appeal. On the other hand, the responsibility of the artist to maintain an audience has to be balanced by her responsibility to explore new worlds, to plumb new depths.' After the clichés, her conclusion all those years ago was that she wanted to write the music she wanted to hear.

There had been one guy in her year who had composed a sound piece recorded from various live concerts on Radio Three. He had taped only the intervals *between* the music – the coughing and breathing and, as he said, 'the rattling of jewellery'. He'd intercut these with one or two over-enthusiastic hand claps which had come at the wrong time. He repeated and played about with these sounds, then put the whole thing on a loop. He claimed he could tell, with about 70 per cent accuracy, from inter-movement bustle whose music was being played on the programme. Mozart or Varèse – Mahler or Boulez.

She blew on the surface of the milk and tried to sip it, but it was still too hot and burned her lip. She set the cup down on the hearth. She had never seen Malcolm Black smile, let alone laugh. In the pub one time with a bunch of people from the choir Catherine had put it to him that she should compose a Haydn Sonata, much the same way as John Cage had composed 4'33". In the programme it would appear as *Joseph Haydn's Piano Sonata, Hob.XVI:49 by Catherine McKenna.*

She claimed that an audience would listen more carefully — just as they did to silence in John Cage's four minutes thirty-three seconds of coughs and tummy rumbles and distant traffic. They would really *hear* Catherine McKenna's Haydn with new ears because it was *exactly* the same as the one Haydn had written. It would be listened to with renewed attention. Malcolm Black nodded and thought it an interesting idea but 'a bit gimmicky'. He also rejected without a smile her proposal to write *A Surprise Sonata for Unprepared Piano.* They were such an ivory-tower bunch the real world passed them by. Another time in the pub she overheard Malcolm Black and a student arguing about Britain and Ireland being at loggerheads. She nose-dived into the argument, rolling up her political sleeves, only to find that they were talking about Benjamin Britten and the disagreements he had with his composition teacher, John Ireland, at the Royal College of Music.

In a different tea-chest she had packed printed scores. Her own handwritten compositions she kept separately in cardboard wallets which would travel with her. The piece which had the working title *By the Sea's Edge* was well under way, its blue folder fattening day by day. *A Suite for Trumpetists and Tromboners* had had a repeat on radio and

222

the reaction was so good that Graeme McNicol had phoned her to congratulate her. When he heard she was working on something he suggested that he should commission it. If it was finished in time, he said, it could be included in the prestigious *Cutting Edge* series. Ideally, it should have a folk element or folk instrument in it. It had shaped itself into two long movements – the *yin* and the *yang*, so to speak. The first was male, the second definitely female. She was excited by the way it was going and annoyed that she had to move house in the middle of, what was for her, such a big piece of work.

There was an unmarked wallet and she looked inside it. It was the *Canon* manuscript she had worked on with Melnichuck. It was her last visit to them and Anatoli had asked to see any orchestral score she was currently working on. She produced the autograph sheets of *A Canon for Ulster* for small orchestra, which was unfinished. In places it was a mirror canon, two parts appearing simultaneously the right way up and upside down, one being the reflection of the other. He sat on a sofa – the waistband of his trousers nearly up to his chest – wheezing and turning the pages. Occasionally he nodded. He laughed once. Then explained himself to Olga. Olga nodded but had to consult the dictionary to find the proper word in English. 'He says he likes your sense of irony.' When he had finished the score he took it to the piano. He played and talked, through his wife, about the music he was reading. Sometimes he hummed the string parts.

'He says this is not resolved,' said Olga and Melnichuck played the phrase. 'Would you think about this?' He hummed, then waggled his fingers as if to indicate he didn't much like what he was suggesting. He tried something else. Humming loudly.

'*Meilleur*,' he said. He seemed embarrassed to be saying a foreign word.

'Better,' said Olga.

'Yes – I mean *Oui, oui*.' Catherine was excited by what she was hearing. '*C'est bon*.' And they were all laughing with embarrassment at their attempts at pidgin French. Melnichuck said with a grin, 'Messiaen. Ravel, *peut-être?*'

Catherine took a pencil from her bag and began to make notes. Olga listened to what her husband said, 'The end is not a movement for orchestra – it is thought of in the piano.' Olga tapped the lid of the piano with her finger, as if Catherine could not understand. 'And then it is arranged for the orchestra . . . the orchestra *is* instrument.'

While they worked Olga ran backwards and forwards to the kitchen translating one moment, the next boiling potatoes and preparing the midday meal. At one point Catherine tried to defend herself and called Olga to say to Melnichuck that in this section she was trying to experiment with tone and texture. Melnichuck replied that tone and texture by themselves were 'mood music'. Real music was about form. Once that was right then the composer could think about other things. But if the form was right, ninety-nine times out of a hundred the tone and texture would be right too. Olga put her hands to her head and claimed that she had forgotten to salt the potatoes. She rushed out of the room. Melnichuck smiled and weighed out the halting English words with his hands.

'*Peut-être?* Form – potatoes. Tone unt texture – salt.'
Catherine nodded and laughed.

When they sat down at the table Melnichuck opened a bottle of vodka with a small penknife which had a fork attached and they drank toasts. Catherine was surprised by the formality with which it was done. Melnichuck stood and recited an address to Catherine while Olga translated. In her turn Olga stood and in halting English welcomed Catherine into her house and her affections. Catherine knew only one toast and stood and said it.

'May we all be happy – and may our enemies know it.' When Olga translated it for Melnichuck he threw back his head and laughed.

After eating, it was Olga's suggestion that they go for a stroll. Catherine asked why the bottoms of the trees were white. Olga told her that fruit trees were painted white to fool the insects into thinking the trees were walls so they would not bother to eat them. Olga said it so seriously that Catherine burst out laughing. She took a fit of hysterics and held on to Olga's arm as she laughed and laughed at the idea. It was only then she realised how drunk she was.

Later with Olga's help she bought a postcard to send home. She wrote,

Dear Mum and Dad,

Hope you got my Christmas card. Sorry I couldn't be there but I had to prepare manuscripts etc. for this trip. Hope this reaches you.

All the best,

Catherine

'I should have gone home at Christmas.' Catherine said. 'It was the first time I missed it. In Ireland Christmas is *big*. Family.'

'Your parents were sad?'

Catherine nodded. Olga reached out and gave her a kiss on the cheek. She pointed to the card.

'Give it for postage at hotel.'

Catherine felt much better when they came back to the house. The discomfort of the drunk and dizzy feeling had gone. She asked Melnichuck to play something and he seemed flattered. He chose his Suite of Ukrainian Folksongs for Piano. And oh . . . the sound he made. The room filled with pain and love, joy and loss. Thousands of years were compressed into these sounds.

His fingers were square, like chisels, as they moved on the keys. This was music of the highest order, of Bach-like proportions – architectural, controlled – but it also cut at the heart. The vodka had made her very emotional. As he played Catherine watched Olga and was struck by her beauty. She was old and must have heard her husband's music so many times – but still she listened with intensity, stock still, as if any movement of her body, however slight, would affect her hearing. Catherine wanted Olga to put her arms around her, to be held by her. To be mothered by her.

When he had finished Catherine shook her head in disbelief and stood and bowed to him – it seemed foolish to applaud being an audience of one. Melnichuck in return asked her to play the Preludes and Fugues, she'd talked of – things she'd written in her final year at University. She apologised for them in advance. At the beginning of the Prelude in G the phone rang in the hallway and Olga went to answer it. Catherine stopped playing and waited. Olga popped her head back into the room and said that it was her daughter from Moscow and that she would be a long time and for Catherine to continue playing. She closed the doors so that her voice would not interrupt the music. Melnichuck stood and indicated that Catherine should go on playing. He made a face and, with a clenched fist rapped his chest. It was almost the same gesture her father made when saying the prayer *Mea culpa, mea culpa, mea maxima culpa*. She started the Prelude in G again. Melnichuck belched and muttered some sort of an apology. He walked to the window, then around behind her in a kind of heel-trailing gait. She was very much aware of him standing there and for some reason she felt distinctly nervous. It was something to do with the way he had looked at her earlier – through those glasses and the way he had breathed with his mouth open. She started hitting wrong notes but he seemed not to notice. There was a mirror on the wall opposite and she glimpsed his face in it. His breathing was becoming louder. She didn't want to look round at him as if she was accusing him of something. It would be rude, would show a lack of trust. After all the hospitality they had shown her. His breathing began to sound like panting. What the hell was he doing? She kept trying to play as best she could. Then she felt him touch her. He was pressing himself against her back. His full weight. In the name of God, she thought – this was going too far.

She spun round and there he was standing and panting, staring at her. He crumpled and went down on one knee beside the piano stool. Then he collapsed on to the floor, his glasses skittering across the boards beneath the piano. The skin of his face was the colour of cement and his lips were blue-black. His eyes were rolling in his head. Catherine didn't know what to do. Jesus. She opened the button of his collar but that seemed such a useless gesture. His breath rasped up his throat. She ran for Olga.

'Quick, there is something wrong.'

Olga shouted goodbye, dropped the phone back in its cradle and took charge. She laid him properly on the floor with a cushion under his head. She forced a tablet into the side of his mouth. She phoned for a doctor.

'This has happened too much. He is a sick man.'

Catherine gathered up her music but stayed with Olga until the doctor arrived.

When she got home to Glasgow she wrote Olga a thank you note which enquired after her husband's health. But she got no reply. Maybe the post in Kiev *was* as notorious as Olga had told her. Then about a year later there was a live performance on radio of Melnichuck's Second Symphony from Birmingham with Rattle conducting – and when she listened to it there was no mention of the composer being dead. So he must have survived.

His name was on a framed poster on the floor in front of her, leaning against a tea-chest – Anatoli Melnichuck – *The Masters of Classical Music*. Around its margins was written the same thing in different languages. *Maîtres – Meister – MACPEPA – Maestri*.

No matter what the language – French, Italian or

Russian – it was male. Masters not Mistresses. Vivaldi's women and girls were known as *Maestra* – so the term was not unknown – just infrequently used. History was represented as a tree with green leaves and brown branches springing up from the eighth and ninth centuries and radiating all the way up to people like Luigi Dallapiccola, Arvo Pärt, Toru Takemitsu, Einojuhani Rautavaara. Helmut Lemberg was there also. Each composer's life was ludicrously compressed into a letter-box shaped slot about an inch long. They were the Masters all right, there was no doubt about it. Three hundred men and one woman. Only the most important of the composers were illustrated. Their oval portraits grew like nuts on the branches of the tree, an array of beards and wigs and whiskers and nearer the top of the chart moustaches and spectacles. What a testosterone brigade. The only woman, at the very bottom of the tree trunk, did not have a picture. Hildegard of Bingen, 1098–1179.

That was how the poster had been printed, but when she was teaching Catherine had changed it. At the top right-hand corner she had, with a mapping pen, printed with extreme neatness her own name and a brief biography. It was in the tone of the other entries and she stuck it into a gap between Harrison Birtwistle and Karlheinz Stockhausen, just above Luigi Nono.

Catherine Anne McKenna. Irish composer. Much sought-after teacher of music during free periods. Main compositions *A Suite for Trumpetists and Tromboners: String Trios*; *A Canon for Ulster: Preludes and Fugues*; *A SET OF 9 SYMPHONIES*.

She hadn't written any symphonies yet but it amused her to include such a fact in the letter box of her life.

She thought that Luigi Nono should be Ulster's favourite composer, if the province was ever to take an interest in such things. Twice the price. Orangemen on marches could chant *Nono Surrender* and daub their walls with such slogans as *ULSTER SAYS NONO*.

A disc of skin had formed on the milk. She lifted it with the rubbered end of a pencil and shook it into the fire. It hissed loudly and made the peat glow for a moment.

She tried to imagine a furniture van being buffeted on a mainland quay – its driver white-knuckled with the delay. No ferry had ventured out for the past thirty-six hours. She was all packed up with nowhere to go.

She wondered if she needed a van at all. She could have, maybe should have, abandoned these things but she hadn't the heart to leave them behind – especially if Dave was going to benefit. She'd become used to her possessions and they had adjusted to her. There was stuff she needed for Anna – the buggy, the cot, her clothes and toys. Medicines and creams and stuff for teething. Bits and pieces about the house she did not want to give up – rugs, her oil lamp, a few pictures, that kind of thing. Her shells which she loved, pot plants she had watered and nursed, her own cases full of clothes, household stuff like brushes and shovels and buckets and basins and dish racks which she would have to buy again *wherever* she ended up. And of course the piano. After three years she had accumulated enough junk to need a removal van to flee the place.

She looked around in disbelief. She was finally going. When she'd been packing her papers she'd come across the Purcell Catch Variations. It was still unfinished. For a whole year – since Anna's arrival – she had not written anything. She had been so busy with looking after the baby, she had felt so awful about herself, the last thing she wanted to do was to put dots on a page. Fat, black tics. Anybody who composes dark music, music without hope, is still a million miles better off than somebody like her. Sitting too tired, too dejected to even lift a pencil. Railing and screaming against the universe is such a positive thing compared to the transfixed nightmare of her condition. Total inaction. I truly, deeply can't be bothered. What's the point? She just couldn't raise herself. Radio Three remained switched off because it was too painful to know she was doing nothing herself. You commit suicide because it results in an improvement of your situation. Better off dead. The silent composer, the blind painter, the dried-up writer. At night Dave would ask her if she was all right and when she would say yes he would go to the pub and she would sit for hours in the dark crying silently. Her tears dripping off the end of her nose. Once they dripped on to Anna's tummy when she was changing her. Another time, when she was feeding her, they fell on her fontanelle like a salt baptism.

But the day of the beach walk was a turning point. It had not felt like it at the time – it was so gradual. She had not asked for it, but the music had come. She sketched out the idea that night, biting her swollen lip. And added a little to it the next day. And the next. She had found small gaps in each day to put down what she was hearing inside her head. And that in turn gave her the confidence to make this move – away from Dave.

There was a time, before they started going out together, when Dave came into a room at a party and it felt as if someone had switched on extra lights. He would not address her immediately, but she knew he would eventually get around to her. And she would be the one with whom he would end the night sitting on the floor, a glass in his hand, talking up to her, telling his jokes.

This last year she had been living with a man whose control over his own life was zero. Of late he couldn't even wake himself in the mornings for work. In the evenings he didn't know how much he could drink. Between these times she didn't see him because she had her child, their child, to look after. She was waking a man with a hangover and sending him out to work and later receiving a drunk back into her house. She tried to hide what was wrong with her and it was easy.

Sundays were no different. He went shooting with the boys. And drinking. She never knew which came first. He always arrived home late, despite assurances, with a hare or a rabbit or a haunch of venison to hang in the shed and would fall asleep in the chair.

'Why don't you bring me some scallops?'

'Because I *sell* scallops.'

She hated cartridges almost as much as she hated him. Squat, fat, red. Lead shot spraying at things which crouched or ran in the heather. One of the first times they ate something he had killed, her teeth almost broke on the bite – she thought a filling from her tooth had fallen out. Thereafter she chewed the food he brought gingerly. 'Feeding his family,' he called it. By ten in the evening he had a headache and would stumble out to cure it. She would go to bed, after assuring herself of the breathing from the baby's room.

She decided to leave before they released him from the mainland clinic. She knew he intended to come back to her, having dried out, saying he had reformed, but she would not be here to meet him. The bird would have flown. Her life had changed – would change.

The rain crackled against the window and occasional rapping noises made her think twigs were hitting it. With storms like this, in the morning the glass was covered with a diced green salad. And the barbed-wire fences had streamers of straw. When the rain came the gusts seemed worse. It was like the child who thought the wind was made by the trees threshing. The window flicked from one plane to another and the drops trembled and ran down and reformed. Without curtains she was more aware of the draughts and more aware of her lack of privacy. Walking out of here with her child the next day, or whatever day it was, she knew she would be a target for their talk. The worst in the world.

She tried to poke some life into the dying fire and a fine white ash whirled upwards. Above, the wind bumbled in the chimney. Earlier she'd noticed that the water see-sawed in the toilet bowl. A half candle, untidy with guttered wax, stood in a saucer on the hearth ready for the next power-cut. There had been two already that day.

Somewhere a clock struck three, muffled inside its cardboard box. She leaned over to plug in the radio and felt with her hand a three-pronged wind coming from the socket. She switched on, hoping to catch the weather forecast at the end of the news. Did they have weather at this time of the morning, apart from what was outside? At home in Northern Ireland it had meant nothing to her, it was either windy or not but since coming here she had learned the nuances, the difference between Force Ten and Eleven, between Gale and Storm, what to expect if the wind was from the north-east or the west. From such things you knew whether or not you would have fresh bread the next day. A brief weather summary was given by the newsreader. Nothing had changed.

God knows why, but that first visit to Islay with Liz was enough to bring her back in the summer. She couldn't believe her luck when a job, teaching music, was advertised in the local school. That was when the damage was done.

Dave had lured her with his cheeky English voice, with his wit and his dark good looks. She remembered walking with him to dig peats, their boots rattling through the heather. The bog was like a drum skin, a trampoline and she could feel the vibration of his step walking beside hers. They'd kissed in this wilderness beneath the hugeness of the sky. Indeed it was on the moss where they'd made love for the first time. A place so public, so open that it was private – a place where people could be seen and heard approaching for miles.

She was amazed and impressed by the amount he could drink and still remain articulate and steady. The lore of the island, spoken through him, also seduced her. The stories of fishing boats, of well-known drunks, of turnip-stealing expeditions and the local sergeant who had a head on him 'as square as a biscuit tin' – and McGovern, 'The only reason he has that long beard is because he can't afford a

tie.' She loved the vividness in what he said. But he was a
sham. The next time they made love he admitted he had a
plate and two false front teeth. They'd been snapped off
against the beaten copper counter in a bar-room brawl in
Derby.

But even then she liked his shyness about it, the black
gap in his smile. He said he was the last of six and spoiled
rotten. Everybody gave into him because of his looks.
Despite the fact that he had been born in Derby, the navel
of England as he called it, he boasted of an Irish great-
grandmother on one side and a Scottish grandfather on the
other – she was Donnelly from County Monaghan and he
was Meikle from Dundee. He claimed to have worked at
everything – insurance, labouring, selling, security – and
been everywhere – Derby, Nottingham, London, Dundee
and finally here. He had just been arsing around and stayed
here because he liked it – the space, the lifestyle, the non-
conformity. The only thing he missed was football.
Watching it on TV wasn't the same thing.

'I'm going out to look for bad company to fall into.'

'You *are* the bad company.'

She had felt this way many times – a kind of black
imprisonment but had done nothing about it. She had
hoped that her child, when it came along, would have
helped but it had made things even worse. Having a child
turned into a different problem.

All she felt now was a sense of vague satisfaction, having
made the phone-calls, the arrangements, knowing that a
change was under way. She had phoned Liz in Glasgow to
ask her to keep an eye out for somewhere to rent. Liz had
phoned back the next day and said that they had a

basement she could use. Two, admittedly small, rooms.
And if she didn't mind using their bathroom, it could all
work out. She had discussed it with Peter, her husband,
who said he would not mind. Catherine said it would only
be for a few weeks, until they got a place of their own.

One of the things which had drawn her to Liz was her
honesty.

'I can tell a guitar from a trumpet but that's about as
much as I know about music. If it was by Abba now, I'd
be on surer ground.'

Peter was a quantity surveyor. Catherine asked her what
exactly a quantity surveyor did.

'He surveys quantities.'

Catherine wondered how they would react to someone
playing music in their basement. That was how she'd met
Liz in the first place. A Nazi warden of halls had so
harassed her about the volume of her music that Catherine
had answered a small ad in a shop window to share a flat.
Liz turned out to be one of the people in it. But if
someone was constantly practising piano or playing
records in their basement, it might be a different story.

Thoughts of murder had kept her awake many nights –
no, it was wrong to say that – imagining the scene of his
death was more accurate. Some of Dave's cronies or the
sergeant maybe, would come to the door and be unable to
meet her eye. Trying to tell her that he had been injured
in a shooting accident.

'He didn't break his gun climbing the fence.'

Then they would have to summon up all their courage
to tell her the worst – that he was dead.

When the police left she imagined lifting her girl from

her cot and hugging her. This would unite them. Or would she weep? Maybe from shock, maybe from relief, maybe surprised by a touching memory from the past. The possibility of his accidental death, by whatever means – maybe a drowning – was just another thing that kept her from sleep. During the day, like some witch with her pins, when she pegged the crotch of his underpants on the line she hoped it would hurt. The infantile prodigy.

For a while she cooked meals for Dave at a certain time but they burned or dried up or went cold and she gave up and fed herself. Food was something she didn't worry about – she was happy enough with beans on toast or tomato sandwiches, fish fingers, apples. If he was hungry he could get fish and chips from the van when it came round.

She began to cry. She had no idea how long she cried – it could have been a couple of minutes or an hour. Her chin was on her chest and the tears wet her face. Her nose bubbled. At some point she looked up and saw herself in a mirror propped against the drop-leaf table. It reflected a woman clutching her knees to her chest. A woman dressed in a nightie and overcoat, and in such a position she looked ridiculous. She stopped crying and blew her nose.

She hoped that on this occasion Dave could manage to pull himself round but very much doubted it. She could write him a piece of music, call it *Anthem for an Exhumed Drouth*. A man with problems as big as his, needed a goal, needed something to look forward to, something to keep him afloat. His daughter, for instance. But he'd blown it, totally and absolutely.

After the bout of crying she moved to the armchair and wrapped her coat around her more tightly. That interminable weekend before they took him away, even he realised there was something wrong. Drinking for a week non-stop – she had no idea where the money had come from. The stomach pains at night and the shakes in the morning – he was the colour of putty. Then he began throwing up blood. He aged ten years in as many days. Throughout he was self-righteous, scornful of her warnings. She meant it when she shouted at him, 'I hope this time you kill yourself.'

In a strange way it was *he* who'd helped *her*. The night he first hit her – she saw that time as a turning point. It was the next day she'd slipped out of the house and walked the beach with Anna for most of the day. At tea-time when she came back she had switched Anna's sling to her front and the baby was asleep between her breasts. Dave was cooking, getting something greasy into him before going out to the pub – 'a good lining' he called it. He stared at her because he had never seen Catherine carry the baby like that before.

'What happened to your mouth?' he said.

'Are you trying to take the piss?'

'Naw – what happened you?'

'You hit me,' she said quietly.

'What?' When he truly didn't understand things there was an area between his eyebrows wrinkled into a V shape.

'With the back of your hand. Do you not remember?'

'Naw – you got too much sun today. You're gonna be like a lobster.'

'If you ever do that again,' she said, 'never – never come back to this house.'

'You're talking a lotta crap.' He was frying some bacon and he broke an egg, crackling, into the fat. He chased it around the pan with a fork, streaking the egg-white with yellow.

'Are you trying to tell me you were so drunk you don't remember?'

He nodded, unsure now. He refused to look at her but concentrated on the contents of the pan.

She didn't go out for a couple of days – until the swelling had gone down and the cut on her lip had reduced to something she could call a cold sore. Dave apologised, said he had never hit anyone before in his life, except assholes in pubs. He couldn't imagine doing it to someone he loved.

But he did it again. And again. It was as if, having broken the taboo once, he could do it any time – when he'd come in from the pub at midnight or whenever. It became the way he settled arguments, particularly if they were arguments about his drinking. And sober, when he saw the evidence of what he'd done, he'd apologise. Once he wept. The morning after the door incident.

By the light of a single lamp she had been playing the piano – softly because the baby was in bed. The door opened and Dave came in. He seemed to spend a long time in the hall – cursing under his breath, fumbling. She stopped playing but did not turn to face the doorway. He came in and slumped into an armchair.

'Jesus,' he said.

'Well?'

'Well what?'

'I don't often see you these days,' she said. 'How're you getting on?'

'I'm not getting on – in case you didn't fuckin notice. You fuckin don't let me on.'

'The same old story.'

'Yeah . . .'

'Dave, you're never at home. And when you are you've that much drink taken, you're useless.'

'We never . . . do it, these days.'

'You're inviting me to have sex with a drunk.' Her voice was not shouting – but was still at speaking pitch because of the baby in the other room. She continued to play chords quietly. 'Make an appointment with me sometime when you're sober and we'll talk about it.' She made an arpeggio of the same chord, spreading the notes across her fingers, and answered it with her right hand. Suddenly Dave leapt to his feet and slammed the lid of the piano. It was just instinct that made her pull her hands away in time. She felt the wind of the slam on her fingernails. The bang of the lid was like a gunshot. Every string in the piano vibrated for a long time.

'How dare . . .' Catherine leapt off the stool, but he caught her a sideways blow on the shoulder and, as she tried to run out of the room, she tripped on the rug which covered the threshold. He was on top of her pinning her to the floor. He grabbed her by the wrists and held them above her head.

'You can be so fuckin . . .' He could not find the word – just shook his head in disgust. 'You and your fucking piano playing. So fuckin superior . . .' His breath smelled bad. His chin rasped against her neck. He was strong and heavy, felt like he was hard, like thick rope. He pressed her hand against the jamb of the door. Her fingers were extended trying to fight him off. She did not want to scream and wake the baby. But she was terrified. This was the worst. With his other hand he lunged forward and tried to yank the door shut. She thought clearly and coolly, like the moment before a car crash, that he was trying to crush her fingers in the jamb of the door. But she got together enough strength to resist the pressure of his forcing and inched her hand out of danger.

Remembering this her mouth felt dry and she coughed. She went to the sink and ran some water into a jamjar. The window trembled in the wind. She knew there was a horse out there somewhere in the dark. A new arrival – its coat glossy and brown as a newly shelled chestnut. Something interesting to look at just as she was leaving. She had watched it earlier in the day, its mane flickering as it stood staring over the fence at her washing and packing dishes in newspaper. It could be standing there now in the darkness, curious about the light coming from a kitchen at four in the morning. If it had any sense it would be sheltering in the lee of the brick outhouse on the other side of the field.

She went back to sit by the fire, the half-filled jamjar in her hand. The curved leaves of the spider plant wagged in the draughts. It was as if the house had turned its back on the wind. At the front, where it was calmer, Anna was sleeping.

He had refused to believe the door incident when she told him the next day.

'You'd better go and see about yourself – before you kill me,' she had said.

'I'm more liable to kill myself.'

'That would help a little.'

He was tying up the laces of his boots. His hands were shaking badly.

'Fuck off.'

'Go and see the doctor. Today. He could get you in somewhere – get yourself straightened out.'

'We could go together. You're in more fuckin need of it than me.'

The clock in its tea-chest struck five. Four o'clock must have happened when she'd been crying. She got up and edged her way between the tea-chests to the window. A paleness was coming into the sky to the east over the mountain. *Taglied.* Day song. Like Schumann's *Gesänge der Frühe* which she had played many times at College. In English there were very few examples of morning songs. Anglo-Saxon guilt prevented any kind of celebration, tuneful or otherwise, after a night spent with a lover. Dawn grew and she saw from the tops of the trees that the storm was dying. The branches no longer threshed but waved. Perhaps the ferry would sail. She turned from the window and moved again to the fireplace. Some of the tea-chests had metal strips along their edges which could rip clothes or worse, cut flesh. She had to be very careful to keep Anna well away from them, because these days she was into everything, toddling everywhere. Even if the boat did sail the furniture van would not arrive until mid-day. In the growing light, she saw her friend, the horse, facing the dawn. Its tail blew around its legs and over its chestnut back. Enough there for a few violin bows. With plenty of pernambuca wood you could go into business. A bread wrapper from the bin whirled up into the air and fell on the horse's side of the fence. It stooped to nose the paper, then looked up at her again. Its mane flamed off to one side of its curved neck. Such grace in everything it did.

Beyond the horse, at the field's end, the slate-coloured sea had fewer white caps. The wind was definitely dropping. Suddenly she was convinced there would be a sailing today. She would get away from here.

In the bath Anna enjoyed splashing, soaking the whole of Liz's bathroom. Catherine wore a plastic apron and sat on the closed toilet seat watching her. Sometimes they played games, Catherine blowing bubbles out of the heel of her cupped hands. She bought a bubble kit and blew large iridescent bubbles from a tiny plastic circle on a stem. Anna loved to burst them and would blink if they popped too near her face and the atomised soap solution got into her eyes. Then she would cry. They ran bubble baths. A drop of liquid churned into mountains of froth which could be scooped up and blown from the hand.

'In my day,' Catherine said to Anna, 'if I wanted a bubble bath we had to use Fairy Liquid and an egg whisk.' Catherine pulled the baby's wet hair up into a peak. 'It was murder on the eyes. Would you look at the unicorn. Here, Silent O'Moyle – look at yourself.' She lifted the slippery baby from the bath and held her up to the mirror. The water wasn't hot enough to steam it over. Anna grinned at her reflection.

'I got my first bubble bath for my birthday.' Catherine remembered being in the bath and her mother trying to read the tiny print of the instructions on the side of the bottle.

'Mum the water's too hot.'

'Row it round you.' The right hand clawed the water backwards, the left pushed it forwards. Sometimes she got bath salts to perfume the water. They were like pink flints and they rattled around the enamel floor of the bath until they dissolved. But this stuff was different. Her mother poured the bubble bath into the water pounding down from the two taps. Gradually the white foam rose to cover the long turquoise stain beneath the cold tap, then to the height of her chin. The roar of the taps going full volume was followed by silence when her mother turned them off. She went out of the bathroom to get a fresh towel and the only sound was the faint fizz as the foam began to disappear. Catherine loved the almost no-feel of it as she lifted it in handfuls, made a Santa Claus beard for her chin so that her mother would laugh when she came back.

She thought of another idea and when her mother did come back with the towel Catherine pretended to be a Hollywood actress in her bubble bath with her hand behind her head. Instead of being amused her mother said, 'How dare you compare yourself to those brazen huzzies? Don't let me see you at that *ever* again.'

'Come on you brazen wee huzzie. I've work to do.' But Catherine couldn't be bothered to pick Anna up. Let her stay when she's happy. The work could wait. She had gone off the idea of calling it *By the Seas's Edge*. It was too literal and it said nothing about the music. Then one day in an Oxfam shop she saw a book, *The Scallop*. Because of the connection with Dave she took it from the shelf to flick through it. She read that medieval pilgrims who had been to the shrine of Santiago de Compostela in Spain wore a scallop-shaped badge on their caps. To prove they had been where they said. She bought the book for twenty pence. Later in the evening she read that St James had never really been to Spain. It was a myth, a made-up thing, but it seemed to make no difference to the fervour of the medieval pilgrims. They went there in their droves. The whole thing was a mistake or a deliberate fabrication – like St Cecilia being the patron saint of music. What if everyone had conspired to lie? Santiago de Compostela, that's what. Each important shrine in Europe produced its own badge – a vernicle. The word appealed to her – it had a good ring to it. Proof that you'd been there. In a land of devastation. At the bottom of the world. And come through it – just. She'd brought back evidence in the shape of a piece of music. *Vernicle.* A feather in her cap – for full orchestra. From the shrine of desolation.

She looked the word up in the dictionary and found it was also a representation of the face of Christ impressed on Veronica's handkerchief. Or any image of Christ's face made by an artist and used for devotional purposes. But she didn't allow this to put her off using the word for a title.

'You've been in there far too long. You'll get prune skin.' Catherine picked up her baby in a towel which had been warming on Liz's chrome rail. She enveloped her in it and played a game of pretending the baby was lost.

'Where did I put her? Who's taken her away?'

She held her close and nuzzled the top of her damp head. She imagined a day when she would hear the door bell ring distantly. Liz would shout into the basement, 'It's for you.'

And she would climb the stairs and see Dave standing there.

'You fucked off.'

'I did not. I moved to Glasgow with my baby.'

'I have rights, y'know.'

'Drunks forfeit their rights.'

'I've been sober since I last saw you.'

'Bully for you.'

It would happen sometime. She'd better have a plan. Would she slam the door in his face? Communicate by letter? Or should both of them use solicitors? Could they not settle it like sensible adults – after all they had been sensible enough not to get married.

There was another possibility – that he would take to the drink again and she'd never hear another word from him. That would be the best thing.

She carried the bundle down to the basement and dumped Anna down on the sofa.

'Where did I put her?'

She groped for her and dried her and finally found her head as it poked out of the large bath towel.

'There you are.' She dried her and covered her with baby powder. It plopped softly inside the container and formed a grey perfumed smoke in the air.

'You're smelling like a rose, m'girl.' She blew raspberries with her lips against the baby's bare tummy before she put her nappy on her for the night. Catherine carried her from the living-room into the bedroom. Anna sucked her thumb and made little noises of satisfaction. Both rooms were a mess. Most of the cardboard boxes were stored in the bedroom. She had labelled them with a black marker pen – KITCHEN THINGS or BEDCLOTHES – but now when they were crushed together like this she couldn't see the labels.

'There isn't a wink of sleep on you.' She looked around for something to amuse her. There was a plastic rattle and she shook it a couple of times and set it into the cot beside her. She popped the dummy into the baby's mouth and said night-night. Then went back and kissed her.

She tiptoed into the other room and although it was not yet dark switched on the Anglepoise lamp and sat in its cone of light, staring at the folder of papers in front of her on the table. She pulled out the staff sheets and began to look over them. As she did so she took a 3B pencil, octagonal in section, from the desk drawer and sharpened it with a one-sided razor blade. Little crescents of pale wood fell on to the table surface. It smelled like Christmas trees or was it cedar wood? She pared the black soft lead to a square end, as if for calligraphy, so that when she put the lead to the paper it would make a square mark in one stroke. Her manuscripts looked more medieval than modern. Plain chant with square notes. Distantly she could hear Anna still moving the rattle. Like a muted rain-stick.

For two months now she had written every day at this table beneath the window, looking up at people's feet as they passed by. Raiding her own bank was how she thought of it. Going down into herself, into the strong-room and seeing what she could come up with. *A method of employing the mind, without the effort of thinking* was what Dr Johnson said. One thing leads to another – was how she characterised it herself. Music was what happened next. Sculpting in sound.

She missed the sea to look at. How it changed constantly. Grey one day, the colour of slate the next. Blue-blown, white-capped. She told herself that having the sea so close was a distraction, like a television, just something else to keep her back from what really mattered – actually writing the notes down. She knew she had embarked on a huge work – by far the biggest thing she'd ever attempted. It took a hell of a lot of notes to keep an orchestra playing for that length of time. The skills gained in past work were of little use in solving the problems of the present. She had to begin to learn all over again for the new thing she was setting out to make. So she felt always a beginner. Getting down to new work was hard for her but this piece was in the final stages. In it she had found a voice of her own.

Whether it was shadows of people passing or the various lights of reflected water which were on her page she had to concentrate, to wear blinkers.

There were two periods in the day when she could work. In the evenings and for an hour or so during the day. Anna still needed a sleep in the afternoon. Catherine had everything prepared to go to work immediately the child hit the pillow. Working was a way of getting rid of time. Once she became absorbed correcting, improving, adding texture, exploring new sequences of notes, time disappeared. Stravinsky once described it as 'like an animal grubbing around'. But for her it was more of a refinement of the original idea, a focusing of what she'd aspired to or heard in the first place but had not managed to achieve. Notes in their perfect places.

In the evenings she found she was tired. She'd been up from Anna's first rattling of the balls on her cot – six o'clock, seven if she was lucky. All she wanted to do at night was to switch on the television and watch some junk. To feel her eyes sagging. To sleep. She felt the best work she did came in that intense hour in the middle of the day.

The pencil rolled with a little purr when she touched it. She picked it up and began to work on the closing section. She was four bars into the work when she heard a footstep on the stairs. It was bloody Liz.

'Hi Kate – how's it going?'

'Fine.' Catherine set her pencil down with a click.

'Peter's in London.'

'Oh?' Catherine stayed sitting over her work.

'He'll be back about eight – I don't know whether to eat or not . . .'

Catherine turned slightly in the chair. Liz sank into the sofa and encircled her knees with her arms, settling herself. Catherine said, 'And you want some advice . . .?'

'What?'

'You came down for some advice on whether to eat or not . . .?'

'I just came down to see how you were getting on, for God's sake.' Catherine nodded her head slowly. She pushed the staff sheets away from her. When Liz spoke again the indignation had gone from her voice, 'Saw on the news – the IRA have started shooting people in the elbows as well as the knees. But you have to be anti-social to qualify.'

'To do the shooting or to be shot?'

Liz smiled and looked up at her.

'I must be getting old.'

'Why?'

'I saw an outfit today in the cancer shop window I liked. Are you working?'

'Trying to.'

There was a long silence between them. Liz waited for some encouragement to stay. But Catherine continued to stare at the sheets on the table in front of her.

'Then I'd better go.' Someone walked past the window and Catherine looked up.

'It's just that I need to get this thing finished.'

She picked up her pencil again. Liz stood and walked towards the door. She closed it sharply. Catherine sighed and put her head in her hands.

'Oh God . . .'

The bang of the door must have wakened Anna. The baby's voice wailed out from the bedroom. The rattle clicked and fell on the floor. The crying went on and on. Catherine held the pencil between her fists, braced against her thumbs and leaned her forehead on the table. She sat waiting for Anna to stop. When the baby cried hard like this she gave herself wind. It was better to give in sooner rather than later. The pencil snapped in two.

'Shit . . .' She flung the halves down on the table, got up and went in and lifted her from the cot. Anna stopped crying immediately. 'What *is* wrong with you tonight?'

She carried her into the other room and sat her on the floor.

'Amuse yourself.' She slid her legs beneath the table and stared at the broken pencil and the scattering of manuscript paper. She thought and made a face. 'Awww no,' she said. 'OK – let's go up and say night-night to your Auntie Liz.' She picked Anna up in one arm and her purse in the other. The baby sat on her hip, one leg to the front, one to the back. Catherine climbed the stairs from the basement.

'Liz?' Liz was sitting in front of the TV. She barely looked round as Catherine came in. 'I'm sorry.' Liz went on watching the screen, her brow wrinkled in concentration. 'For being so . . . but I'm getting uptight about this commission thing. It's just that I . . .' There was a long silence and then something in Catherine's voice that made Liz turn round. Catherine's face was distorted, trying to fight against tears. She stood there weeping, holding on to her baby. Liz jumped up and took Anna from her.

'Hey! What's wrong? What's wrong, Kate?' It was difficult to hug with the baby between them. 'Sit down. Take it easy.' With her free arm Liz reached out and put it about Catherine's shoulder. She guided her down into an armchair and sat above her on the upholstered arm.

'What is it?'

'This girl . . . this girl . . . would like to say . . . good night to you.' Her voice was filled with gasps and shudders. Her speech was distorted.

'What's wrong, Kate?'

'Nothing – this is me . . . normal.' She wailed and covered her wet face with her hands. Her nose was dripping as she sniffed in wetly. Liz handed her a tissue. 'When I came here first . . . I thought I was doing so well. I was so good . . . those first four weeks . . . Then it all came back.'

'What did?'

'This.'

'What's this?'

'Fuckin *this*.'

Catherine gave a suppressed wail and sat there, her face running with tears. It seemed useless to apply the tiny tissue Liz had handed her. Liz got up and came back with an ironed handkerchief of Peter's.

'Thanks.'

'It might help if you could explain to me what *this* is.'

'Crying and . . . getting depressed again.'

'I've never seen you crying before.'

'It's been happening for ages.'

'I didn't know. How awful. You poor thing.'

'It started happening after her.'

'Don't you listen, sweetheart,' Liz said in a lowered voice to the baby. Then nuzzled her into her neck. 'You're all right by me.' Despite the crying face Catherine started to laugh.

'Poor wee Anna. Getting the blame. Put her down on the floor, Liz – she'll be all right.'

'Oh, I love the smell of them.'

'Come down and smell her first thing in the morning.'

'No thanks.'

'I'm sorry . . . for speaking to you the way I did. You've been so good to me.' Catherine dabbed her cheeks dry.

She felt that the skin of her face had sagged and would never lift again. The tears stopped.

'I wish I was artistic,' said Liz, 'then I could be temperamental.'

'That is awful – don't say stupid things like that.'

'I'm sorry. I take that back.'

'The doctor says it'll go away eventually. He's given me these things to take.' Liz reached out and put her hand over Catherine's hand and made a sympathetic face.

'Your hanky smells nice,' said Catherine. 'Like ironing.'

'Have you been to our doctor here?'

'With Anna.' Catherine nodded.' He's nice. I told him the situation. When I feel like this I try to think of other things.'

Liz's hand tightened over hers. Catherine blew her nose. Liz said, 'Are you manic depressive?'

'I wish I was – I'd be happy now and again if that was the case.' Liz laughed at her.

'What about a cup of tea?'

'Yeah. Tea would be nice. I'll make it and you can entertain the lovely Anna.' Catherine stood and filled the kettle and switched it on. Liz dandled the baby on her knee. She said, 'No words yet, Anna?'

'Not a one,' said Catherine. 'Silent O'Moyle.'

'What?'

'It's a thing my mother used to say.' Catherine set out the china mugs and put a tea-bag in each. Liz said, 'Imagine you hurting all that time and not telling anyone.'

'Maybe we should talk about something else.'

'Whatever helps.'

'Oh yes – today I put in a claim for Housing Benefit.

You might have to sign a form for me. To say I'm a tenant.'

'But you're only here on a temporary basis. As a friend.'

'You might as well have the money.'

'The tax man might want to ask Peter about it. Any sign of a job?'

'Naw . . .'

'Not even a subbing job?'

'No – in a time of cuts, music jobs are the first to go. Arty-farty stuff – of no practical use. Anyway, I prefer it this way. At the moment – until I finish this piece.'

'How *is* it going?'

'So–so.'

'As good as that?' Catherine laughed.

Liz said, 'Tell me about so–so?'

'It's hard to talk about music. This thing . . .'

'Called?'

'I don't know yet. Maybe *Vernicle*. Everybody's into one-word titles nowadays.'

'Sounds more like an ailment. Half-way between a verruca and a cuticle.'

'At least it's *my* ailment.'

'Kate's *Vernicle*. And how much do you get paid?'

'Two thousand.'

'Wow – that's not bad.' The kettle began to make tickling sounds.

'It's not great when you consider it as a year's salary.'

'I suppose not.'

'But this one's so important I'd have done it for nothing – the third thing to get broadcast.'

'Why's that so important?'

'I get to join the Performing Rights Society. The men let me in. It's like Equity for actors. After this I can write composer on my passport.'

The kettle boiled. Catherine filled both cups and waited for the revolving tea-bags to darken the water. Liz played *Round and round the garden* with the baby. 'How do you like your tea?'

'Now,' said Liz. She banged the table with the flat of her hand. 'I don't care if it's weak or strong, I want it *now.*' Liz's joke frightened Anna and the baby's lip dropped and she began to howl. Catherine took her.

'It's OK, love – that big bad woman shouldn't have shouted. There, there.'

The child stopped crying but stayed close to Catherine's neck, holding on tightly.

'Don't be so clingy – let me drink my tea. I'm sorry Liz – about the crying. Me, not the baby. I don't like laying it on you.'

'Not at all. Come and lay it on me any time you like.'

When Peter came home Catherine went back downstairs. She put Anna down in her cot and this time the child slept almost immediately. She went back to the table and looked down at her work. The broken cross section of the pencil had a central black spindle of graphite embedded in the cedar wood. She smiled. If she cut it carefully she could make two pencils. And do twice the work. She shuddered and rubbed her face with both hands. Then she switched on the television to see what was on.

Catherine knew that, given her luck, she would get her period on the first day of rehearsal. She had stood in front of the largely male orchestra, her knees trembling, her back aching. She'd wanted to run away and curl up somewhere, to be anywhere but there, doing anything but that. If Andy the Flute said he didn't like his part then she'd have agreed to scrap it. If Robert Percussion complained that it was all too much for him she'd have given in and rewritten the part for tambourine. I am a nobody, a pain in the ass. Who am I to be on this podium talking to these talented people? The conductor, Randal Kresner, had made a suggestion about the entry of the cellos. If he'd suggested that, then he must have hated the way it was before. Look Randal, she wanted to say, why don't we scrap the whole thing? It's nothing but a piece of pretentious crap with a pretentious bloody title. *Vernicle*. It's hard to believe. Why don't we jack it in and everybody can go home. I'll do better next time. But it's more likely, given the way I feel at the moment, that I'll never write another note. I just want to go to my bed. I want my hot-water bottle.

Now, on the evening of the concert, it was a different angst. Her confidence had come back in like a tide. The music was good – what was bad were her nerves. She sat on the toilet, her head held in her hands. She felt as if her stomach had fallen out of her and only wind remained. She was dying for a swig of Nurse Harvey's Gripe Mixture – stuff she'd poured into Anna for the colic. Then she could have a good belch. She was on the verge of nausea. Earlier, before the concert, her mouth had flooded with saliva and she'd dashed to the toilet and hunkered down beside the bowl. But nothing had come. A dry boke. She'd swallowed again and again until the spasm passed.

Now on this second visit she'd just had evidence that she was suffering from diarrhoea. She closed her eyes and covered them with her hands. What would happen if she threw up in the bloody concert hall? Or shat herself on the radio? She started to laugh. There was no need for this. The piece had been well rehearsed. She and the conductor had talked long and hard about it. Indeed Randal, in various subtle ways, had made it sound better than when she'd first imagined it.

Above the noise of cisterns refilling she could distantly hear instruments being tuned. Stuttering trumpets, violins being sawed, flutes tootling, a tuba pomping. Above all she could hear someone working with a Lambeg drum. She had watched the drums being tuned before rehearsal – the Ulster men called it 'pulling them'. One held the drum firm while the other used his knee as a brace to pull each linen rope in turn.

'The long journey,' said the big man as he worked his way round. He wore gloves and pulled hard until the skin of the drum was the right tension.

The four Orangemen from Portadown had arrived mid-week in a mini-bus. They had been offered an hotel but had preferred to stay with friends in Bridgeton. One of the things that had enticed them over had been the thought of seeing Rangers playing at Ibrox on Saturday. They had driven straight from Stranraer to the first rehearsal. Catherine shook hands with the man who seemed to be the leader.

'The name's Sandy Foster. And this is Billy McIlwham. Norman Hutchinson. And last but definitely least, Cameron Lawlor.' They seemed sheepish. And a bit nervous. Without thinking, Cameron Lawlor rubbed his hand on the backside of his jeans after shaking Catherine's hand. He said, 'Where's the composer?'

'That's me.'

'You ...' his voice almost screeched. 'You're too young to be anything.' The leader said, 'Pay no attention to Cammy – he's always like this.'

'Any danger of a cuppa tea?' said Cammy.

'I'll put the kettle on,' Catherine said. The echo of the hard skin of Cammy's hand was still with her. Scar tissue. She heard her father.

They bleed their wrists. Against the rim. Sheer bloody bigotry.

The handshakes had taken place at the back of the hall. While Catherine went off to the kitchen all four men began to look around them. At the stained-glass windows, the pulpit, the water font. When she came back Sandy said, 'What kind of a church is it?'

'It's not a church any longer.'

'But what was it – in its day?'

'Church of Scotland, I think,' said Catherine. Cammy wiped imaginary sweat off his brow.

'Whew!'

The first time all four Lambegs had come on in rehearsal Catherine watched the faces of the players in the orchestra. They were genuinely astonished. They looked at one another in disbelief. The building resonated to the enormous blattering. The air vibrated.

'We very rarely bate a trevally on the drums indoors,' Cammy said. 'Because the buildings fall down afterwards.'

258

At break-time the members of the orchestra, mostly the men, gathered round to poke and finger the drums and ask questions.

'The shell's of oak,' said Sandy, 'and the drum heads are goat skin. I've seen brass shells as well.'

'How long have you been playing?'

'Since his arsehole wasn't the size of a shirt button,' said Cammy.

'Mind your tongue,' hissed Sandy, 'there's ladies about.'

'You mean me?' Catherine said, coming into the circle. 'What about the sticks?'

'Sticks?' Cammy's voice went up. 'Malucca canes, if you don't mind.'

'They say you play tunes,' said Robert Percussion.

'Not so's you'd notice. In the beginning it was always the fife and drum. The fife played the tune, the drum bate a trevally along with it. Then over the years the fifing fell away. But the drumming went on. It'll go on for ever, if you ask me.'

'You're accompanying a tune which doesn't exist any more,' said Catherine.

'You might be right.'

She looked down at his wrists. 'Any scars?'

'Nonsense – a good drummer's wrists never touch the rim.' Cammy looked at her. 'That's Roman Catholic propaganda – to make us look like fanatics.'

The concert was sponsored by the European Broadcasting Union and was being transmitted live to about twenty European countries. Earlier, she could hardly get in by the dressing-room door for BBC vans and strewn cables. And there was an audience of people out there buzzing with talk and expectation. Her anonymity would disappear. She knew, however well- or ill-received it was, she would have to go up to the rostrum and take the applause. Bad and all as that was, it wasn't the worst thing – the worst thing was that her notes were going to be played to people who might hate them, might ridicule them. They might say, *who does she think she is?* She shuddered. This was the unknown. It was like the blind man diving. What if everyone had conspired to lie? And her piece *Vernicle* was awful? Pain for fuck all, as Marge had said. An act of no creation. Alasdair Kirkpatrick at the Royal Scottish Academy of Music and Drama had said, 'Composers seek praise in exact proportion to how unsure they are of themselves. An artist who is sure doesn't need any praise, he knows. Whereas someone who's unsure, hearing the applause, says to himself – maybe it's better than I thought.'

What if the audience reacted to her the way she had reacted to Schoenberg or Stockhausen? She had heard a performance of Stockhausen's *Gruppen*, for three orchestras under three conductors, and had thought it a complete waste of time and space – so much musical talent thrown away. This was what happened when everyone had conspired to lie. Something ugly got no better when viewed in three mirrors, something ineffectual got no better when tripled, like Olga blessing herself. Stockhausen's was music written without regard for the ear – a totally abstract concept. Because one theme was a retrograde inversion of another didn't automatically make it good. It was theoretical music. But in some circles it was so highly regarded. How different to Messiaen and Stravinsky.

The buzzer for the end of the interval sounded. A harsh jagged electric sound. But still she sat on the toilet. The first half of the concert had been two works, Lyell Creswell's *Dragspil*, which was really a concerto for accordion (the programme note pointed out that *dragspil* was Icelandic for accordion) and Eddie McGuire's *Calgacus*, which climaxed with the entrance of a piper in full Highland regalia, walking up the middle aisle of the church giving it everything he'd got, vying with the orchestra. When the European Broadcasting Union had invited submissions, it had said it would look favourably on works which included an instrument more associated with music of ethnic origins. The Lambeg drum was not normally associated with Irish folk music but it was undoubtedly ethnic.

Her piece had played in rehearsal at twenty-eight minutes and formed the whole second half of the programme. The first half of the concert had all gone over her head. She'd sat as still as she could but found it impossible to concentrate. Her mind was on her own piece. Its shortcomings, how it could have been improved.

The sound the men from Portadown made at rehearsal was exactly what Catherine had hoped for. Now she was ridiculously worried about how they would look on the night of the performance. She had always hated evening dress on the platform. They were the only profession whose working clothes were ball-gowns. The men, she said, should have black-leather elbows fitted – to make their duds last longer. Randal had talked to the guest

261

musicians of the three pieces about what they would wear. Lyell Creswell's accordionist matched the orchestra in black tie and evening suit. His accordion was an unobtrusive gun-metal grey. In Eddie McGuire's *Calgacus* the piper had looked great in Highland regalia. But there was no equivalent for Northern Ireland. To dress the Lambeg drummers in black tie and tails for their entrance would have been ludicrous. Randal insisted that he didn't want them coming on in jeans and shirt-sleeves. It was Cammy who said they were members of the same band so why didn't they wear band uniforms. His friends in Bridgeton were members of a flute band and they could borrow four uniforms. No bother.

'Thank God it's radio,' said Catherine. Cammy winked at her. She considered her music to be of high seriousness – why did something always come up at the last minute to trivialise the whole thing. The argument about the title of *Trumpetists and Tromboners*, now this – who cared how it would *look*? She cared. It would probably be acceptable to everyone else in the hall except herself. All she would see was a Kick the Pope band. So she resolved to keep her eyes down. She heard the outer door of the LADIES open and someone come in.

'Kate?' It was Liz. 'Kate, are you there?'

'I'm in here.'

'Are you all right?'

'I'm OK.' She stood and flushed the toilet.

'We didn't know where you were.'

Catherine unsnibbed the door and came out. She smiled bravely and went to wash her hands.

'They're beginning to move in for the second half. Your half.'

'Don't,' said Catherine. She looked at herself in the mirror, tilting her head a little. Even here in the toilets it was obvious that the place was a converted church – pointed archways, columns, a rose window high on the wall.

'Do I look OK? Am I too pale?'

'All that matters is you're late.'

She reached her hand beneath the soap dispenser and pressed. It deposited a white splurge in her palm. She showed it to Liz and laughed.

'Don't say a word.'

'You're awful,' said Liz. The final buzzer was giving a long dithering screech. Catherine washed her hands thoroughly, as if she were going to an operating theatre rather than a concert hall.

'Come on, Kate.'

'Don't panic.'

She shook the drops from her hands and went to the towel machine and tugged a new area of white cloth into position. The buzzer ceased. Catherine dried her hands slowly. Liz took her by the elbow and half dragged, half hurried her out of the door, past the Christmas tree in the foyer and into the hall.

'Face the music,' she said.

Liz's husband Peter was looking round for them. He grinned as they excuse me'd their way to where he sat in the middle of the row. They were among the last to be seated. Liz still held on to Catherine's arm. She squeezed it as the audience went quiet. Catherine covered Liz's hand

and squeezed back in thanks. There were two microphone booms, like huge fishing rods dangling over the orchestra. And one hung over the audience for recording applause.

She found it hard to believe that *Vernicle* was about to have its first performance. She picked up the printed sheets being used as a handout. She was shaking. The paper fluttering in her hand. She steadied her hand against her thigh. There was a brief biographical note and an interview with each of the composers in the programme. She'd avoided reading her contribution during the first half.

Catherine Anne McKenna *was born in Co. Derry, and studied composition at Queen's University, Belfast and later at the Royal Scottish Academy of Music and Drama in Glasgow. Winner of the Moncrieff-Hewitt Travel Award she studied composition briefly with Anatoli Melnichuck in Kiev. She has now left teaching to devote herself to full-time composition. She lives in Glasgow.*

Principal Compositions: *A Suite for Trumpetists and Tromboners* for orchestral brass; *The Goat Paths* – a song cycle for high voice and piano – text of poems by James Stephens; Three Piano Trios; Preludes and Fugues for piano.

How can I say what I go through writing an instrumental composition? The same as a poet except that he uses words. It is a kind of musical confession. Told from the head, full of musical ideas. Except that music is far richer, much more subtle than words. It can scourge the heart. Music comes from pre-hearing.

You sit down to your desk and listen to what's inside your head. Things appear suddenly and unexpectedly. I don't mean it's like inspiration or anything like that but, put it this way, you are there with a 3B pencil in your hand should you hear anything good. If you are in a notion of working, the idea takes root and won't let you go. It puts out twigs and branches. These twigs get leaves and thorns and maybe, if you are lucky, blossoms. And fruit. Occasionally you get fruit to sustain you. And then grey lichens grow on the branches and so on and so on. Maybe a ladybird comes. Maybe a woodcutter comes if it's a fairy-tale. The problem is that the seed must appear at the right time – you can only carry so much in your head until the next time you come across pencil and paper. The baby must be in bed. And asleep. The washing must be done. And the dishes and God knows what else. When it's going well there's a kind of joy to it – even if you are writing something which is sombre, something really dark. You sort of lose touch with the world around you, your body ceases to be of any importance. One musical idea comes hard on the heels of another. Sometimes I shake when it's going well. But that's rare. The worst thing that can happen at a time like this is an interruption. The baby starts crying. The phone rings. I get so mad when that happens. It's like interrupted sex. When the interruption is over it's very hard to get the same momentum going again.

Catherine's eye slid over the page. Jesus, did she really say that? She had laughed a lot during the interview – but that hadn't come out. Where was the irony, the self-deprecation? Only some of what she had said was true. The studying composition with Melnichuck was a bit of an exaggeration – although he was a good name to have on her CV. But she didn't dare mention the worst thing of all. To write something really dark, despairing even, is so much better than being silent. If you're depressed your mind says there's no point in writing anything. You just want to sit with your mouth hanging open – your mind full of scorpions. There was no formula for getting around that.

Liz was reading her copy of the programme. She broke off and leaned over, 'Kate, what's this about interrupted sex?'

Catherine laughed and shrugged. 'My sex life has been interrupted.'

'You're shaking,' said Liz, her eyes widening.

'You think I haven't noticed? It's all the orgasms I've missed.'

Liz grinned and squeezed her arm. She continued to stare all around her. 'What's that?' Liz nodded at the wall. Multi-faceted boxes were set at intervals all over its surface.

'It's baffling.'

'I know – that's why I'm asking.' Liz squealed too loudly at her own joke and covered her mouth with her hand. Catherine rolled her eyes at her then looked away again. Where the altar used to be was the orchestral platform. Above it soared two stained-glass windows, elongated and black. During rehearsals the sun had made the Victorian windows vivid. Flecks of colour shone on the walls and floor, on the cloth of the practising musicians' shoulders. The windows depicted Victorian religious sentiments. Apostles. Old Testament types. Wycliffe. Erasmus. Catherine said she would like to have seen one devoted to the Twelve Apostates. Written words appeared here and there. TRUTH & TOLERANCE. FERVOUR &

FAITH. And above all TO THE GLORY OF GOD. But now the windows were featureless and dead, facing out into the night. To see them properly you would have to be outside the church.

Suddenly there was a hand-clap and then everyone was applauding, including herself. The players of the orchestra were coming on from both sides of the transept. The applause stopped and the audience noise died down. It was a kind of embarrassing silence because nothing seemed to be happening. Someone was talking somewhere. An indistinct but loud single voice. Catherine panicked – was something wrong? Was the conductor refusing at the last moment? Was there an argument with one of the Orangemen? Then she remembered the same thing had happened in the first half and that what she was hearing was the voice of the announcer. Then she noticed the red light was on. Like a BBC sacristy lamp. Out of the listening silence she heard her own name. The voice said *Catherine Anne McKenna* but she could make out little else. In embarrassment she put her hand to her face and smelled the strange liquid soap she had just used.

She thought of the radio at home in her parents' kitchen. It sat to one side of the cooker and was almost always tuned to Radio Eireann. After mass her mother listened to *Sunday Miscellany* and the house would be filled with the rich talking voice of Benedict Kiely. It was a tape-cassette and radio combined – the tape part of it had ceased to function long ago. When new it had a matt aluminium finish with two round speakers of dark mesh on the front. Over the years the mesh had become clogged with flour dust and fat japped from the pan. It was operated by levers, more trendy than knobs at the time. The air in the kitchen left an atomic layer of grease on anything which didn't move. And the radio hadn't been moved in years. Its satin aluminium finish had dulled and the levers were sticky to the touch so her parents just switched it on and off at the plug. But it gave them the news and *Sunday Miscellany* and any important Gaelic football matches.

She should have told them. Even a polite card to say she was having a piece performed on radio. But she'd delayed too long. And there had been last-minute revisions suggested by Randal. She hadn't done it, and that was that. A girl who doesn't tell her parents of her success is more estranged than one who conceals her mistakes. Would there have been any chance that someone in the know would have told them? Maybe Miss Bingham – she used to go through the *Radio Times* with a red pen circling the programmes. And seeing Catherine's name maybe she would have phoned and they would be listening? Both of them, sitting now in the kitchen, nervous as she was? Nervous *for* her. Anyway they would hate what she had written. John McCormack and 'I Hear You Calling Me' it was not.

It was unheard of. For an only child to walk out like that. An only girl.

It sounded now like the announcer was rhyming off the names of all the places where the broadcast was being received. She made out the words Germany, Greece, Hungary, Iceland, Italy, Poland, Portugal. Liz leaned across and said, 'This is the only bit a geographer like me understands.'

She wondered if Huang Xaio Gang could be performing or teaching in any of these places. Would he hear *Vernicle*? Not that he would know in a million years who it was by. She hoped he would be intrigued and listen, keeping time with his greying head.

It was the last concert in the *Cutting Edge* series given by the BBC Scottish Symphony Orchestra from the Henry Wood Hall, Glasgow. Before the beginning a nice BBC man had asked them to make sure that their watch alarms were not set to go off in the midst of the broadcast.

'They don't want them to drown out your Lambeg drums, Kate,' said Liz.

The announcement after the interval finished and again the hush came. Everything seemed to take an interminable amount of time. Catherine stared at the backs of people's heads. The intricacy of hair – the way it curls and grows and disappears. Different kinds and stages of baldness. One man had the track of his hat band still on his hair. It was odd to be sitting like this, row upon row in the light. In the cinema it was dark. The only equivalent, she thought, was sitting in church. But this *was* church. One of the few Scottish poems they'd done in school was 'To a Louse'. Applause as Randal strode on to the platform. He went straight to the podium, faced the orchestra with his baton upraised and waited for absolute silence.

It began with a wisp of music, barely there – a whispered five-note phrase on the violins and she was right back on that beach with her baby. If the audience thought themselves mistaken she would be well pleased. Did I hear that correctly? Like the artist's hand which moves to begin a drawing but makes no mark. Preliminary footering – throat clearing. Then the phrase repeated an eyelash louder. I did hear something. The listeners feel that they must pay absolute attention to hear anything more. But the pause is longer, seems interminable before the music begins again. Is it over? they should be saying. Or, have they not started yet? The phrase repeats a third time on the violas. They sound like violins with a cold. Yes, it has started, that there is something there is undeniable. But it is so very ordinary. Everyday stuff. Nevertheless starting friction has been overcome and now the phrase unravels and strengthens, becomes louder – becomes a fugue-like figure and is joined by the cellos, then the basses. Darkening and growing, rising and falling by the narrowest of intervals. Plaiting bread. Her mother's hands, three pallid strands, pale fingers over and under, in and out. Weaving. Like ornament in the Book of Kells. Under and over, out and in. Like pale fingers interlocked in prayer. Grace notes with a vaguely Celtic flavour. More and more threads slowly and imperceptibly surround what the violins are saying, repeating over and over again to themselves. This is the ascent. This is the climbing of steps.

The music is simple. A simple idea, the way life is simple – a woman produces an egg and receives a man's seed into her womb and grows a baby and brings another person into the world. Utterly simple. Or so amazingly complex that it cannot be understood. So far beyond us that it is a mystery. And yet it happens every minute of every day. How can something be utterly simple and amazingly complex at the same time? Things are simple or complex according to how much attention is paid to them. She has reached down into the tabernacle of herself

for this music and feels something sacred in its performance.

Gradually the great arch of the movement begins to take
shape. She is absorbed in her own music – its drama. Her
shaking has stopped. How can a thing have drama if you
know what is going to happen? Like football on television.
Dave always knew the result but the drama of how it was
achieved was never diminished. He knew the score. Ha-
ha. She was absorbed in what would be next even though
she *knew* what would be next. She was paying attention
with her whole body. She was now utterly still. Reacting
to the mystery. Filling herself with her own grace. And yet
she was walking again the firm sand in bare feet. Step by
step. One foot after the other. She closed her eyes. Testing
her bravery, her faith. Trusting that the wind would not
turn to rock.

Randal was perfect – in his phrasing, in his tempi and
textures. All her self-criticism had been put aside. It was as
if her nervousness had evaporated the moment the music
began. And she was into it – working at listening.
Eavesdropping on her own life.

The strings begin to converge and insist on the one
note, F sharp, until everyone is pulled into the wake of this
note. The ascent is complete, the climactic point is
reached. But there is no vista from the top. Suddenly
everything is cut short by the entrance of the Lambegs. It
is almost like machine-gun fire. A short burst – enough to
kill and maim. Silence. It's the kind of silence induced by a
slap in the face or the roarings of a drunk. Catherine keeps
her eyes closed. She cannot bear to look and see the four
men in band uniform emerging from both sides of the

transept. It could be, would be ludicrous. The strings try again but darken. The sections of the orchestra begin to ask who or what is this – what is going on? What right have they to elbow their way in here? She feels a remembered angst and is momentarily afraid the music will induce it again for real. Oh Jesus. Even a memory of the blackness of her depression startles her. It was that bad. It was *worse* than that bad. For a second time the Lambegs open fire. This time it is a sustained burst. The subsequent silence is longer. The vault throbbing with the echoes of the huge drums. The orchestra begins again, stating and restating an inversion of the five-note motif of the opening. Annoyance has crept in. The orchestra is angry and shrill now as it has a post-mortem on the intervention and what can be done if it happens again. Clarinets and flutes squeal, the trombones rasp. Then, almost with nonchalance, with a swagger one drum begins, then the second, then the third and fourth. Insistent, cacophonous rhythm. Disintegration. The tormented orchestra tries to keep its head above the din of these strangers. The black blood of hatred stains every ear. The brass, like hatchets, chopping into the noise. Eventually, after an intense struggle, the orchestra falls away section by section until only the drums are left pulsing. It reminds her of the candle flames snuffing out beneath the invisible tide of suffocating gas. Step after step. Dark after dark. Four toads ballooning out their throats, blattering the air above them and leaving it throbbing. She was amazed at how well the drums sounded as the four men gave it everything, raw – improvised almost, exactly as she'd imagined. Their aggression, their swagger put her in mind of Fascism. She

272

was not trying to copy the vulgarity of Shostakovitch Seven – the march of the Nazis on Leningrad – but that was the effect. A brutalising of the body, the spirit, humanity. Thundering and thundering and thundering and thundering. When the drums stopped on a signal from Randal the only thing that remained was a feeling of depression and darkness. Utter despair.

The audience remained petrified for some moments. Intimidated. Stunned. Then the throat clearing began. The shuffling. Catherine tried to interpret the agitation. Were they annoyed? Did they hate it? Was it naïvely simple? She looked up at Liz who made a face, like the Man in the Moon, her mouth an open O. What did that mean? Was she impressed by the racket the musicians had made? Beyond Liz, Peter nodded and winked at her. At the end of the row a man sat, his knuckles to his forehead. He was frowning. He was definitely frowning. Catherine turned her eyes to the floor and kept them fixed there. She felt a trickle of sweat run from her armpit down past her bra, down the folds of skin of her left side. She held her elbows tight to her body to trap any further perspiration and keep it in its place. Randal raised his baton again and all the fidgeting stopped.

The second movement is the other side of the arch – she hoped it would have the bilateral symmetry of a scallop shell – again starting quietly, the strings meandering almost. The music still quiet enough for the flutes to be breathy. There is a feeling that the music is messing around. Where to? It is as if the orchestra has not forgotten what happened on the first side of the arch and are playing, looking over their shoulders, waiting for the reappearance of the Lambegs. The first real textural difference is the introduction of the bells. Small sharp raps of the wooden hammer playing a clarion call of seven notes. A bright hard sound, as if heard at some distance over ice. A statement sounded out, remembered from the bell tower in Kiev. The bitter cold of her fingers as she wrote it down. The tower reverberating in the soles of her shoes. Tintinnabulation. Hearing with her sternum – listening with the bones of her head, paying attention with her heart. Visceral music. Sound shaking the blood from the walls of her womb. The rhythm of a woman's life is synchronised with the moon and the moon is synchronised with the sea, ergo – a woman is synchronised with the tides. She had made the raid and come away with something significant. The organism was a spore – conditions had come right. It was flowering in front of her ears. She had been to the hard shell at her centre. The iron room – the safe place, the tabernacle. And come away with gold.

Now the listeners know they are going somewhere. They cannot see their destination but they know they are on a journey. Through snow. Then the bell figure is inverted and repeated on the strings, but distorted. Sizzled, in descending leaps, swoops. Back to the child in the playground who preferred climbing the steps to sliding down the shute. Next a slalom. Bowed near the bridge to produce a glassy, metallic effect. The bell theme is taken up by everyone. It grows in confidence and in volume. Gradually the horror of the first movement falls away, is forgotten. There is a new feeling in the air. It is urgent and hopeful and the tempo quickens. Things are possible.

Work can be done – good work, at that. Love is not lost or wasted. The music builds, laying down substantial foundations, the strength of which signal to the listener the size of the crescendo to come. It sweeps everyone along, draws the reluctant into its slipstream.

What happens next is difficult to explain. It is in sound terms like counterpoint – the ability unique to music to say two or more things at once. But it is not like counterpoint – more like an optical illusion in sound. The drawing was in psychology books – either an old woman or a girl. The eye could not accommodate both images at once. Either one or the other. The mind flicked. Grandmother? Girl? Girl. Grandmother. Another one was a chalice or was it two profiles staring at each other? The same thing could be two things. Transubstantiation. How could the drum battering of the first movement be the same as the drum battering of the second movement – how could the same drumming in a different context produce a totally opposite effect? The sound has transformed itself. Homophones. Linseed oil. Lynn C. Doyle. Bar talk. Bartók – the same sound but with a different meaning. Catherine heard it inside her head and knew that it was possible to achieve it, once the idea was conceived. At the moment when the music comes to its climax, a carillon of bells and brass, the Lambegs make another entry at maximum volume. The effect this time is not one of terror or depression but the opposite. Like scalloped curtains being raised, like a cascade of suffocation being drawn back to the point it came from and lights reappearing. The great drone bell sets the beat and the treble bells yell the melody. The whole church reverberates. The Lambegs have been stripped of their bigotry and have become pure sound. The black sea withdraws. So too the trappings of the church – they have nothing to do with belief and exist as colour and form. It is infectious. On this accumulating wave the drumming has a fierce joy about it. Exhilaration comes from nowhere. The bell-beat, the slabs of brass, the whooping of the horns, the battering of the drums. Sheer fucking unadulterated joy. Passion and pattern. An orchestra at full tilt – going fortissimo – the bows, up and down, jigging and sawing in parallel – the cellos and basses sideways. The brass shining and shouting at the back. The orchestra has become a machine, a stitching machine. The purpose of training an army is to dehumanise, to make a machine of people yet here all this discipline, all this conformity was to express the individuality and uniqueness of one human being. Catherine Anne's vision. A joy that celebrates being human. A joy that celebrates its own reflection, its own ability to make joy. To reproduce.

The orchestra soars in conjunction with the Lambegs, and the Lambegs roar in response to the orchestra and the effect is as she had hoped for. Her baby. *Deo Gratias.* Anna's song.

Her face is wet. Catherine is weeping. Her eyes are streaming yet again. But this time the tears are different. Just as the drum sound could be two things – so too could the tears. Anna. Vernicle. Music, her faith.

One final lurch and the orchestra stops. The Orangemen continue drumming but now they are walking away.

Diminuendo. The Lambegs continue to sound in the sacristy, distantly. On a signal from Randal they stop.

There was a moment's silence which was broken by a man's voice shouting. Then the hall was full of applause. Bravo. Catherine stared at her knees. Her nerves returned. She wondered if she would shake visibly if she stood up. Would her legs bear her weight? Still the applause went on. Some people whistled. Others shouted and cheered. Liz leaned over and squeezed Catherine's arm.

'Good for you,' Liz said looking around. 'There's no booing. They really liked it. I've no idea why, but they really liked it. Hey – you've been crying. It wasn't that bad.' Both of them were laughing. A male voice shouted bravo again. Catherine shouted, 'Did *you* like it?'

'Yes, yes.' Liz nodded her head. And Catherine knew that it didn't matter whether her friend liked it or not. As long as she liked *her*. Liz said, 'Linguists would insist on that man shouting *brava*.'

Randal came back and pointed to the various sections of the orchestra and they stood. He looked down into the audience and beckoned Catherine with a high wave to the podium. *Bravo*.

She rose.